Matt Miller in the Colonies

MATT MILLER IN THE COLONIES

Book Three: Virginian

MARK J. ROSE

The Skydenn Looking Glass

Simi Valley

The Skydenn Looking Glass
508 Longbranch Rd.
Simi Valley, CA 93065

Printed in the United States of America

Library of Congress Cataloging-in-Publication Data
Rose, Mark J., 1965 –
Matt Miller in the Colonies : Book Three: Virginian /
Mark J. Rose.
ISBN 978-0-9975554-5-5
1. Science Fiction. 2. Historical Fiction.
Title: Matt Miller in the Colonies : Book Three:
Virginian

First Edition, Edit: 04/2019

MAJOR FERGUSON

Major Patrick Ferguson did his best to remain hidden as he approached the smoking wreckage that was barely visible through the trees. His training was hardly necessary here in the Tennessee countryside, but the habits he'd developed during two tours in Iraq were hard to break. Destruction was rarely a singularity in that desert hellhole; another bomb was always ready to go off, another jihadi waiting around the corner. Patrick scanned the surrounding woods and then stopped to watch the rays of sun filtering through the thick canopy of leaves. It reminded him of a proper English forest, then of the home he had left behind. He'd been away for four months, participating in a high-tech weapons transfer at Oak Ridge Laboratories, and would stay until the end of the year.

Patrick looked again at the trees and realized why they'd stopped him. The leaves were green. Tennessee had been at the peak of fall color the last time he could remember. He surveyed the forest wondering if his splitting headache was making him hallucinate. The strong smell of smoke pulled his eyes back to the ground and he moved toward the fire, stooping low as he approached the burning rubble. He smiled through the thundering in his head at the idea that anything of consequence had happened in the countryside of the sleepy town of Oak Ridge. The smoke was doubtlessly some Tennessee redneck burning his trash, or kids playing with matches.

Patrick stood higher as he moved closer, and another volcano erupted in his skull, forcing him to his knees. The immobilizing pain took him into some far-off and unrecognizable world. He hugged the ground and held as still as possible while his mind went haywire with flashing images. The Special Forces had trained him well enough to take cover when he was injured.

Patrick lost track of time as the pain engulfed him and he could only crouch there waiting for his vision to clear enough for him to struggle to his feet. His head seared and he almost went down again. It took all his effort to put one foot in front of the other and move forward. Straining through the pain, he could see four burning wagons on a dirt road that ran along the edge of the forest. He was close enough to feel the heat. He knew he was in Tennessee, but something here hinted of war. He scanned the forest again.

Patrick looked past the blazing wagons at the sound of moaning. He forced himself to the ground and worked his way around the flames to where he could see into a clearing. He ducked into a depression as he got across the road, his head thundering, and rested for a moment to press on his temples.

When Patrick stood, he moved forward until he saw bodies on the ground. *Drug dealers?* Everyone knew there was methamphetamine in the hills of Tennessee. It crossed his mind that he should go back to his pack and call the police. But he heard another moan and any thought of retreat disappeared. He pressed forward and saw a dozen or so bodies in the short grass. They were dressed like Mennonites or Pennsylvania Dutch. Their faces were bloody and their bodies riddled with arrows.

Arrows?

Their bloody faces struck him as odd, and then he realized that they'd been scalped. Patrick had seen too many mutilated bodies in the Gulf to count, but taking a scalp was particularly brutal. Someone had dragged these bodies into the clearing and arranged them in a line. From the amount of blood, he suspected that some were alive when the scalping started. Patrick grimaced. Another moan; a woman's body shuddered on the ground.

"Help me," she whispered through a bloody mouth.

Patrick crouched to her. Bright red blood soaked the front of her dress around the arrow protruding from her chest. "Help me," she said again.

Patrick knelt beside her. "What happened?"

"Savages," she whispered. "Took the horses."

Patrick scanned the perimeter in response to this bizarre explanation. "Can I pull this out?" he asked, motioning to the arrow. "You'll be fine." She had already lost too much blood. Removing the arrow would help her breathe in the time she had left.

"Please," she said. Thick blood oozed from her skull.

"Where are you from?" he asked, studying the arrow, thinking about how he could remove it in one clean motion.

"We left Philadelphia but a week ago," she gasped, "for the Ohio country."

"You were taking these wagons to Ohio?"

"We had a grant. Please, I cannot breathe."

He wrapped his fingers gently around the shaft and slid it quickly out of her chest. Bright red spurted from the hole as she inhaled.

"God bless," she gasped. Patrick watched her shudder and die. He let the bloody shaft fall from his grasp and reached down to close her eyes. He had never gotten used to watching a human life end.

He heard a noise and instinctively ducked. There was only a hint of motion at first, barely visible through the smoke, but as the movement closed, Patrick registered a man on horseback. He had a camouflaged face and held a spear. Patrick knew the rider had seen him. He grabbed the bloody arrow and slunk back into the thick, choking smoke, pressing low to the ground, hoping he was out of the horse's path.

The rider thundered through the smoke and his spear missed Patrick by inches. Patrick sprang to his feet and snatched him from his horse as he rode, pulling him crashing to the ground. The attacker struggled in Patrick's arms to face him with a red and black striped face.

Warpaint?

The man threw his fists and elbows repeatedly as Patrick worked him into a jujitsu hold. Patrick squeezed until the attacker went limp. The man struggled until the end. Patrick felt no remorse in ending a man he knew was responsible for the death of innocent travelers. He eased his arms from the dead rider and pushed him away into a heap on the ground. He reached for the spear and crouched in place, but no one else came.

Patrick searched the body and found only a knife. He

tucked it into his shorts and returned to the trees to retrieve his mountain bike. When he pulled his phone from his saddlebag to call the police, there was no signal. This was as bizarre as anything else that was happening. Quantum phones work if there is a tower within a thousand miles, and towers are all over the East Coast.

Patrick straddled his bike and started pedaling down the country road. He had woken up in the dirt next to his bike, in a place with no phone signal, and killed a painted man on horseback. To top it off, this splitting headache was about to drive him mad.

PART I.

ENGLISHMAN

"Every man's life ends the same way. It is only the details of how he lived and how he died that distinguish one man from another." ~ Ernest Hemingway

CHAPTER 1.

REPRESENTATIVE MATTHEW MILLER

It was a game of cat and mouse, and the crew's agitation grew over the week that the ship had matched their speed and course. They'd catch enough wind to press their pursuer into the horizon only to see the vessel materialize, magically, hours later. The ship would disappear long enough to give them hope, but like Chinese water torture, it would pop unexpectedly into view and bring their anxiety rushing back.

Matt sat on the deck of the *Norfolk* reading his third book of the journey. The *Norfolk* was a twenty-gun, sixth-rate frigate with a complement of one hundred and sixty souls. Matt glanced up at the sounding of four bells to watch Captain Pearce, a tall grey man, shouting orders to the crew as he tried to harvest every bit of speed from the robust winds. The bells signaled the midpoint of the afternoon watch; the men on deck had another two hours before they'd be replaced.

The seamen jumped to the captain's commands as they crawled about the masts and rigging like so many ants to adjust the positioning of the weathered canvas sails. Matt had spent enough time assessing the captain to know he was smart, experienced, and respected. He trusted the captain's judgment.

Captain Pearce caught Matt watching him, stepped closer, and looked down at him with humor. "You don't appear vexed by this pirate nonsense, Mr. Miller," he said. "Perhaps you could do us the service of reading one of your books aloud to the crew if they impart such calm."

"I hardly think medicinal plants would interest them, Captain," Matt replied. "But if you think."

"Probably not," Pearce murmured gruffly. "Only the end of this dogged pursuit will set them at ease. This chase has lasted overlong by half. Better you should work on their swordplay." He gave a throaty chuckle.

The crew, and the marines, especially, had been fascinated by Matt's daily practice. Matt began every morning on the deck by moving through tae kwon do forms and finished each practice with the saber. He had vowed more than a decade ago, after his first disastrous fight in the colonies, never again to let his combat skills lapse. Matt had trained regularly since then, either by himself or with Richmond's most famous gentleman, dancer, and swordsman, Henry Duncan. Matt smiled when he thought back to the day that he met Henry, and the assumptions he'd made of a man who described London fashion in terms used only by the most flamboyant designers of the twenty-first century. Matt's preconceptions were almost immediately shattered, and he and Henry had become close friends.

"I was hoping that we wouldn't need to fight," Matt said to the captain. "They told me this was the fastest ship in the colonies."

"And so we believed," Pearce replied as he looked toward the tiny sails on the edge of the horizon.

"You're surprised by their speed," Matt observed.

The captain nodded. "They should have melted into the sea by now."

"They have a fast ship, too," Matt said, shrugging.

"Or a skillful fellow at their helm," Pearce replied. "Such a man flying a pirate banner vexes me heartily."

"You're sure it's a pirate ship?" Matt asked. They had never gotten near enough to see the ship's colors.

"I'll not let her close," Pearce answered. He went quiet as he looked off into the distance and up at the wispy blue skies. "It's a keen, clear wind. It'll hold."

Matt glanced up at the full sails, each stretched tight like the skin of a drum, and then down to the frothing sea that sped past them. The straining of the sailcloth and the whoosh of the rushing water told him they were moving fast. "What happens when the winds go?" he asked.

"The same for that piece of shite," Pearce replied. He looked again toward the chasing ship. "Ah! We shall drink the claret tonight, that's to be certain."

Matt smiled. "Excellent plan, sir," he replied, but Pearce had already walked away to shout more orders at his crew.

"Look alive, there!" Matt heard him yell.

****

The ship's officers and the surgeon gathered around the captain's table in full dress that night. Matt watched the porter fill his goblet. The wine was strong, and like the others sitting there, Matt was beginning to feel its effects. The jovial debate that jumped around the table was proof that

Pearce's instinct to pull the best bottles from his cabinet was correct. The *Norfolk's* officers seemed thankful for a diversion from the threat that loomed on the horizon.

Their respite ended abruptly, though, when First Lieutenant Daniel Jay entered the captain's mess to resume his place at the table. Jay took a drink from his full goblet, wiped his mouth, and measured their faces. He knew they expected him to speak, but he stared doggedly at his plate and finally took a savage bite of the butter-soaked chicken cooling there.

"What report from the deck?" Lieutenant John Creighton stammered. He was third in command and often at the helm or plotting their course.

Since the appearance of the pirate ship, the crew had split into three groups, as far as Matt could discern. The first was anxious to fight; the *Norfolk* couldn't stop fast enough. The second didn't pay much attention at all and went about their tasks as usual. The third group consisted of men who were visibly agitated and spent the days staring soberly aft. Creighton, Matt knew, was definitely in the third group.

"Report?" Jay asked. He picked up his goblet and drank.

"The pirates!" Creighton cried.

"That business?" Jay said nonchalantly after making Creighton wait for what seemed like an eternity. "Their topsails are lit by the moon."

"Why am I not surprised?" moaned Captain Pearce. He was contemplating his wine as he swirled it around in the goblet. He had been quiet during dinner, happy to relax and nod at the tales his men told as they emptied their glasses.

"We're a good ship with a damn fine crew," Pearce said. "God willing, we shouldn't make the acquaintance of our sea brothers any time soon, but should they come, so be it." He gave a satisfied grunt.

"With all due respect, Captain," Creighton said. "They're not brothers. They're pirate scum!"

"A bunch of drunken cutthroats, I suspect," Jay declared. "We should teach them the price of tangling with Virginia seamen. Our marines are itching for a fight."

"The *Norfolk* is the fastest ship in the colonies, but she has paid that price in cannon," the captain said. "Deliver our cargo and our passengers. Those are our orders, Mr. Jay." He looked at Matt. "We should not want Mr. Miller to miss his appointments in London."

The men turned to Matt and the room became quiet. Matt was a special guest among the passengers. Besides being a member of the Virginia House of Burgesses and having paid a premium for the largest guest cabin, he had spent much of his time on deck talking with the men, reading, or training. He knew most of the crew by name and moved easily among seamen and officers. The ability to endear himself to people of all stations was something he had learned from Benjamin Franklin. Adopting Ben's skills had helped Matt navigate many of the complexities that governed the eighteenth century.

Like Pearce, Matt had been happy to remain quiet. Matt scanned their fresh faces. "Don't let me be your excuse," he said. "I'm no longer a young man, but as you've seen, I prepare for a fight every day." He gave the table a knowing smile. "My fighting master was the toughest man I've ever met . . . aside from many of you, of course." A forced laugh went around the table. Matt could see that none of the men felt particularly potent in the present situation. "My master said there was no disgrace in avoiding a fight, especially when there's nothing to gain. If by mastery of the sea we can leave your drunken cutthroats behind, then we have defeated them."

"You'd join us if they *were* to come?" Jay asked.

Matt nodded. "You've seen me."

"Lettered men," Jay declared. "They choose talking o'er fighting, almost always."

"If we do our best to avoid this fight and it still comes, I'll be at your side."

"We'll fight if we must," Captain Pearce said. "For now, we'll stay ahead of 'em."

The table went quiet to ponder this. Midshipman James Carlton, a yellow-haired man with a reddish face, interrupted the silence. His voice was unsure until he found his pitch, but then his words rang clear.

'There once was a lofty ship, from . . . Virginia she did hail,
Blow high, blow low, and so sailed we.
From the . . . south of Hampton and she did sail,
A-cruising down the coast of the High Barbary.'

The sailor gave a clever smile at the changes he had made in their shanty. Captain Pearce took up the next verse in a voice that resonated like an old, slow sandstone wheel touching the dull blade of an ax. It took one line from the captain for the rest of the exuberant voices to join, lubricated with extra gulps from their goblets.

'Aloft there, aloft!' our jolly bosun cried.
Blow high, blow low, and so sailed we;
'Look ahead, look astern, look windward and a-lee,
A-cruising down the coast of the High Barbary.'

'There's naught upon the stern, sir, there's naught upon the lee.'
Blow high, blow low, and so sailed we;
'But there's a lofty ship to windward, and she's sailing fast and free,
A-cruising down the coast of High Barbary.'

'O hail her! O hail her!' our gallant captain cried.
Blow high, blow low, and so sailed we;
'Are you a man-o'-war or a privateer?' asked he,
'A-cruising down the coast of High Barbary?'

'O, I am not a man-o'-war nor privateer,' said he.
Blow high, blow low, and so sailed we;
'But I'm a salt-sea pirate a-looking for my fee,
A-cruising down the coast of High Barbary.'

'O, 'twas broadside to broadside a long time we lay,
Blow high, blow low, and so sailed we;
Until the . . . Norfolk shot the pirate's mast away.
A-cruising down the coast of High Barbary.'

'O quarter! O quarter!' those pirates then did cry.
   Blow high, blow low, and so sailed we;
   But the quarter that we gave them was we sunk them in
the sea,
   A-cruising down the coast of High Barbary.'

They broke out in roaring laughter and Matt joined heartily in their cheer. "Huzzah! Huzzah! Huzzah!"

CHAPTER 2.

MADAM GRACE MILLER

Grace stopped to gather herself for the next exercise. She used the silence to pick up a full strand of barley that lay at her feet. Hay bales hadn't been stored in this barn for many years, but hay still managed to find its way to the polished wooden practice floor. Grace suspected that an angel sat up there somewhere and flicked chaff from the rafters to remind them of who they were. She looked at the walls and then up at the roof and its skylights, hoping for some tangible proof of the God she knew permeated a building that had remained central to her family's life.

Grace watched the hypnotic flapping of the faded green strand of barley as she rolled it between her thumb and finger, and her mind filled with images from long ago, when her passion and fancy had been almost overwhelming. It was a time when an unconscious young stranger laid on a bench roughly where she stood now. She remembered feeling that there was something different about him, something unexplained.

Even her younger brothers had felt it. They told stories of this newcomer being from an exotic country, and their certainty grew as he walked the farm and spoke to them in his unrecognizable accent. Her youngest brother, Jonathan, thought he was a pirate running from the English, but her other brother, Jeb, guessed that he was a French deserter escaping the war on the frontier. Grace had scoffed. She was sure that the soft-handed young man was a drunkard.

It had unsettled her that her father put their family's fame at risk by bringing a drifter onto their farm, and she had told him as much. Back in those days, her father often made her very angry. She recalled her frustration when his only reaction was to shrug. Grace and her mother had grown used to Thomas Taylor's fits of compassion and his need for redemption for whatsoever he had done in his past. Much of the Taylors' silver went to help the poor, but this was the first time he had opened their home to a pauper. Drifters were common where they lived, and farmers mostly ignored them.

Grace was a haughty young girl then, and she stole into the barn to investigate the stranger as he lay sleeping. She tried to guess where he was from and why he was dressed so peculiarly. When he first awoke, this young intruder insisted he had been born and raised in Philadelphia, but it was clear he was hiding something. Grace saw how he looked at the simplest of things as if he was seeing them for the first time.

The more she interacted with the young man, though, the more she wished her brothers were right. Soon, Grace had joined Jonathan on his mission to discover the stranger's identity. She encouraged her youngest brother to visit Matthew Miller, as he called himself, every day and report back so they could clandestinely work through the possibilities of his existence. In a week, though, Jonathan forgot the alliance with his sister and embarked upon an original mission to help this stranger. Jonathan's reports disappeared almost entirely, which obliged Grace to discover the man's intentions on her own.

To Grace, there was nothing worse than a lettered city boy, and the young man irritated her right from the start. She saw how quickly he used words to win her family over. He was handsome in an odd sort of way, but so were the other suitors who came to the farm to ingratiate themselves to her father, and the great men who came to buy their horses.

There was much about her father that Grace admired, but his obsession with elevating their family by means of her marriage had put a wedge between them. Grace's vexation with her father deepened after her sister had passed and his ambitions fell entirely on her. She loved her father and knew he wanted what was best, but being a pawn in his pursuit of status was hard to accept. It made it worse, too, that even when Kathryn was alive, Grace had been singular in challenging their father. Her sister had been madly in love with a wealthy Virginia horseman, and there could have been no better family alliance in her father's eyes.

Grace was now far enough from those years to realize that her rebellion had made her drop her guard. A penniless commoner with a dark past was all she needed to teach her father a lesson. As hard as she tried now, though, she couldn't remember what lesson she'd been trying to teach. Grace had planned to keep the stranger at arm's length and flirt with him enough to concern her father, but she lost control of the situation while the uncouth young man worked on their farm and gained her family's favor. Even the dog, who had growled at the man inexplicably for an entire week, started to follow him around—and even slept with him in the barn.

Matthew Miller had refused to be the rascal she needed him to be. He had empty pockets but he didn't act poor; he worked hard despite the blisters he hid on his hands; hands that gave him away as someone who hadn't labored a day in his life. His white smile and his arrogant nature irritated her to her soul, and even more so when her family began conspiring against her to treat him as an equal. Who did he think he was, strolling proudly about their farm? What was he hiding?

****

Grace looked up from the strand of barley in her hands and crossed to the edge of the room to drop it into a small waste-bin by the rack of swords. She returned to the center of the floor and moved into her ready stance. With a shout, she stepped to the front target, went into a spinning sidekick, and connected squarely with the thick wool pad twelve inches above her head. The target teetered across the floor, rocking rigidly on its sand-filled pedestal. She snapped into motion, spun in a full circle, and drove the target back to where it started. The feeling of satisfaction she experienced every time she connected was something that remained unexplained.

Grace moved to the center of the polished floor and began her final flurry of kicks and punches against the targets and leather bags positioned about the barn. Afterwards, she stood there to catch her breath and reached down to feel the hardening bump in her belly. It would be awhile before the swelling was enough to restrict her movements. The thought of a new baby in her arms flooded her with joy and she felt her breasts flush. The mood was fleeting, though, and readily replaced with concern for everything she needed to do before the new arrival.

Plans always bounced endlessly around in her head after training, and even when they concerned some care, she welcomed them. She came to the barn in the late afternoons, shut and latched the big sliding door, changed into her white robe, wrapped the black belt around her waist, and practiced for an hour. She'd step through her poomsae and stalk the perimeter in imaginary combat to become what her husband described humorously as "the primal mother." On the best days, the feeling intoxicated her, and she fancied herself having the prowess to protect all the children of the world. Somewhere near the end of each workout, though, she shifted from enraged mother grizzly to anxious mother hen.

She felt her belly again for the movement that was likely still a month away. Grace hoped Matthew would return from England in time. Sometimes he was overly involved with the children, almost like a woman, and she wished merely that he'd go away, like when Grace hired a wet nurse for Katie. She still could not understand his aversion to something so ordinary. But despite her husband's stubbornness, Grace had come to depend on him during childbirth, when she was bruised, bloody, and hopelessly weak.

Grace touched her belly and looked upward again for the

angel in the rafters. She felt uneasy all of a sudden, like some chaos lay around the corner.

A knock on the barn door interrupted Grace's meditation and shocked her back into the present. Everyone knew she was not to be disturbed during practice, but a quick glance at the clock in the corner told her that she had been there long past her usual time.

"Yes," she called, letting some irritation into her voice.

"Madam," came the response.

Grace crossed to the door and opened it. "Yes?"

Rachael, the pretty young wife of Charles, their farm foreman, gazed quietly into Grace's eyes for a long moment before she spoke. "With child again, madam?"

Grace peered back at her, surprised. "Is it that noticeable?"

Rachael offered a knowing smile. "The Jefferson party is here," she said. Her smile turned to something else.

Grace ignored the scrutiny and checked the clock again. "He was expected this evening."

Rachael shrugged. "Mr. Jefferson can be . . . enthusiastic."

Grace cut a glance at Rachael, but the judgment had left the younger woman's face. "Delay him until I can bathe and dress for dinner."

"Yes, madam."

CHAPTER 3.

SEA DOG

Matt opened his eyes to the dim grey light sifting through the porthole of his stateroom. Despite overdrinking the night before, his sleep had been heavy and refreshing. The tossing waves usually woke him many times during the night.

Calm seas!

Matt jumped from his hammock in stocking feet to the horizontal wooden floor. Until today, there hadn't been a time since their journey began that he didn't need to grab the rail for support after leaving his hammock. He looked out the porthole to see the *Norfolk* stopped in the water and engulfed in a dense grey fog. He pulled his shoes on, grabbed a jacket, and rushed topside, surprised that there hadn't been a call to quarters. He stepped outside into a grey soup that obscured the entire deck. The mist made it difficult to tell whether any crewmen were about at all.

Matt scanned the sea looking for a shadow of the pirate ship, but he couldn't even see the water. He pulled his jacket on against the cold wet air and made his way to the quarterdeck. The captain was looking through a folding telescope as he turned on the deck. He and his first lieutenant put their fingers to their lips in unison. Neither said a word until Matt was directly under the station.

"Top of the morning, Mr. Miller," First Lieutenant Jay said in a low voice. "Capital you could join us."

"No one woke me," Matt said in a hushed tone. "How long have we been stopped?"

"Three hours, thereabouts," Jay replied. "Since sunrise, anyway."

"Shouldn't there be an alarm or something?"

The captain took the telescope from his eye and looked down at him. "Let them finish their berth," he answered. "Once we beat quarters, all hands until the wind returns."

Matt crept up the steps to the quarterdeck. "Any sight of the pirate ship?"

"No," Captain Pearce replied, shrugging. "They could be next to us in this fog, and we'd not know until their hooks were set."

Matt looked around in alarm.

Jay snickered. "Our heading is unchanged," he said. "Not likely they'd circle full 'round us." He pointed to port.

Matt followed the man's finger. He smiled, thinking of how he had once relied on Google Maps to tell him where he was going. Now he was with men who navigated an entire ocean with only a clock, a compass, and a sextant. Finding London after ten weeks in the open sea seemed nearly impossible with the simple instruments they possessed.

"Mr. Jay," Pearce whispered. "Pick three men. Take a jolly to see what you can see."

"Aye, aye, sir," Jay replied. "Have some rowing in you, Mr. Miller?"

Captain Pearce shook his head. "Paying passenger."

"With all respect, Captain," Matt replied. "I'd appreciate accompanying Mr. Jay."

Pearce nodded. "Very well, carry on." He looked at Jay. "Return him safe and dry."

"Some salt in his clothes would do him well, sir."

"Safe and dry, Mr. Jay," Pearce repeated. "And not a sound."

Jay motioned for Matt to follow him across the deck to enlist two seamen.

"Porter . . . Grey," Jay whispered, motioning to the young men. "We're taking a jolly to find our pirates." The crewmen stopped what they were doing and followed Jay to a longboat rigged to the side of the ship. Both sailors were boys in Matt's eyes.

"They are strong lads, Mr. Miller," Jay said, noticing Matt's expression. "They'll take care of the rowing. Pray, are your eyes sharp enough to scout?"

"Good enough," Matt replied.

They watched the young sailors lower the boat into the water. Matt searched his memory for this event, but there was nothing. It had been a long time since he'd been able to see the future with any sort of clarity. He concentrated again, desperate, and felt a hint of connected images and shadows. Then, suddenly, there it was: a dark ship in the fog flying pirate colors, rushing toward him at full speed.

"Mr. Miller!" Jay said. "Are you ill?"

Jay's voice stunned Matt back to the present. Matt had

no idea how long he had been lost in his vision. "Not ill, Mr. Jay," Matt said. "Only thinking. Let there be no doubt that this is a pirate ship. We will confront them before day's end."

"They are leagues away," one of the young sailors said.

"They are as lost in this soup as us," the other added.

"There's some truth in it," Jay corrected. "Arm yourselves."

"Aye, aye, sir," they replied. The young men scurried off.

Jay motioned to Matt. "Best take your sword. I intend only to scout, but I too feel we'll meet these rascals before the light has gone. My mind is heavy with it."

Matt nodded and hurried back to his cabin for his sheathed saber and a knife that he slipped onto his belt. When he returned topside, the two sailors had already descended the rope ladder into the boat. Jay waved Matt over to help lower a cache of oilcloth-wrapped muskets down to the jolly. Once ready, the sailors held the boat steady against the hull of the *Norfolk* while Matt and Jay climbed down. Matt felt a twinge of regret at having left his Walther back in Virginia, but there was no way to use a modern handgun without arousing suspicion.

Matt dropped onto the rowboat, steadied himself, and lowered himself onto a bench that was wet with fog. He tried to sweep the water away with his hand and Jay threw him a cloth.

"No sense soaking your arse all at once," he said. "We may be rowing for a while."

Matt nodded thanks and wiped the bench. He sat down

and checked his knife, then set the sword at his feet within reach. It was a quality weapon, made of the hardest steel, a gift from his instructor, Henry Duncan. It was as familiar to him as his own hand.

The two young men sat one behind the other in the middle of the boat and each grabbed a set of oars. Jay motioned them to be quiet as they dipped the paddles into the water and began rowing away from the port side of the *Norfolk*. After a few minutes of rowing, the *Norfolk* disappeared into the fog on the smooth, glassy waters of the Atlantic. Even in the company of his three shipmates, Matt found the desolation and loneliness of the open sea overwhelming.

CHAPTER 4.

OVERLONG

Grace was walking Thomas Jefferson through her unfinished home, showing him the renovations they'd completed since he last visited Miller Grange. When they entered the library, Jefferson stepped to the canvas-covered shelves, then looked over his shoulder at Grace.

"Go ahead," she said. She could feel Jefferson linger as he considered her in his backward stare.

He lifted the canvas to take stock of the titles and a bright smile filled his face. "Are they all this impressive?" he asked with respect.

"Some," Grace replied. She fought back a smirk and kept herself from shaking her head until he had turned back to the shelves. He was leaking charm again, and she reminded herself as she had many times in the past not to succumb. Rachael's assessment of Jefferson was entirely accurate, and her suspicion was justified. Jefferson's enthusiasm was sincere, but flattery and allure always accompanied his fervor. He managed to seduce everyone around him.

Jefferson moved his hand across the books' spines, touching them as he named them. "Marcus Aurelius . . . and you have the Englishmen. Locke, Bacon, Newton." He moved to the next shelf. "Another for the Scots. Frances Hutcheson, Adam Smith—I've heard John Witherspoon speak." He pulled down *The Treatise of Human Nature* by David Hume. He looked at Grace with his flecked grey eyes. "Are you familiar?"

"'Tis *my* library, after all," she replied.

Jefferson opened the volume. "With Hume?"

She shrugged.

"Does reason govern human behavior?"

"Men think so," Grace replied. "Hume believed 'twas passion."

"And you?"

Grace smiled.

Jefferson returned it to the shelf and pulled down another volume. "Speaking of passion," he said as he held it for her to read the cover: *The Complete Works of William Shakespeare.*

"My husband oft quotes Lord Hamlet," Grace said. "I sometimes question his obsession."

"Certainly, Lord Hamlet is in almost everything he says and does."

"You see tragedy in my husband?" Grace asked, intrigued.

"Humanity and its suffering," Jefferson declared. "It frustrates him."

"As it does everyone," she replied.

Jefferson shrugged. "Some. Most have their families or their religion. They are happy, but who knows?"

Grace looked at him questioningly.

Jefferson frowned. "Don't pretend that the scriptures comfort *you* or your husband."

Grace raised her eyebrows. "Matthew believes they should," she replied. "He becomes caught, it seems, on every word. But no, they almost never comfort him."

"Maybe Lord Hamlet was scowling at the Bible as he turned the pages and exclaimed, 'Words, words, words!'" Jefferson smiled. "Matthew would cure the human experience if he could only discover the potion in his laboratories. He's an alchemist in his manner, but surely you've seen that."

"He oft insists that he's no wizard," Grace replied with humor.

Jefferson glanced down at the book in his hands and grinned slyly. "The lady doth protest too much, methinks."

"My husband's medicines have saved many, but it has not been through magic or consultation with the stars."

Jefferson again studied her face. She turned away from the seduction she saw repeated in his eyes. "I've heard him pray," he said.

"You do not pray, Mr. Jefferson?"

"Not so specifically," he answered. "And certainly not to cure humanity of ills that can never be cured."

Jefferson hefted the leather-bound book in his hands and flipped the pages as if he was verifying that the plays were all in there. "Are you familiar?"

"Not so much as my husband or father," Grace replied. "For Father during his last years, 'twas Henry the Fifth," she explained. "I fancy though that sometimes he memorized it less for his own passion and more to foil my husband's ruminations."

"You make me jealous not to have been akin to such a duel," Jefferson replied, "though I'd not have wished to take sides." He smiled and again gazed profoundly at her.

Grace was willing to meet his gaze long enough to map the crinkled lines around his eyes that screamed intellect, and to discern the hazel flecks that interrupted their grey. Maybe she *was* uncomfortable with his stare, the one that screamed of impropriety and woke her body unconsciously and unexpectedly.

Her husband's confidence in Jefferson had never been justified in her mind. Matthew was either willing to ignore or unable to see the insecurity in a man who judged his worth by those around him. Grace saw it as Jefferson's greatest weakness and the one thing that held his powers of seduction at bay. There was no denying Jefferson's abilities when it came to ladies, though; he had been at the center of at least two scandals that Grace knew of. His recent marriage to Martha Wales Skelton had done nothing to shrink the net of allure he cast over everyone around him. He was tall, handsome, and charming, and Grace fancied that more chaste women than she could fall victim to his captivating grin.

Grace went to speak again, but Jefferson put his finger up to silence her. He paged back through the book and gave her a challenging smirk. "Men of a few words are . . . ?"

"The best men," she finished.

He paged again. "Every subject's duty is the king."

"But every subject's soul is his own."

Jefferson paged through the book a third time. "This above all."

"To thine own self be true."

"You know the bard well."

"You did pick the most elementary passages."

"Your intellect astounds me."

"For a woman, you surely meant to add," she replied.

"I said what I meant."

She saw, maybe, a hint of respect in his expression.

"I know now of your father's and husband's passions, but still nothing of yours. Which play is *your* favorite?"

Grace held his eye, thinking that it would take more than this simple creature and his two years at William and Mary to make her yield to a duel of wills. "Of course 'tis *The Taming of the Shrew*," she answered.

He looked back at her for an explanation.

Grace mustered her most seductive look. "I'm overwhelmed by Katherine's willingness to surrender to the passions of a charming, smart, and commanding man." She smiled heartily and saw Jefferson's fair complexion blush. She was immediately satisfied and ashamed of what she had just done. He'd not soon patronize her again, but it made her question why she'd had to demonstrate anything at all.

Jefferson recovered and the smile returned to his face. When the moment between them had passed, she motioned for him to follow her to the dining room and she waited for him to join her. Jefferson reached up, made a space for the volume, and slid it solidly back onto the shelf. He spent one last moment scanning the books as if he was hoping to discover some clue there. He glanced up to the ceiling for longer than a moment, almost as if he was saying a prayer, before he turned to follow Grace to the dining room.

CHAPTER 5.

WHERE'S WILLIAM?

The Taylors were conversing around the dinner table when Grace and Thomas Jefferson entered the room. Everyone stood to greet their visitor and Jefferson moved around the table, kissing and shaking hands. It was clear that he relished his role as a son of Virginia. Much like Matt, he had built his fame during the past couple of years as a firm advocate for the colony. Jefferson was a flirt, to be sure, but he was also a charming dinner guest, and Grace suspected that the two were connected. Either way, he was a friend to her family, and much to Grace's chagrin, Scout liked him.

Servants in livery brought trays from the kitchen and heaped each plate with roast beef, carrots, and boiled potatoes. After they had passed the bread, Grace said, "Mr. Jefferson, would you do the honor?"

Jefferson nodded, bowed his head and began to speak.

Almighty God, Who has given us this good land for our heritage, we humbly beseech Thee,
We desire to prove ourselves a people mindful of Thy favor.

Bless our land with honorable ministry, sound learning,
and pure manners.
Save us from violence, discord, and confusion,
Save us from pride and arrogance, and from every evil
way.
Defend our liberties, and fashion us into one united
people,
Though we are the multitude brought hither out of many
kindreds and tongues.
In a time of prosperity, fill our hearts with thankfulness,
But, in the day of trouble, suffer not our trust in Thee to
fail;
We ask all of this through Jesus Christ our Lord.
Amen.

Tears welled up in Grace's eyes. She looked up and saw that her mother was also wiping away tears. "Mr. Jefferson," Grace said, "you honor our table."

"This fine estate and family deserve no less," Jefferson proclaimed.

"I do not know how anyone can resist such flattery," Grace's mother, Mary, said. "I too appreciate your blessing."

"The pleasure is mine, madam," Jefferson replied. "I am honored to be invited to dine and singularly thankful not to suffer eating alone at my estate. Speaking of, where are William and his lovely family? I expected to debate my favorite Tory."

"We rarely see him," Jonathan replied, scowling. "He's

across the ocean, no doubt long since given up the title of Virginian."

"Do not judge your relation so harshly," Jefferson warned. "The Old Dominion runs deep in him. In the end, though, we are all British subjects."

"And yet no Virginian sits in Parliament," Jonathan replied.

"Maybe your brother can, someday, be such a man."

"He'd have no use for us if that time ever comes."

"Jonathan!" Mary exclaimed. "What would your father say?"

"He'd tell my brother to stay away from the bloody English and return to his farm."

"Jonathan!" Grace repeated. "We have company."

"Mr. Jefferson's aware of my brother's loyalties. 'Twill be no surprise to him." Jonathan sat back in his chair and raised his hand to wave them off. "William shall follow his passions and so shall I."

"Let us change the subject, then," Jefferson offered. "How are Richmond's coffee houses these days?"

"They are the only places where verity can be heard," Jonathan replied.

"And which verity is this?" Jefferson asked.

"The British troops we support are a pox on this land."

"The Crown believes differently. 'Tis certain we've not managed to muster any sort of militia to provide for our own defense."

"A militia is a simple thing. I am sore weary of old nobles, thousands of miles away, telling me what is best.

I've had my fill of soldiers on this farm. It makes me ill to gaze upon them."

"I'm acquainted with many of these old nobles," Jefferson said. "They are lettered and influential, and 'twill take an equally lettered treatise to shake their hold on our affairs. When do you begin at William and Mary?"

"I have not decided whether I will go," Jonathan replied.

Mary gasped. "After all Dr. Franklin did to gain your admittance?" she demanded.

"I never wanted to go," Jonathan declared. "I've more to do for the cause."

"And which cause is this?" Grace asked.

"Independence," Jonathan replied. "Virginia and the other American colonies are destined. God has ordained it!"

"Do not speak so simply of such things," Jefferson replied. "The laws that have suffered this family to attain their prosperity should not be cast aside for light and transient causes."

"And if the laws are unjust?" Jonathan asked.

"'Tis rare, indeed, to encounter a fellow who has run afoul of the law who does not think he has been incriminated unjustly. A wise man would lay a new foundation before abolishing laws that function better than most. Else new chains will quickly replace those he has broken. Your greatest prosecution, this day, should be to further your education. Know what other men have already proposed."

Jonathan rolled his eyes and resumed eating. Jefferson, too, looked down at his plate.

"I oft wish to talk only of art, music, fine horses, or maybe theatre at this table," Grace said, laughing.

Jefferson gave her a knowing smile. "Your husband has accepted a role in the governing of the colony. Discussing statecraft in the Miller household should be as natural as breathing the air. I am reminded—how are your plans coming for hosting the royal governor?"

"The invitations will be sent with the post tomorrow," Grace replied. "It should be a splendid occasion." She glanced at her younger brother, but Jonathan continued to inspect his food.

CHAPTER 6.

SIR PATRICK

There seemed to be no end to the obstructionism the average English official would commit in the name of bureaucracy. Patrick Ferguson reminded himself to keep his cool as he watched an impossibly young inspector crawling through his shipments. Patrick had no desire to intimidate some underling who was simply trying to do his job; he knew the Crown needed to squeeze every bit of revenue out of English businesses to stay afloat. Some of its procedures made sense, but often, like today, they were complete and utter nonsense. The only consolation was that Patrick could watch this economic debacle from the sidelines; he'd sold all his stock positions at the peak and was entirely invested in hard assets.

"Can I help you with anything?" Patrick asked.

"I think I have it, Sir Patrick," the young man replied. "We're almost finished."

"I'm not sending these crates anywhere else," Patrick said. "You know that, do you not?"

"Sorry, yes, sir," the man replied. "Still, they must be stamped and recorded. You may speak to Lord Cantor if you believe there is some impropriety."

"My shipping manager has already spoken to Cantor,"

Patrick said. "I didn't believe him when he told me how long this would take."

"I beg your pardon, sir." The inspector motioned for Patrick to step back so he could check another crate.

"Gah!" Patrick said, moving aside. "Don't let me delay you."

The inspector moved among the crates, stamping each one with a fist-sized red crown, then painting a number under the crown and recording it in a ledger next to the crate's contents. Patrick eventually walked away. He was already late for his meeting with his secretary and chief foreman, Nathan Trent. Anyway, a delayed shipment of muskets didn't matter in the scheme of things. His factory was running at full capacity; machines were rolling off the assembly line at a rapid pace. No bureaucrat could divert him from his goals.

****

When Patrick got back to his office, he began checking items off the list he'd prepared at the start of the day. His plans were at the very edge of fruition. He'd built a production line that would make Henry Ford envious. When it became necessary, he'd convert his factories and turn out weapons that would fuel British power and bring about a peace to last a thousand years. The inspector he'd just met was a reminder, though, of his present and future struggles. Bureaucracy and nepotism remained his biggest hurdle.

Damn nobles!

His breech-loading flintlock alone should have been enough to gain audiences with the most influential men in the military, but jealous war profiteers had thwarted him at every turn. Patrick did his best to ferret them out, but even he could not predict the sway these men held in the British government and how quickly they could ostracize an outsider. They had acted decisively and destroyed his character among the top brass.

Repairing his reputation had been difficult even with the money he was willing to spend. He knew, though, that it was only a matter of time before they'd be buying his weapons and his influence. In the interim, he collected a cadre determined to run an empire with the power to change the world. Despite some superficial reservations, Nathan Trent was of the same stock as Patrick Ferguson. He was the perfect man to staff Ferguson Industries, which would soon be able to bend the government to its will and help Great Britain lead Europe into a thousand years of peace and prosperity. There'd be no world wars, and the globe would finally see its utopia.

Patrick took a moment to rub his headache away and then reached for the mail. The second letter he opened was a report from his spies: They were pleased to inform him that Mr. Matthew Miller had booked passage on an American frigate, the *Norfolk*, sailing out of Hampton Roads, and would be arriving in London very soon.

The thought filled Patrick with anticipation. Since he started the treatments, he had precious few surprises left in life, but there were four people who were only shadows, even in his most intense visions. One shadow, he knew, was somewhere close and another would arrive in London within the month. The game was afoot.

CHAPTER 7.

NATHAN TRENT

Nathan Trent and Patrick Ferguson met in Patrick's office and settled down on either side of Patrick's large mahogany desk.

"Well, Mr. Trent, who do we have today?" Patrick asked.

"Former captain of an East India merchant vessel. Lost his commission six months ago. He'd be a capable supervisor of the line."

"Details," Patrick insisted. He reached up and rubbed his temples.

Nathan would wait until Patrick was looking straight at him. His boss's eyes had glazed, and he was somewhere far away. Nathan knew how to navigate powerful, idiosyncratic men and had become singularly wealthy based on his own parts. He gave his masters precisely what they wanted, exactly when they wanted it.

"He's comfortable with command," Nathan replied once his boss's eyes had cleared. "He never suffered that they took his commission."

"You don't like them much," Patrick said.

"Don't like who, sir?" Nathan replied softly. He prided himself on his ability to disguise his emotions, and it perplexed him when Patrick saw right through his mask. Sometimes it was as if the man knew what he was thinking before he knew it himself.

"You don't like the East India folks," Patrick clarified, looking at Nathan expectantly.

Nathan was recruiting new men every week for Ferguson Industries, and one in three had come from the company. "Distasteful manner about them," Nathan replied. "Too entitled. I'm vexed to fill our ranks with mercenaries. They'll make their gold any way they can and damn the consequences."

"They have an air," Patrick said. "I will allow."

Nathan nodded. "You can only employ so many of them before they corrupt the lot."

"Shattered ambitions. They'll not put a period to it until they taste fortune again."

"I know their designs, but ultimately, it'll be destructive."

"No doubt."

"You fear this too?"

Patrick half-nodded. "For now, we should be ready to take advantage of their ambition without placing ourselves at risk."

"I understand, Sir Patrick," Nathan finally said.

"That all, then?"

"We must discuss the profit report."

Patrick stared back silently.

"Can our manufacturing endeavor to lose money for three years?" Nathan asked.

"Let me worry about that."

"Our hiring is precipitous, and at too high of a wage."

"I can operate for years without a profit."

"It's not certain why you'd want to," Nathan replied.

Patrick waved him off. "Hire ambitious men at the going rate and let me worry about the cost. Anything else?"

"No, sir."

Patrick opened his desk drawer, pulled out a heavy leather purse, and handed it to Nathan. Its weight squelched Nathan's other questions.

"Thank you, sir," Nathan said, bowing slightly.

Patrick smiled. "Hire this new man. Ferguson Enterprises should be filled with such men."

"Yes, sir."

Patrick spoke as Nathan put his hand on the door to leave. "If Mr. Hawke is out there, you can tell him to come in."

Nathan opened the door to an anteroom that was almost the size of Patrick's office and closed the door behind him. He saw Hawke, an enormous man stuffed into a wool suit and silk stockings, sitting in a padded chair that he had pulled from a nearby writing desk. Nathan said, "He's ready for you now."

Hawke slowly rose to his feet as he glared heavily into Nathan's face. He always filled Nathan with trepidation, but Nathan did his best to meet him with as much nonchalance as he could muster. Hawke slipped past him without saying a word and let himself into Patrick's office.

Nathan pulled the chair back to the writing desk and sat down when he heard the click of the door. He hoped to complete his notes and retire before he heard Hawke count one.

CHAPTER 8.

THE BLACK SHIP

Matt lost track of time as Tom Porter and Ebenezer Grey rowed hypnotically through the smooth, cold Atlantic. They'd bring the boat to full speed, stop to let it glide silently through the water, scan the fog for shadows, and listen for sounds through the grey mist. Their oars would touch the water again before the boat stalled and the cycle of row, glide, and observe would repeat. First Lieutenant Jay, kneeling in the front of the craft, checked his compass, whispered corrections to their course, blinked, and peered ahead into the fog.

Matt couldn't see beyond Jay, so he focused on listening. He was the first to signal. The oars came out of the water and the four men froze, holding their breath as Matt cupped his hand to his ear again. The sounds that carried in the fog would have been mistaken for the splashing of waves, but not today, when the water was a sheet of glass.

Jay motioned for them to stay low as they silently drifted forward. He pointed with two fingers to the faint outline off their port bow, then put one finger to his lips. The soft sounds of a man calling out strokes were distinct under the layer of fog. Jay pulled a collapsible telescope from a case on his belt and fixed it upon the tiny dark shadow that appeared between concealing strands of drifting grey fog.

"By God, that's it," Jay whispered. "Capital, Mr. Miller."

"Colors?" Matt asked quietly.

"Matters not," Jay replied, taking his eye from the brass tube. "What do you make of her?" He handed the telescope to Matt.

Matt could just make out her masts and the front of her bow. She was headed straight for them. There was a wide smudge in front of the ship that first presented itself as an illusion in the shimmering fog, but then became two long-boats. The vessels were far enough away to fade in and out of the flowing grey mist. "Are they towing her?" Matt asked softly.

"Seems," Jay said.

"We should return to warn the *Norfolk*."

"Not until we come around her," Jay said. "She's big. We want her guns."

Matt looked out into the distance and estimated the cir-cumference they'd need to row to have a view of the ship's side. It seemed impossibly long. "How're we gonna do that?" he whispered.

Jay pointed off to the starboard of the approaching ship like it was no big deal, but Matt wasn't convinced.

"She'll be on the *Norfolk* before we have a chance to warn them," Matt said.

Jay waved him off. "They've been at it all night, and it's church work. They'll come close and wait out the fog." He stooped to direct Porter and Grey where to row and to do it quietly. They set their oars in the water, doing their best to break and leave its surface with a smooth and silent transition. Jay put the glass back up to his eye.

Matt reached down to touch the scabbard of his saber where it lay on the floor. His senses, supercharged with adrenaline, made the rhythm of the oars as loud as a steam locomotive. Jay handed Matt his telescope to get his compass from his pocket and Matt assessed their assailant. They could almost count her cannons now. Porter and Grey let the boat glide and Matt dropped the telescope to listen. The fog hissed as it melted into the water.

"They've stopped rowing," Matt said.

"Resting," Jay replied. He checked his compass and looked back in the direction of the *Norfolk*.

Matt raised the telescope to his eye. "We're getting there. I can almost see her starboard."

"They've changed course?" Jay whispered, surprised.

"I'll be able to count her guns in a moment."

Jay snatched the telescope from Matt's eye. Matt scowled at him, but Jay already had the brass tube to his face. There were flashes on the horizon.

"Down!" Jay shouted as he turned and dived into his shipmates, nearly capsizing the boat. The frantic boom was followed by cannonballs that whistled all around them and dropped into the water. The jolly rocked violently.

"Fifth-rate!" Jay shouted. "She's turned on us. Take us out of here!" He pointed back at the *Norfolk*. The boys grabbed their oars in a panic and were rowing full speed almost immediately.

Matt stooped as Jay scanned aft through the glass.

"Down!" he yelled again, and they all dropped to the wet floor of the rowboat. The cannonballs from this second broadside fell short, but a few skipped across the water to splash close behind them.

"Look alive," Jay commanded. The young sailors sat up and resumed their frenzied rowing as swells from the broadside rocked the boat. The pirate ship was already melting into the fog. They heard the cannons fire twice more, but the splashes fell harmlessly into the sea. The fog engulfed them again. There was silence except for the heavy breathing of the young men and the slosh of their oars on the water.

"How big?" Matt asked finally.

"Thirty-six guns," Jay replied.

"Can we match her?"

Jay shook his head. "We should run."

CHAPTER 9.

THERAPIST

Patrick's head was searing with pain after Hawke left, but it gave him nothing but smiles. Hawke had earned his gold. The rush of visions hit Patrick like a tidal wave, and he sloshed and rolled in a froth of events and people. He had long since learned to surf the waves; it was a productive session filled with images he expected to see again. An anomaly on the horizon taunted him, though. He was sure it was Matthew Miller, and he was impatient to meet this shadow.

"Mrs. Crane," he called from his desk.

The woman came bounding in, quill in hand. Patrick liked this about her; she was all business.

"I want a grand party at the manor," he said. "Create a stir."

"We'll want a few weeks to plan," she said. "How big?"

"Fill it."

"Pretty penny," she said. "Anyone in particular?"

Patrick waved his hand. "The American delegation. Whoever's in London."

She looked at him knowingly. "Tell me who, specifically."

"You know me too well," he proclaimed. "Benjamin

Franklin. Franklin is expecting a guest from America, a man named Matthew Miller, who should be strongly encouraged to attend the party. None should know they are singular in any way."

She nodded. "The invitations will go out and our agents will create a stir. Do you have a theme?"

The anticipation was almost too much to bear. Patrick knew he would challenge the unknown for as long as possible.

"A masquerade!"

CHAPTER 10.

SARAH MORRIS MIFFLIN

"It's at the home of Sir Patrick," Thomas Mifflin said, showing his wife the invitation she had somehow known to expect. "That estate that fascinates you so." He scrutinized her face. "Do you find his wealth attractive?"

"Husband," Sarah said. "I am proud of the life you have made for me."

"And yet I have not surpassed the success enjoyed by the widow Morris and her beautiful daughter."

"'Tis only a matter of time," Sarah replied.

He looked at her with doubt and she stepped forward to kiss him passionately. She lingered at his lips. "The widow Morris's daughter cherishes much more about you than your considerable success, and 'twill still be thus." It was the truth, and she hoped that her husband was reassured. She respected and loved him deeply, and had no admiration whatsoever for Patrick Ferguson. In fact, she wanted to scream when she thought about the trouble he could cause, but there was no way to explain that to her husband.

Patrick Ferguson's estate had long played an active part in her dreams. She'd gotten better at interpreting her visions of the future and sometimes could predict events almost perfectly. She considered this a victory over the universe that had thrust her through a wormhole to colonial America against her will. Unfortunately, the events that involved Patrick were cloudy. Her dreams swirled around him like colors of paint mixing in a can. She had filled entire journals with the stories she saw in her head, but when it came to Patrick, her visions were clear as mud.

Matt Miller was less cloudy, so she spent weeks piecing together his future in an attempt to define Patrick's, but nothing was certain. Lately, too, some shadow had crossed in front of them all. It was only a glimpse, but it made her suspect that someone else had been caught in the reactor accident, someone they hadn't met. The ambiguity had driven her crazy enough to convince her husband that she should accompany him on his trip to London so she could "help his business."

Thomas Mifflin's import-export business relied heavily on English traffic, and efforts to strengthen his partnerships were essential. When she wasn't busy with the Morris bakeries, Sarah had demonstrated her worth on a number of occasions by working through the wives and families of his associates. She took supreme satisfaction in being a dutiful wife in public—then shepherding her sisters aside to discuss the possibilities of a ladies' future in a burgeoning America.

The future she talked about was one that many eighteenth-century women hoped for but feared to discuss. Wives and mothers, once they were comfortable enough to speak, inundated her with their dreams for their daughters. It satisfied Sarah to plant a seed of constructive discontent in their minds, but she also enjoyed the benefit of their wisdom. Older women, especially, taught Sarah about religion, marriage, and family, and she envied their keen sense of community. Friendships with other women fulfilled them in a way that had been foreign to Sarah and her mother.

"We shall want costumes," Thomas said, interrupting Sarah's thoughts.

"Costumes?"

"It's a masquerade."

Nothing in her visions had told her to expect a costume party, which was vexing. Sarah and her mother had befriended Patrick Ferguson in Philadelphia a decade earlier when he found them using the same cell phone they all brought from the future. He had left their home suddenly and returned to England to escape his gambling enemies. It took Sarah days to realize he'd stolen her backpack containing four college textbooks. She'd had maybe a dozen visions since then predicting that harm would come from these books.

The theft didn't bother Sarah much at the time; she didn't need textbooks to build a bakery business. Matt Miller was the one who had made her realize the danger of them falling into the wrong hands. Patrick, an Englishman from her own time with delusions of grandeur and notions of preventing the American Revolution, was the epitome of the wrong hands.

Sarah had hoped to melt into Philadelphia society and forget about Patrick forever, but any chance of that disappeared when Benjamin Franklin walked into their lives. As Ben and her mother grew closer, Ben became a fixture at the Morris bakeries and coffee shops across the city. His fame alone was enough for them to draw politicians, merchants, and community leaders in Philadelphia.

Ben, a lightning rod for discourse, was a staunch Loyalist who always argued the Crown's case. It had seemed natural one day for Sarah to listen to one of these heated exchanges. She met the men's frowns with the excuse that she needed to get off her feet; they swiftly forgot about her as they argued the issues of the day. When the stunningly handsome and passionate Thomas Mifflin stood up to state his case for an autonomous American government, Sarah's eyes filled with stars.

They had been married five years now and she feared for their lives almost every day. Her love for Thomas made her rue the day she let her guard down and allowed Patrick Ferguson to steal her books, one of which was entitled *The American Experiment*. It contained names, dates, and actions of every man and woman essential to the American Revolution. It told of acts of treason punishable by death. She couldn't remember her husband being explicitly named in the book, but she knew many of their friends were.

Sarah's intent to join her husband in London was more than fact-finding. She was determined to seek out Patrick Ferguson and retrieve her textbooks. She was prepared to do whatever it took.

CHAPTER 11.

THOMAS MIFFLIN

Thomas Mifflin studied his wife while he held her waist in his hands. Some days she seemed the opposite of everything he was supposed to think attractive in a woman, and yet she lit a fire in his very soul. She was two women: one in public, another behind closed doors. The public Sarah was a dutiful wife and socialite who talked of trivial things and endeared herself to all. She attended quilting parties and organized events to raise silver to care for the orphans of Philadelphia.

Behind closed doors, though, she was a tigress. Thomas knew she was better educated than himself, and that she could go toe to toe with any man on those rare occasions when she dropped her façade. It was only he, her mother, and Benjamin Franklin who knew the real Sarah. He learned of her close connection with Ben one day when he overheard Sarah letting loose with him about an indiscretion involving William Allen, the mayor of Philadelphia. Thomas had proved her often, since, by asking detailed questions about current events, and it was rare when there wasn't an advanced understanding to be found in her answers.

Sarah leaned against him in her thin silk dress and he

thought of their marriage bed. She had taken him on journeys of marital bliss that he durst not hint of to his fellows in the pub. He knew Sarah had a secret. Despite her attempts to hide her intellect from the world, her uncommon letters were unmistakable, made the more secretive by some pact she had with Ben and her mother. Thomas had asked Sarah about her connection with Ben before, and she had reacted the same every time. She'd pull him close, kiss him passionately, and explain that it as an old family issue that concerned her father. "And you want not to fret," she'd say. "'Tis nothing that would bring us disgrace."

This was usually enough, and his suspicions would fade rapidly for the simple reason that he felt her love. He could see the adoration in her eyes when he stood to speak at the Philadelphia gatherings. Sarah's affection was so overwhelming, her physical presence so intoxicating; the taste of her lips drove him so mad with hunger and the blessing of her intellect so enthralled him that he vowed repeatedly never to care about her past. Only their future mattered.

Sarah slept fitfully on some nights, though, and it was after these nights of tossing and turning that she'd spend the morning writing in her diaries. She had asked him not to read them since they were merely the "trivial musings of a woman." He had mostly kept his pledge. There were times, though, when she was away, that he'd pull them from their hiding spot behind the dining room shelves.

Even knowing her as he did, he had been surprised to see half the pages filled with elaborate diagrams, pictures, and phrases connected by lines. There were representations of daily events, some names he recognized and others he didn't. Some pages were, indeed, the thoughts of a young woman, but others belonged to a strategist or a politician. Some bordered on treason. Sarah wrote of revolution, war, and independence. She knew prominent men in far-off colonies. She knew more than seemed possible. Two initials were common in her early scribblings, and then these initials disappeared from her writing entirely, replaced by either an empty square or an empty triangle. The square represented a man whose initials were P.F., and the triangle was someone whose initials were M. M. Thomas learned early that M. M. was Matthew Miller, a Virginia horseman, politician, and scientist. Either as initials or shapes, Sarah always framed them similarly, obscuring much of the page around with random words and phrases. Thomas had never discussed these men with his wife, not wanting her to know that he had read her journals.

Sarah's enthusiasm about his trip to London immediately aroused his suspicion. She had declined his last invitation, saying that living aboard a ship was not ladylike and their interests were best served with her in Pennsylvania. He had waited for her to retire from the house on the day that she asked to go to London, and then he pulled out her journal. There it was, clear as day: a picture of a ship; the word "England"; and two arrows pointing to a triangle, a square, and a pair of round eyeglasses. She expected to encounter the man he now knew to be Patrick Ferguson, as well as Matthew Miller and Benjamin Franklin, at the end of their journey. From the thick scribbles around their names, it looked like she knew little else.

The first real shiver he felt, though, was on the day that she had asked him to walk through London and they had looked up to see an engraved archway that read "Ferguson Manor." He'd said a prayer, and she had noticed. He explained his reaction by pretending he was overwhelmed by an estate undoubtedly built by angels. In truth, he suspected the entire opposite.

His second shiver was when they received the invitation to Sir Patrick Ferguson's party. Thomas had said another prayer, and almost tore the note to pieces. He stood there for the longest time, guessing at how she had known. Thomas knew he was one American businessman among a thousand in London, hardly worth the deliberation of a prominent manufacturer. Yet there it was: an invitation to Ferguson Manor.

Thomas had chided her about her fascination with Sir Patrick, acting jealous, but he was nothing of the sort. He'd continue to poke for some rationale explaining her motivation to come to England and her premonition that she'd encounter Patrick. She seemed satisfied now that they were going to the party and he recognized that singular look in her eyes when she was considering possibilities.

"There should be a few Americans there," Thomas said. "Do you think we'll encounter anyone we know?"

He knew she was lying when she replied, "I know not, husband."

"I heard that Dr. Franklin is in London."

"There is a chance he'd be invited."

"I'm still much impressed that *we've* been invited."

"Is it not true that this Sir Patrick is a manufacturer?" she asked. "He must wish to attract exporters like yourself to further his business."

Thomas held his tongue. He did not want her to know now or ever that he had read her journals. Thomas still hoped she might be telling him the truth. "Anyone else you may know?"

Sarah looked at him suspiciously, but then her expression softened. "I must tell you something. I want no secrets between us." She fell quiet, as if deciding what to say.

"You must tell me, wife," he replied. He was afraid then and whispered another prayer.

"You have oft been curious how such an eminent man as Dr. Franklin began to frequent our coffee houses," she began.

"His love for your mother is manifest to everyone."

"But you don't know how the friendship began."

He looked at her anxiously and pressed his hands at his sides to keep them from shaking. "I do not."

"He came with another man," she explained. "Mr. Matthew Miller."

"And what business does Miller have with us?"

"He is an intimate fellow and business partner of Dr. Franklin. He's the one who introduced us to Dr. Franklin."

"How did you meet Matthew Miller?"

"We came from the same place—Virginia. Miller sought us out and brought Dr. Franklin. We've all been friends ever since."

He took the chance to smile at her. "Friends?"

Everyone knew that Anne Morris and Benjamin

Franklin were parties in a passionate love affair. Thomas's mischievous smile broke the tension.

Sarah reached out to embrace him. "Tell me that you will still love me at the end of this, no matter what."

"What in God's name should make me not love you?"

"I cannot tell," she said. "Not yet."

"Then when?" he demanded.

"I have some history with Patrick Ferguson," she confessed.

"History!" he exclaimed. He realized that of all the things he feared Sarah might say, the possibility that she had loved another was the most vexing.

"'Tis nothing intimate, you jealous man!"

His shoulders relaxed and his fists unclenched. "Then what?" He suddenly grinned, realizing that discovering his wife was a witch who could navigate the depths of hell would be superior to learning that she'd had relations with Patrick Ferguson.

"We . . . my mother and I helped Patrick Ferguson," she said. "Long ago."

"Helped him?"

"He was penniless and alone in Philadelphia. We took him in."

"Why have you never confessed this?" he said, perplexed.

"I had hoped never to see Patrick Ferguson again."

"Then why were you so keen to come to London?"

"He stole something," she explained. "I want it back."

"Stole?"

"Books."

"Why are these books singular?"

"They tell the history of my family," she replied, "and they have my father's inventions."

"Sir Patrick has used this information?"

She nodded.

"For his success?"

She nodded again.

"We'll book passage on the next ship back to America and never talk of the man again," he proclaimed.

"These books are my property, and I will have them back."

"And what if he won't return them? Then what?"

"I don't intend to ask."

"You plan to hook them at the party?"

"Yes."

"How do you intend this?"

"I don't know . . . yet."

Thomas raised his eyebrows and scrutinized his wife.

"I've bared my soul to you these last years," she entreated him. "You think me a thief?"

"I don't know what I think you are."

There were tears in her eyes. "You must help me."

"Help you?" he exclaimed. "I want to shackle you to a ship's hold and return you to Pennsylvania."

"These books will be used against us and many of our allies."

"How do you know this?"

"Please trust me," she said, tears running down her face. "I just know."

He studied her, hoping for some indication that she was

mad, but her eyes, even red and glassy, were calculating. He wasn't sure why, but a question formed in his mind. "Does Patrick Ferguson suspect that you will try to retrieve these books?"

"He may."

"After all this time?"

"Maybe he has dreams," she suggested, unsure. "He too keeps a journal," she said, looking at her husband for some admission that he had read hers. "He draws me not as a square or a triangle, but as a diamond."

"You *are* a diamond," Thomas replied. He wiped the tear that had crawled down her cheek. "I will help you in this fool's errand, but—"

"But what?" she asked quietly.

"You will swear verity! When we are safely back in Philadelphia, you will tell me the truth—all of it."

"You may not believe my story."

He took her hand, pulled her gently into the bedroom, and shut the door behind them.

CHAPTER 12.

HIGH TAILING

On the quarterdeck of the *Norfolk*, Matt and Jay talked in whispers so they would not give their position away to the black ship that waited for them somewhere in the fog.

"What, we're just going to float here?" Matt asked.

"Our longboats aren't big enough to put any sea between us," Jay replied, scanning the fog with his telescope.

"We'll just wait until they run into us?"

Matt was incensed that the *Norfolk*'s captain and crew had so little imagination. The pirates outgunned them handily; they wouldn't survive a firefight in open water. Matt had learned that the captain planned to charge the pirate ship and force a melee between the crews. Matt stood behind his pledge to the officers of the *Norfolk* that he'd fight, but he wasn't going to risk his life until they had exhausted every attempt to put the odds in their favor.

"If you have some plan to outsmart a fifth-rate, speak it," Jay said.

"Aye, Mr. Miller," Captain Pearce said as he emerged from the fog, looking amused.

"Put your heads together," Matt commanded.

"We're outgunned, and she's as quick," Pearce said. "We'll take a good bang at her before she's on us if that's what worries you. She'd be a thundering great prize for us." The sailors were in surprisingly good humor now that they had committed themselves to a fight.

"You don't have some old sea-dog trick?" Matt asked.

Pearce nodded. "They'll not expect us to come about. We'll catch 'em with their pants down." He waved to the sailor in the crow's nest, who replied with the "all clear" sign.

"Until they blow us out of the water," Matt said, disappointed.

"You're a representative of the Virginia government," Pearce said. "You'll be ransomed and returned to the colonies as a hostage."

Matt gave him an icy stare. "You believe me to be a coward?"

"No," Pearce said simply, "which is why I'm surprised that this battle vexes you so."

Matt gazed up at the sailor standing in the crow's nest. He was one of the younger midshipmen, maybe fourteen years old. "Many of your crew are little more than boys."

"We have our marines," Pearce said, "and what are boys will fight like men when the time comes."

"Try something else," Matt said.

Jay grinned. "Like?"

"Torpedoes, mines . . . a submarine."

The sailors regarded Matt with puzzlement.

"Let me draw some pictures," Matt explained.

Pearce looked around at the fog and back up at the crow's nest. "Mr. Jay," he said. "Find him a quill."

Matt took it as a challenge to wipe the captain's smirk away.

****

In the captain's stateroom, Matt sketched a ship alongside exploding underwater mines. He pointed with his quill as he explained the prospect of floating a mine toward the hull of a chasing ship. Black ink splashed from his quill whenever he pointed too vigorously, but it helped to highlight that the mines were supposed to explode.

"I've heard of such a thing," Jay said, "but I don't see how it's possible."

"You said there's a mortar on board," Matt said.

"We could hoist it on deck," Jay replied, "but they'd hit us with a broadside before we're in range."

Matt pointed. "No. Float them on the water as she follows. Rig them to explode when they hit her hull."

"There's no time," Jay said. He pulled the diagram closer, suddenly better engaged. "Put 'em in barrels and light a fuse. They'd have to reach her hull and explode."

Matt looked at the diagram, puzzled. There'd be a lot of ocean between the two ships, and they didn't have time to make an infinite number of floating bombs. Matt could feel his idea crumbling. Making a mechanical detonator would take days, and they had hours.

"Fine," he said. "We make as many barrels as we can, drop them in the water, and hope one hits."

Jay scoffed. "They're not idiots. They'll steer clear."

"Can we sail through some narrow passage, between rocks or in the shallows? Make it so they can't steer away."

"We're in the middle of the sea."

Matt pulled the diagram back and examined it again. "How do we make it so they can't avoid the barrels?"

Jay smiled. "She'll be right up our arse." He put his hand out for the quill and Matt watched as he drew two barrels spanning the bow of a ship, then a line around the ship to a barrel at each end. "Rope. She'll tangle and pull 'em in."

"We want—" The boom of cannons interrupted Matt.

Jay stood. "It's begun."

CHAPTER 13.

BEN FRANKLIN

Ben looked out across the River Thames, ale in hand, trying to stop seething. He wanted to throttle Matthew Miller. In all their discussions, how could Matthew have left out a detail like this? The civilized world was on the brink of economic collapse, and the young Dr. Miller hadn't thought it prudent to include this one crucial detail along with all the useless nonsense about the future he had spewed? There was no excuse for an omission of this magnitude—none!

Ben had met Matt Miller by chance in a Philadelphia pub a few days after Christmas in 1762. His first impression was of a wide-eyed kid who had stumbled into one of the toughest cities in the colonies. Ben took the lad under his wing, hoping to save him from being eaten alive in a town known for separating fools from their money.

A smile came to Ben's face when he thought back to that simpler time. English taxes had been high in the sixties, but so was English investment. Prosperity was there for the taking, not just for the landed elites, but for anyone willing to put in a fair day's labor. It was a boom time for every city in America. Now the banking crisis had overwhelmed England and the world was engulfed in debt. Ben had lived through some banking bubbles in his lifetime, but none so vast as this. Moneyed British families were falling one by one. Estates new and old were liquidated to pay debts accumulated during the excesses of the past decade.

As hard as the economic crisis hit England and Europe, the American colonies were hammered even harder. The credit essential to transatlantic traffic, including tobacco, cotton, and linen, had disappeared and been replaced by a margin call. Men with names like Washington, Hancock, Carter, and Wharton were no longer mentioned for their business acumen, but for their connection to the growing number of delinquencies. English and Scottish creditors estimated that the Americans owed them almost five million pounds. It was an astronomical sum of money.

In all of Ben's discussions with Matthew concerning the independence of the colonies and the coming revolution, young Miller had never mentioned a banking crisis. Monetary strife was now the most significant factor in the rift between Great Britain and her colonies. Ben couldn't believe his protégé had left him so unprepared. Overwhelming debt was a more credible explanation for revolution than all the other drivel. Taxation without representation took on an entirely new meaning when the world was in the middle of a banking disaster.

Ben, like many of his fellows, had suffered personal losses in the crash, and some previous intelligence could have deterred it entirely.

Wasn't this supposed to be the benefit of knowing someone from the future?

Patrick Ferguson, in contrast, had timed the market perfectly. He was an oak now, and among the greatest men in England. "Ah!" Ben said into his mug and then to the water. "'Tis my own fault. After throttling that young man, I should throw myself into the Thames for being so beetle-headed."

Ben took pride in his insight into people and human events. This was the South Sea Bubble all over again, and the signs had been there from the start, yet he had followed the sheep right to the edge of the cliff! Now he was only hanging on. He had been arrogant to believe he had the wit to leave the market before it was too late. "'Tis the game we play," he sighed, studying his beer.

Ben knew his situation wasn't as bad as most. Smarter men than he were already in debtor's prison. All the gold he'd carried to London was gone, though. Luckily, he'd paid six months' rent in advance. He'd be mostly insolvent until he could sell some of his property in Pennsylvania. He'd have to live on credit and his royalties from Miller Head and Stomach Tablets for the remainder of his time in London, and he'd be paying his creditors for years.

One thing Ben couldn't gripe about when it came to his former pupil was that tablet sales were going up like a Chinese rocket. When they had first formed their partnership, Ben had considered his purchase of fifteen percent of Miller Head and Stomach Tablets the musings of a sentimental old man. Matt was highly leveraged while he was trying to build his business, and he left Philadelphia in what Ben had considered a fit of mad passion.

As he sat looking over the Thames, Ben thought back to Matt telling him about the Virginia gentlewoman he wanted for his wife. That chilly Philadelphia afternoon was so vivid in Ben's mind that he shivered.

"You're a madman," he'd said to Matt. "Your affairs are only now profitable, and you want to retire to be a farmhand? Why not bring her hither?"

"I agreed to go there."

"I don't give idle advice," Ben said. He remembered Matt rolling his eyes and thinking how predictable he was at times. Ben had ignored him. "You must complete your affairs in Philadelphia before running off to chase—"

Matt waved him quiet. "I'm not running off."

"Do what you must now, that you may do what you want later."

"I belong in Virginia."

"You know less about horses than I do," Ben said.

"My laboratory's done," Matt replied.

"They're finished with that?"

Matt nodded.

"I still have trouble imagining this future you say we share," Ben had declared. "Carriages that move by themselves. You were pulled into a hole between centuries and shot like a lead ball through a piece of rotted parchment?"

"It was a reactor accident," Matt said, thinking for a moment, "but for all intents, that's about right."

"I would expect a man from two hundred and fifty years in the future to be smarter," Ben said. "He wouldn't throw away a successful business to chase a woman." He still remembered the fire in Matt's eyes then. It had made Ben jealous of Matt's youth.

"I know it sounds stupid," Matt replied. "I'm willing to take the risk."

"Rethink this!" he'd cried, trying his best to keep a grim face although he wanted to smile. "Bring her here."

Matt had shaken his head. "I'd be lying in a gutter somewhere if not for them."

"You'll be married with five children, speculating about how you're going to pay the debt collector."

"I hardly think God transported me two hundred and fifty years into the past to let me become a beggar."

"Arrogance!" Ben cried. "It's the easiest way to hear God laugh."

"Ever since I arrived in this century, everyone has said 'Trust in God.' I finally decide to trust in God, and now I'm arrogant?"

"How do you know this lady will take you as her husband?" Ben asked.

Matt gave him a dirty look. "You've met her. Nothing is guaranteed. Who said that?"

"Some old fool," Ben replied. "How much money *do* you have?"

"Enough," Matt said.

"Do you want help or not?"

"Seven hundred pounds, give or take."

"Tell me why—exactly—you're going there," Ben demanded.

"To collect my wife, help the farm, and start manufacturing."

"While you're helping these kind people with *their* farm,

how will you be supporting *your* family?" Ben asked, giving Matt a hard look. Ben's humor had disappeared.

"I'll be starting the aspirin synthesis," Matt said. "I don't have all the details."

"You expect her family to support you?"

"Seven hundred pounds will last me a long time."

"Purchase a piece of that farm."

"Seven hundred pounds won't buy much."

"Another two thousand pounds?"

"I already owe Ricken too much," Matt replied.

Ben's offer had slipped out of his mouth. "Furnish collateral and I'll lend it to you."

"I don't have anything worth two thousand pounds. Except the business."

"With your debt?" Ben replied seriously. "It's worth nothing."

"I employ seven people," Matt said. "Hardly worthless."

"Leave the dog," Ben said, smiling. He looked down at Scout, Matt's shepherd, who was between them, following the conversation with his head.

"It'd break his heart if he couldn't be with his horse," Matt said.

A peculiar fellowship had developed between Scout and Thunder, Matt's Thoroughbred stallion. Ben had rarely seen Matt without one or both of his animals, and the three of them had achieved storybook proportions in Ben's fantasies. Ben still romanticized this dashing young man from the future, accompanied by his two animal comrades, traipsing about the colonies curing human ills and confronting injustice.

Ben gazed down at the dog and let out a sigh. "Who will walk with me when you're gone?"

"He's not even mine, Ben. He's a loaner from the Taylors."

Ben had shaken his head in mock disgust. "I cannot fancy how you became so entwined with these people in so little time. How did you manage to quit them when you did?"

"Needed to make my fortune," Matt replied. "Do what you must *now* so—"

"You have absolutely nothing of value?"

"Besides a business that employs seven people," Matt repeated, irritated.

Ben had come to think of Matt as a son, so he had to fight the urge to give him the money outright. "I want fifteen percent of all future profits on those fizzing tablets everyone is griping about."

"Only when they eat them like candy," Matt replied. "Fifteen percent? Are you mad?"

"You're confusing me with one of your fellow farmhands," Ben declared. "'Tis a fair price. I may never see you again."

"Twenty-five hundred pounds for fifteen percent of future earnings," Matt countered. "And you will see me again."

"Two thousand," Ben insisted.

"An extra five hundred pounds would take the pressure off."

"Fine," Ben said, resigned. "I'll have the papers drawn

on the morrow. I can't fancy you'll leave before then." He shrugged and turned to go.

"I want your opinion on a few things," Matt called.

Ben waved him off. "You know the future. Figure it out. I plan to take my stroll with the Taylors' dog. Maybe they'd be willing to sell."

"Come down to Richmond with me and ask," Matt implored him.

Ben had seriously considered taking another journey with the young man and the animals that had become a part of his life, but he resisted the temptation.

"Go ahead," Matt said to the dog, who was looking up for permission to follow Ben. Scout trotted to catch up to the older man's side as he opened the door.

"Ben," Matt called.

Ben placed his hand on the door and finally turned to face him. "What now?"

"Thanks."

"You're welcome."

Ben remembered the intense melancholy he'd felt that day as the dog strutted happily at his side through the hills over Philadelphia. Even now, he missed both Matt and Scout dearly.

CHAPTER 14.

LIMEYS

The sun worked with the growing gusts to disperse the protective fog that had shrouded the *Norfolk*. The sails were filling with a stiff breeze, and this was enough to foster a new sense of purpose among the crew as they rushed about the deck. Matt watched the sails swell, heard the stretching and straining of the canvas and rigging, and felt the ship lurch forward. It was a rousing symphony of human ingenuity, and Matt suddenly knew why men took to the seas. The ship's transformation had put a satisfied smile on his face.

"I get it," he thought.

Captain Pearce shouted down at him from the quarterdeck. "A good seaman is only happy when his lady is pregnant with the wind."

The *Norfolk* began to pick up speed. Pearce raised his telescope to his eye to assess their attacker while Second Lieutenant Creighton spun the wheel to catch the wind. The pirate ship, having fired her starboard guns, took time to come about and start the chase, and the *Norfolk* had a head start. Pearce peered through his brass telescope, then dropped the glass from his eye and called, "Look alive! They have a long nine."

The pirate ship was equipped with a chase gun, a long, forward-pointing cannon that could fire a nine-pound ball. This ball was relatively small compared to those used in her main battery guns, which were probably from eighteen to thirty-six pounds. The long nine could strike from a mile away. The *Norfolk*'s two rear-facing four-pounders were no match.

"They'll pick us apart if we let 'em," the captain said.

"We've a scheme, Captain, to blow her from the water," Jay replied.

They heard cannon fire and saw a ball splash far off their stern. It was a range-finding shot; the next one would be closer.

"Lose not a moment," Pearce said. "I'll not let 'em chew us apart before we have a go."

Matt almost saluted, thrilled to have a chance to try their plan.

"Mr. Miller," Jay commanded, waving Matt impatiently toward the hold. "I'll want your help."

They descended a ladder through three levels to the ship's hold. The first level held the sleeping quarters for the crew. The second, lit by portholes, contained bags of flour, bread, fruits, and vegetables. Matt noted with relief some open crates that held lemons. Citrus was an essential part of a seaman's diet because vitamin C prevented scurvy on a long sea voyage.

Every sailor feared scurvy and the lethargy, muscle weakness, and loose teeth it brought. The disease was so prevalent that it was the basis for the old seaman's taunt, "Ye scurvy dogs." They called British sailors "limeys" in reference to the British Navy's dictate that limes be stocked plentifully on British vessels. Hindsight would recognize this as a poor decision; limes contain about half as much vitamin C as lemons and oranges.

Common Name: Vitamin C

Chemical Name: Ascorbic Acid

Chemical Formula: $C_6H_8O_6$

Molecular Weight: 176.1

Natural Source: Citrus, Kale, Berries

There was livestock in pens on the third deck, including pigs and chickens. Jay lit a lantern on this third deck, closed the protective glass window, and carried it with him as he descended the ladder to the very bottom of the ship. The *Norfolk* was a new vessel, so its hold was not as bad as the lower decks of some older rat-infested ships, but it was still dark, damp, and musty. The murkiness, the creaking of the wooden hull, and the intermittent sound of cannon fire did nothing to make Matt comfortable in its shadowy confines.

Jay set the lantern down as he stepped off the ladder and

pointed at a stack of empty barrels. "The large ones," he instructed as he turned away to look for something else. When Matt pulled the top one from the stack, dirt and debris littered his head as he tilted the barrel. He hefted it to the ladder and then bent over to brush off whatever had fallen into his hair. Pieces of chewed wood and rodent droppings fell onto the floor. He shuddered in disgust.

"Damn rats," Jay said beside him.

Jay dropped two long coils of rope next to the barrel and went back for additional supplies. Matt lifted another barrel, but not before clearing its top this time. He and Jay stacked everything on the elevator: six wooden barrels, three coils of rope, and a crate of carpenter's tools.

As they climbed back to the top deck, the ship was swaying broadly. They had to work to keep from falling back down into the hold. They reached the deck in time to hear cannon fire, followed almost instantly by the sound of a ripping mainsail. They turned their heads to the sails, realized concurrently that the damage was mild, and then returned their attention to the ship's deck.

Matt hurried behind Jay to the wooden crane to haul up their supplies. Before reaching the crane, Jay tapped a seaman on the shoulder and then waved to two others. When the three had assembled, he gave them instructions. They headed in Matt's direction, making him step aside, and then continued to the hold.

Matt helped Jay work the pulleys on the crane as the pirates' cannon fired again. They ducked and watched a ball crash into the water off the *Norfolk*'s stern. The booming of the long nine was coming at five-minute intervals, so they used the intermittent quiet to return to their task until they had to duck another cannonball. When the pallet reached the main deck, Jay locked the rope into the wood pulley and they worked in unison to move the supplies from the crane.

By the time they emptied the pallet onto the deck, the sailors had returned from the ship's magazine with crates of mortar shells and a small box of fuses. The shells were impressively large and had removable inserts packed with gunpowder and a hole for a fuse. The three sailors set the crates down and then hurried back to their posts.

Jay swiftly set the barrels in pairs along the deck and placed a rope coil between each. Matt's respect for the first lieutenant increased as he watched him in action. Matt's suggestion to throw mines in the water had been vague at best, but Jay had filled in the missing pieces.

"I'll set the fuses," Jay said. He pointed to the barrels. "Nail the ends of the rope. They'll hit her hull hard, so the leash should be solid." He was already placing fuses into the mortar shells.

Another blast sounded from the pirate ship, followed by the crash of a ball smashing into the deck beside them, knocking Matt to the floor in a shower of splinters. Captain Pearce spun the wheel sharply to move out of the pirates' sights and the ship tilted hard to starboard, sending the six barrels straight for Matt, who was trying to regain his feet while brushing splinters from his face. He dodged, but a barrel smacked his forehead and opened a gash above his eyebrow. The next thing he knew, Jay was pulling him to his feet.

"You fine?" Jay asked, gripping Matt's arm to keep him upright.

Matt wiped the blood from his eye and looked for the barrels. His head was jittery and his vision was being interrupted by intermittent pictures.

"Crap," he said aloud as he pressed his temples. The last thing he needed was to lose his sight. He relaxed enough to bring himself back into the present. It was something he hadn't done for almost two years. He was relieved when the aura dulled and he could take stock of the five barrels on the deck. "One's missing," he yelled.

"Overboard," Jay shouted. "We'll make do."

"Shit, shit . . . shit," Matt swore loudly.

He looked back at the expanse between the vessels. Hitting the pirate ship with tethered barrels tossed from the stern had already seemed unlikely, and now they had one less chance. Matt and Jay dashed for the four barrels and carried them back to the coils of rope. Matt wedged the fifth barrel against the side of the ship so it wouldn't come rolling at him the next time the captain turned the wheel. He swiped blood away from his eye.

Matt picked up the rope, made a loop around the remaining four barrels, and tied a knot, spattering the barrels with blood as he worked. He hammered six nails into each barrel along the length of wrapped rope and then bent the nails to secure the rope, pulling hard to test each one. The knots were tight and the rope was solid, but he hammered another four nails for good measure. The rope would have to hold and the barrels had to be strong enough not to be smashed to bits before the fuses could burn down to the powder.

They ducked as a cannonball ripped into the mast above their heads. Pieces of wood and sail dropped all around them. Jay walked low as he returned with a hand wagon containing two bales of straw. He crouched down to pry off the top of a barrel and begin filling it with straw. Matt used his knife to pry open another barrel. "How much?" he shouted.

"Half," Jay yelled as he ducked at the sound of a cannon and the whoosh of a ball rushing through the sails. The *Norfolk* veered hard again, but this time they were ready and managed to keep the barrels upright. It was a meager victory, but enough to bring back their sense of control. When the deck leveled, Matt wiped blood from his eye.

"You'll want the surgeon," Jay said. He stooped to lift two mortar shells from a crate onto the beds of straw in the barrels.

Matt laid the long fuses to the sides and they packed the barrels with straw. The weight of the first barrel surprised Matt when he hefted it. A shiver of regret went up his spine. "They're too heavy," he yelled. They ducked at the sound of another cannon shot that tore through the sails. Only the sail on the mizzenmast, the rearmost of three masts, was intact.

"They'll float," Jay called back. Jay swept the last of the straw from the wagon with his arms and they lifted the barrels onto the rolling wooden platform to move them to the edge of the stern and drop them into the sea.

Pearce had been watching their activities from the helm. "Look alive," he yelled. "They're targeting our main."

CHAPTER 15.

A PALPABLE MISS

Matt and Jay were standing at the stern, trying to move anything that could interfere with the barrels as they threw them overboard. They'd roll the barrels aft, one to port and the other to starboard, hoping they'd float with the rope high enough to catch the bow of the pirate ship behind them. It seemed more possible now that the ship was gaining.

Once the fuses were lit, they had seven minutes. The crew would have to light them in unison, lay them on top of a piece of tin over the hay, stuff the fuses into the barrels, coat the opening with pitch, pound the covers onto the barrels, and roll them off the back. Jay enlisted Tom Porter and Ebenezer Grey, the young men who had rowed the jolly, along with another seaman named John Turner, to help them heft the sealed barrels off the stern.

Tom Porter stood next to them with a glowing cannon rod and doubled as their lookout for cannon fire. Jay put his hand up as they waited for the next cannon shot to pass through the sails, then sprang into action. Tom touched the rod to the fuses and they hissed. Ebenezer coated the tops of the barrels with thick black tar, Matt dropped the lids onto the barrels, and Jay hammered them tight. It was the point of no return.

Matt and Jay heaved one of the barrels and Tom and Ebenezer another. John Turner hefted a generous loop of rope between them. Together they hurried stern and looked expectantly down at the water. A cannonball smashed the wood between them, sending razor-sharp splinters everywhere and blowing John off his feet.

He landed on his rear and sat dazed. "On your feet, seaman!" Jay yelled.

Turner looked around, trying to figure out where he was, then pulled himself up and lifted the spool of rope in his hands.

They set the barrels on the deck and Jay brushed splinters from his shirt and pulled out some that had lodged in his arm. Matt leaned over the railing. There were three wooden protrusions and a wooden mermaid that could snag the rope. The barrels had an easy path off the corners, but the rope had to be thrown perfectly to keep from snagging.

Damn mermaid!

Matt tapped John on the shoulder and pointed at the four snag points. "Can you clear them?"

John waved broadly and pointed. "If I throw it that way," he said.

"Hard as you can."

"Aye, aye, Mr. Miller."

"You'll do fine."

Matt said a quick prayer, hoping things did not go so poorly that they blew a hole in the *Norfolk* instead of the pirate ship. At the very least, they could tow the barrels behind them and stall the ship long enough to allow the pirates to catch them.

At Jay's signal, they all lifted their packages into the air.

"On three," he said, and they heaved the barrels overboard in a throw that was perfect in all respects. The barrels entered the water cleanly and the rope only glanced off the carved stern before dropping into the sea. Matt looked to the sky and said another prayer as the barrels disappeared into the water. After half a minute the rope sank, too. Another cannonball ripped above their heads.

When they looked back at the ocean, there was no sign of barrels or rope. "They sank," Matt said. "Shit!"

"Give 'em a moment," Jay replied. He opened his telescope and scanned the water.

"Well?" Matt asked, on the verge of panic.

"There," Jay finally said. He pointed and handed the telescope to Matt. The very tops of the barrels were bobbing to the surface. They hadn't drifted far apart, but they were almost dead in the path of the pirate ship.

"Can't see the rope," Matt said, "but they're headed straight for it." He handed the telescope back.

Jay fixed the telescope again. "She's got 'em."

Matt clenched his fist and checked his watch. There was another minute before they exploded. A cannonball came crashing into the rear of the ship, almost at the waterline.

"Mr. Jay!" Captain Pearce called. "Report."

"Less than a minute," Matt shouted.

They saw the explosions before they heard them. The pirate ship was sandwiched between two geysers of water.

"Yes," Matt cheered. Jay still had the glass up to his eye.

"Well done!"

"A miss," Jay exclaimed, looking through the scope. "The explosions were behind her."

"Mr. Jay!" the captain shouted.

"Missed 'em, Captain," Jay yelled.

"Time to have a bang at the bastards," Pearce said.

"We've another, Captain," Matt shouted.

Pearce ignored him as he turned the wheel. The ship veered starboard and Matt held the barrels in place.

"What went wrong?" Matt asked Jay.

"She went right between," Jay proclaimed, "then skidded o'er."

Matt ran toward the hold.

"Where the hell are you off to?" Jay yelled.

Matt hurried back a moment later, awkwardly hefting the fifth barrel he'd lodged against the ship's rail. The barrel slammed against the deck as he thrust it down. He pointed to the last set of tethered barrels.

"Find the rope's center," he yelled. Another cannonball crashed into the deck and they went sprawling.

"Mr. Jay," Captain Pearce shouted from the wheel. "Do what you'll do!"

Jay was busy scrolling through the rope. At its center, he handed it to Matt, who set it against the fifth barrel and pulled four nails from his mouth as he hammered the rope to the barrel. It looked sloppy at best.

"It'll never hold," Jay said.

"Just needs to float the rope above her waterline."

Tom was already standing with the glowing rod. Lighting the fuses and sealing the barrels went faster the second time and they were soon at the stern with the live mines set to throw. John was struggling to hold the barrel and the rope.

"Can you handle it?" Matt asked.

"I can do it," John replied.

"On three again," Jay yelled. They tossed all three barrels astern. Events unfolded in slow motion in Matt's vision as he watched. The barrels containing the mines cleared the bow, but the center barrel snapped back and bounced awkwardly off the stern toward the port before it hit the water. The rope slid across the rear of the ship and snagged on the mermaid's head and tail. The mines were now dragging in the water behind them. Matt rushed to the center of the stern for a closer look.

"My fault, sir," John said to Matt. "I'll fix it."

"How?" Matt said, looking toward the pirate ship, but the young man had already disappeared. Another cannonball slammed into the deck, sending large splinters and knocking Matt back. His ears rang. The captain veered hard to port.

"Keep her straight, Captain," Matt yelled. He looked at his watch; the barrels had four minutes before they exploded.

"Drop sails to come about, Mr. Lewis," the captain yelled. "Quarters!" Ten seconds later, the drum sounded, signaling the men to quarters.

Matt crossed over the railing and climbed down to help untangle the rope, but John was almost there. Musket balls spattered the stern and Matt ducked under the rail. He looked for Jay, but the drum had called him away. The

Norfolk shuddered as half its sails dropped and the ship slowed. Matt leaned over the rail again, trying to keep his feet on the tilting deck.

Dropping sails put slack in the rope and Turner was frantically trying to unravel it. The rope came loose from the mermaid's tail, but her head was out of reach. The pirate's cannon fired again; another hit to the stern threw Matt back. He pulled himself to the rail and saw Tom bobbing in the water, hanging onto the rope that was towing the two barrels. There were two minutes on Matt's watch.

"Man overboard!" Matt yelled.

In the melee, though, there was no one to listen. The pirate ship was now a giant at their stern. Matt tied the last rope around his waist and the other end to the rail, then stepped overboard to finish what Tom had started. It was no longer a matter of trapping the pirate ship. Now their own rigs could blow the backside off the *Norfolk* and kill John Turner.

Matt spotted John nearly engulfed in whitecaps, hanging desperately to the rope. Matt scrambled over to the mermaid, which wore the fateful rope like a string of pearls. There was no way to lift the rope over her head while hanging onto the ship. Matt reached for the rope, resigned to falling into the water, and hoisted hard.

I've got you!

The rope came loose as another cannonball exploded above him. Matt snapped back like an arrow shot from a bow. He hit the water, and his world turned dark green.

CHAPTER 16.

CELIA FERGUSON

The great hall of Ferguson Manor was a polished-marble monstrosity. Glass panes rose from floor to vaulted ceiling along its entire northern wall and looked out onto a fountain at the center of a topiary garden surrounded by cherry trees. An enormous fireplace dominated the far western end. Lady Celia Ferguson stood in the middle of the light-grey marble floor watching two servants hang a life-sized painting of her late father, Charles, Duke of Fairchild. Celia hoped that hanging the portrait would help make Ferguson Manor feel like home; something that had eluded her thus far.

"Ferguson Manor," she whispered to herself with scorn.

No matter how she said it, bile filled her mouth. This building wasn't anything like the homes of her childhood. It had no fame or legacy. Nothing that lingered in the air, no laudable spirits haunting the halls, and not a single lord or lady had ever walked its new marble floor.

Fairchild Manor, her home until her marriage to Sir Patrick Ferguson, was a proper seat for a noble family, not this empty shell. Ferguson Manor's legacy consisted of a few dust outlines of paintings recently removed and sold at auction. The estate was liquidated before its completion to save the previous owner from debtor's prison. The seats of noble families did not pass one to another with the stroke of a pen. It took centuries to make a proper manor, and this was no more than one man's ode to pomp and largess.

"Is it to your satisfaction, Lady Celia?" Cavener called from the platform.

Celia shook her thumb sideways. "Slightly to the right," she called back.

They adjusted the portrait and looked at her for approval. She gave a thumbs-up this time. "Lovely, Mr. Cavener."

The men climbed down the ladder and moved the platform away from the mantel. Celia gazed up at the portrait of her late father resplendent in a full matador's costume. He was in his late thirties at the time. It was her mother's favorite portrait, and Celia knew she would expect it to be conspicuous when she came to visit. Her father had trained in bullfighting in Spain and had retained the hobby when he returned to England. It had eventually killed him.

Celia wanted to hate bullfighting, but the ring was part of her legacy, too. She warmed at the memory of inspecting young bulls with her father, assessing their best qualities. She was a young and idealistic girl back then, and her father had made her feel like anything was possible. Their relationship had turned cold and formal in their last years. She never forgave him for using her to shore up his title and increase his sway.

When she was younger, he took her to places and gave her experiences no English daughter had dreamed of, but in the end, he expected her to do her duty. When a rich man appeared one day and placed a sizable amount of money on the table, wanting to buy his way into the upper echelons of English aristocracy, her father made the deal. In this new industrial England, everything depended on liquidity.

Celia cursed her father again under her breath. She had not been innocent to noble titles being made available to the highest bidder, but she had not expected to become a pariah. People who had once treated her like family now shunned her. To make it worse, before his death her father had confessed that he'd expected as much; the ramifications of marrying her to a man with no family and no ancestry had been unavoidable. To increase her frustration, Celia's husband had no shame about buying titles and influence, so he would never understand how deeply wounded she was by the loss of her support.

To his credit, Patrick Ferguson was handsome, prosperous, and confident, and although they couldn't move among the old families, there were plenty of new ones in London. These families, too, had been able to purchase status. Britain's wrecked economy hadn't opened as many doors as her husband had predicted, but even Celia had been able to sense the vibration of their shifting fortunes.

Celia scanned the great hall of perhaps the grandest English estate in London, thinking that maybe this room, at least, was worthy of hanging the portraits her mother expected to see.

"It looks marvelous, m'lady."

Celia turned to see her attendant gazing up at the portrait. Camille was in her late forties and had been with Celia since before she had learned to walk.

"'Twill do, I think," Celia answered quietly.

"Your father was never happier than when he was in the ring," Camille said. "He liked to put on a shew for you and your mother."

"I expect you're right," Celia replied. "I accompanied him many times to examine the bulls."

"He wanted you with him, m'lady, still."

"It's difficult to understand why."

"He wanted you to know the world of men."

Celia looked sharply at Camille. "He confided this in you?"

"Oh no, m'lady," Camille replied, "but servants talk."

"What things do servants say?"

"He was proud of you."

"Proud?"

"He knew the challenge you'd face. He said you were made of firmer things and that if anyone could bring England's nobility into a new era, it was a Fairchild woman."

Celia felt a tear form in her eye. "Camille, why have you never told me this?"

"Not my place, m'lady."

"And now?"

Camille gazed up at the portrait. "He was still a handsome man."

"So they say."

"Dinner will be served soon."

"Have Mary dress the children in their finest. The Parkers should see 'nobility's new era' even in its children."

"Yes, m'lady." Camille curtsied and retreated toward the kitchen.

"Nobility's new era," Celia whispered up at her father.

She had wanted to say it with more contempt.

CHAPTER 17.

OLD DOMINION

Hosting elaborate dinner parties wasn't Grace's favorite pastime, but there was something satisfying about watching Virginia politics play out at her table. The Economic Congress was in session in Richmond, and it had seemed appropriate to welcome the delegates to the farm and see what they'd say after a few glasses of wine. Thankfully, Rebecca was brilliant at inviting, feeding, and lodging their guests. It was a mixed blessing, too, that Graine had moved her family back to the Martin estate from the Taylor-Miller farm; their house, built to exacting and opulent standards by Graine's father, was usually empty now that Will was spending long periods in England. Even with Will back on the farm this weekend, there were still five luxurious bedrooms available for guests.

Thomas Jefferson detested conforming to anyone else's schedule; he liked solitude once it was time for bed. The last time he visited, he slept in an unfinished guest bedroom in the new Miller house, which they now called Miller Grange. Since Matthew was away, Jefferson's sleeping quarters were removed from the women and children. Etiquette aside, Grace knew it was best to keep Jefferson at arm's length, so she housed him in the Taylors' white farmhouse, where he enjoyed the company of her mother, Mary, and her brothers, Jonathan and Jeb.

Dabney Carr, who was Jefferson's best friend; Edmund Pendleton; George Wythe; George Fleming; and Governor Murray had comfortable lodgings in Will's home with their wives. The Murrays traveled with a squad of soldiers who happily occupied the shacks in front of Uncle David's house, where they could cook and gather around the fire pit. The soldiers would be coming and going as they took watch and would probably stay up late, although Uncle David would try to keep things under control. Overall, despite the complications, everyone seemed to be pleased with their housing arrangements.

Matthew always found at least ten reasons to think of canceling these parties, but Dr. Franklin insisted that members of the House of Burgesses must socialize. Grace had been insisting long before that. Societal intrigue and statecraft would never be among Matthew's strengths. Deep down, he didn't understand that his desire to be left alone to go about his business would never be respected by high-ranking bureaucrats. Grace knew his hopes to stand by while conspirators lurked all around was naïve, so here they were, hosting another party, even in his absence.

Grace was standing in front of a large looking glass in her bedroom while her maid fastened her gown. It was understated, silver, with ruffled sleeves and a white petticoat.

"'Tis an exquisite dress, madam," Patricia said.

"A curious cloth," Grace replied. "'Tis both fancy and simple."

"As are Virginians, madam," Patricia said with a grin. "I suspect Mr. Jefferson's suit will be the same."

"This is our first audience with the governor and Lady Murray," Grace said. "I'm sure they'll be resplendent."

"They say the countess is captivating."

"Make sure the staff understands that they are our honored guests tonight. The countess, especially, should be used with care."

"I will convey your message to the staff."

"That is not to say that *all* the ladies shouldn't be used like royalty," Grace replied.

Patricia's face filled with a broad smile. "I'm sure Mr. Jefferson will provide flattery enough," she said.

"We will not depend on Mr. Jefferson in this regard."

Patricia turned serious. "Of course, madam. All of the staff know too well the expectations of the great families."

"The ladies have much sway on their husbands. I will defer to all this evening. We are new to this world and can afford to let the matrons lead."

"Yes, madam," Patricia said, then asked lightly, "Are you glad to have your brother home?"

Grace looked at Patricia suspiciously. The question broke right to the heart of the matter.

"He may not behave as I'd want," she admitted, "but I believe he will take this time to further our interests. Robert Martin has affected my brother in an astounding fashion." Grace sucked in so Patricia could fasten the last buttons and pull the dress tightly onto her shoulders.

"Anything else, madam?"

Grace shook her head. Patricia curtsied and excused herself.

Grace watched her walk away, appreciating her husband's ability to hire good people. He'd insisted on certain qualities and argued strongly with her when he rejected servants she selected.

"They should have wit," Matthew had said, "and I want trust, and I'm willing to pay for it."

"These are *my* servants," Grace had protested. "You know nothing about the duties of a lady's maid."

"I don't see this one standing with us through tough times," he'd replied. "Scout doesn't like her."

Grace didn't know what he meant by "tough times," and she wasn't sure if he was joking about the dog. She had seen her husband change over the past few years, and she thought it might be because of the children. He talked about how important it was to "walk with God" and the implications of "preparing for the flood." It irritated her because nothing about her family, which she had built on the rocks, was weak. They were close to building a financial wall around their family that few could breach.

Despite her annoyance with his idiosyncrasies, Grace allowed that Matthew had been right about the people they employed. Everyone on the farm was loyal to the Taylors or to Dr. Franklin, or was among Matthew's old Philadelphia business associates. In many cases, husbands, wives, and children from the same family worked together at the Taylor-Miller complex caring for animals or manufacturing medicines. Matthew sent people packing at the slightest hint of ambivalence, but he advanced them, too, when he saw loyalty and ambition. Grace smiled in frustration, thinking she'd soon have to replace Patricia. After all, the dog liked her.

Grace studied herself in the glass and began to work at a braid that was too low. She pulled a string of rubies around her neck and admired how they shone above her silver dress. She smoothed her bodice again, pooched up the folds of her skirt, and walked out of the room satisfied that she was dressed appropriately to chase her ambition.

CHAPTER 18.

JOHN TURNER

"Got you!" John yelled.

Matt thought at first that the pain in his shoulder was part of dying, but it was John Turner's firm grasp pulling him to the surface. The mayhem of crashing water and cannon fire replaced the relative quiet of drowning. Matt coughed saltwater and took his first breath in what had seemed like an eternity. He felt helpless against the overwhelming strength of the sea as he tried to orient himself.

"I'll make it," Matt gasped, struggling to cough the water from his lungs and take a full breath. John held him with one hand and hung onto the rope that tethered them to the *Norfolk* with the other. Matt rose high enough to see the *Norfolk's* stern cannons flash. She had come about and was halfway through a broadside of her ten guns firing at the pirate ship. She was moving slowly enough that they could keep their heads above water.

When the cannons went silent, a white cloud of smoke shrouded the bow of the pirate ship. It was turning in the water to fire its starboard battery. Matt ducked at the bee-like hiss of musket balls biting into the water around them.

"Keep low," John cautioned. "We gotta pull ourselves in."

Matt coughed and nodded. The *Norfolk* seemed miles away. John squeezed his hands around Matt's, urging him to hold tight to the rope, then pushed him toward the ship. Matt's arms burned from fatigue, but he did his best to move one hand in front of the other. John pushed Matt forward every time he reached for another handhold.

Knowing how hard the kid was working to save him, Matt redoubled his efforts and put all temptation out of his mind to rest his arms. Letting go would mean losing the progress they had made. Matt was reaching forward again when a shock wave from two explosions thundered across the surface of the ocean and walloped them. He turned in time to see a geyser off the pirate ship's starboard drop back into the sea in front of a thick cloud of smoke.

"A hit!" John yelled.

"Can't tell," Matt called.

John pointed at the *Norfolk*. All her sails were going up as she tried to make her escape. John looped the rope around himself and checked that Matt was secure. "Keep your head out of the water," he yelled against the crashing waves.

Matt took a deep breath before the *Norfolk* shot forward under full sail and dragged them under the sea again.

CHAPTER 19.

DRY

The breeze was strong and cool and the sun was shining on the deck of the *Norfolk*. Matt was sitting in the shade, writing in the journal he had kept since the day they left Virginia. He looked up to watch a young seaman ritualistically observing the workings of his right arm. David Sutton would bend his arm, turn it, and flex each finger through its complete range of motion, front and back. He'd relax, lean against the railing to look out to sea, then renew the inspection.

Matt closed his journal and tucked it under his jacket on the wooden bench. He crossed the deck to the young sailor. "How's it healing?" he asked.

David turned, surprised and maybe embarrassed. "Only a fleabite, Mr. Miller. Magic, no doubt."

Matt smiled. "It works like magic, but it's pure philosophy." He'd adopted the eighteenth-century use of the word to describe the natural sciences.

"I know you said so, sir," David replied, "but everyone who gets a ball in the arm gets the saw."

David was slightly shorter than Matt, with straight teeth and a fresh and curious grin. His skin was smooth, with no trace of having had smallpox. The intelligence in his face was not surprising to Matt, considering the way he'd been studying his arm, and there looked to be ambition there, too, which made Matt feel a special camaraderie. David reminded Matt of himself when he was the same age.

"You don't get the saw if you take the right medicine," Matt replied.

"Sick as a horse, I was."

"I haven't figured out how to prevent the stomachache."

Matt had experimented for years trying to purify the penicillin powder. He had used different molds from any number of fruits and had even attempted bread mold again, which gave a purer mix of compounds but so paltry a yield as to be useless. He had tried chromatographic columns—long tubes filled with diatomaceous earth—to separate the brown matter from the active penicillin. But in the end, the only setup that worked was the one he started with: mold grown on cantaloupes, extracted into ethanol, and isolated as a brown powder. It worked over seven days to prevent or cure infection, but it made people tragically nauseous. There was always vomiting.

David pulled up his sleeve to show Matt his wound. The bullet hole was thick and red, but the surgeon had done a good job of sewing it closed, and it was healing.

"Careful with that," Matt said. "I don't have more powder if you tear it open."

David nodded and flexed his fingers. "Why did God make a hand thus?" he asked. "Is this in your philosophy?"

Matt nodded. "Some say that the hand is one of the things that separate men from beasts."

David inspected his raised fingers and flexed them up

and down. "I set my mind to it, and my fingers move. Yet there are times when they move together for some task, and I have not commanded them to move at all."

"Have you asked Mr. Callaway if you could learn about such things?" Matt asked. "Maybe even assist him in his surgeries."

"That old loblolly. He'd be on thorns to have me there."

"I'll speak to him on your behalf."

"I could apprentice with a ship's surgeon?" David asked, surprised.

"I think he'd welcome someone who shared his curiosity."

"I'd be much in your debt, sir."

"Even if Mr. Callaway doesn't have the wherewithal, I know a few men who might appreciate someone who is curious and motivated."

"Thank you, sir," David replied happily. "I'd welcome any effort."

Matt looked at his own hand, flexing his fingers. "It *is* a remarkable invention."

****

By Lt. Creighton's calculations, they'd hit land within a week. There was a fair wind, and they'd been traveling near ten knots for the last couple of days. Matt's back-of-the-envelope conversion put them at around two hundred and fifty miles per day. The carpenters repaired almost every hole the pirates had put in the *Norfolk*, and the rest of the crew crawled about the riggings and masts to replace or patch all the sails. She was starting to feel like the sleek vessel that had sailed from Hampton Roads, save for fresh wood patches everywhere that gave her the look of a kid who had lost a fight on the playground. The patches were flush, though, so once painted, the evidence of their ocean battle would disappear.

The loss of their comrades was harder to patch over. Matt stepped forward to speak when they slid Daniel Jay and Ebenezer Grey into the sea, both men having succumbed to cannon fire after they'd finished dropping the exploding barrels into the water. Matt had spent a day writing their epitaphs to do justice to their heroism.

Along with David Sutton, three other sailors survived musket-ball wounds. It took Matt hours to convince Callaway not to amputate, but to remove the balls and clean and sew the wounds. The amputee candidates' arguments had weighed heavily in the surgeon's decision to forego the bone saw. Men rarely survived the infections resulting from small-arms injuries without amputation, but thanks to Matt's penicillin, all four were recovering.

Matt was recovering, too. The surgeon put five stitches in his forehead to close the gash from the rolling barrel. The cut was healing and showed no hint of infection, which was fortunate since he'd needed to stretch the penicillin powder across four musket injuries. His head wound had caused more headaches than he'd experienced in a long time, and he was randomly losing his vision again. Vivid dreams were waking him every night now.

During his first years in the colonies, headaches and the flashing pictures had overloaded his vision, and he'd go blind, sometimes for hours. When this happened, his head became a camera, taking rapid time-lapse photographs of future events. Often, the pictures flashed so briefly that he'd only see bits and pieces that spanned years. Sometimes, usually when he was under stress, he'd been able to anticipate the immediate future. He'd go physically blind, but the pictures in his mind allowed him to predict each footstep, cross a busy street, or even duck to avoid a punch.

Matt's dreams at night were another phenomenon entirely. They could be hard to interpret, but sometimes they narrated a future that was days, weeks, or years away. There was no scientific explanation for it: A wormhole had formed during a reactor accident and propelled him two hundred and fifty years into the past. It defied anything he knew about the human brain that he could have retained a complete timeline of the events he encountered on the journey across time.

Matt had read a paper about brain surgery that claimed it was possible for a human brain to record a lifetime of memories. Doctors had been able to electrically stimulate sections of the brain during an operation and make patients relive forgotten moments in their lives. These people didn't just vaguely remember the days, but experienced them again with every sight, sound, and smell.

Matt had thought little about this in the last couple of years, insomuch as his dreams and visions had diminished. He had ignored the potential tragedy that lay ahead, hoping he'd been wrong or that the future he saw had changed. He smiled as he thought of the bump in Grace's belly as they made love on his last night in Richmond. He hoped to be home in time to see their sixth child's birth.

Early in their courting, he had joked with Grace that he

wanted ten children; she had countered that it would only happen if they had a prosperous horse farm with excellent stables. Through their combined efforts to grow their farm and Matt's pharmaceutical business, they were successful by any standard. Grace saw no reason not to have the large family they joked about almost a decade ago. Matt smiled again, thinking of how irrational the ten-child plan had sounded, but they couldn't keep their hands off each other. He'd sought a woman like Grace his whole life. Her air of superiority from her role as a mother made his love even stronger. She felt sorry for men who could only participate briefly in what she said was "God's greatest gift."

Matt had spent most of a decade walling up his memories of the future, and now a wooden barrel had brought that wall crashing down. The visions had often been debilitating after an accident or a fight, but now that Matt was established, accidents and fights were rare. His ocean voyage had certainly changed that. He felt a cringe of regret as he looked out across the sea.

Why am I here?

Ben Franklin had been adamant that Matt join him in England to counter the imminent threat he saw to the "natural course of humanity." His friend needed his help, and Matt came without question, even though he'd had trouble explaining to Grace why he was leaving on a mission that could take the greater part of a year. Any trip across the Atlantic was fraught with peril.

Ben, it seemed, was doing everything he could to bring the colonies and England closer. It seemed to Matt that Ben was blurring the lines, but really, who knew what the natural course of humanity was supposed to be? Matt hadn't the least idea of how much damage Ben believed Patrick Ferguson could cause. Patrick was a fellow time traveler who had disappeared from America within a year of their arrival. Ben had discovered him in London almost a decade later. Some said Patrick Ferguson was rich and had married into an old and commanding English family. Ben wrote that Patrick was "up to no good" and that Matt needed to join him to determine what his plan entailed.

Now that Matt's visions of the future were strong again in his head, Matt suspected Ben's assessment was accurate. Patrick was working to increase British influence, especially with the French, who were essential to the American colonies' independence. A closer friendship between England and France—or England's domination of France—would prevent the Americans from winning their revolution. A prosperous Great Britain in alliance with France might be able to thwart an American Revolution altogether.

****

It was quiet, even as the wind blew and the *Norfolk* rose on the occasional swell. Out here, a man could be alone with God to think and dream big dreams. Like Patrick, Matt had gained influence in this new time. Could Matt somehow work with Patrick on a compromise? Could they avoid the American Revolution to *everyone's* advantage? Maybe it was selfish, but why should Matt make such a sacrifice? Matt's desire to keep Grace alive and his family together had only grown stronger, and at this point he knew he'd sell his soul for five more years.

Matt looked up into the blue sky. "Damn it all to hell," he said.

CHAPTER 20.

WIVES

Grace walked across the second-floor balcony of Miller Grange and descended the staircase to meet her guests. It probably looked to everyone like she was making a grand entrance, but her choice not to wear hoops had made her dress long enough to tangle in her feet. *Let them think I'm cautious and deliberate.*

Miller Grange wouldn't be finished for a few years yet, and it would never be as breathtaking as the home of Robert Martin, her sister-in-law's father, but it was grand in its own right. The entry and the staircase had been Grace's father's inspiration and his favorite part of the house.

Thomas Taylor had designed most of the Grange, actually, during a time when Matthew was building his business and wanted nothing to do with architecture. One of Thomas's goals was to establish a brilliant estate for his family, and Miller Grange was his gift to them. Grace felt a twinge of melancholy that he'd died before seeing it finished, but she knew he was watching as she stepped cautiously down the stairs of the fine Virginia home he'd promised her since she was a little girl.

Guests skittered excitedly about the marble foyer to her

right and others had gathered in the parlor in front of her. There were eight members of the House of Burgesses in attendance along with their wives, a half-dozen merchants, and two Scottish bankers. All were from influential families or organizations whose reach extended into international government and business. Grace knew everyone was here for personal gain, but also that their interests coincided with the Millers', and Virginia's at large. Even Matthew could be convinced of that.

Jonathan had joined the group dressed in a dark-blue suit with grey silk stockings. She tried to make eye contact, but he looked away. He had not wanted to attend, but Grace had been adamant. "You must represent our family among these people," she had said. "Father would have insisted, and so do I."

Jonathan had replied that he no longer respected the "fine families" and their willingness to subjugate themselves to the British. Grace had to own that she, too, was angry at the townspeople who were offering little help to farmers who were quartering English soldiers.

Grace's brother, Will, was talking to John Alsop, a New York merchant she'd met before. Will had prepared a list of prospects; she knew he'd work through them as the evening progressed, teaching them enough about Thoroughbred horses to spur their interest in husbandry. She expected to give up a number of prize animals over the next fortnight to associates willing to pay an exorbitant price; she suspected that the gold came mostly from the Martins' coffers, but whatever her brother's motives, she was glad to have him there. He was a master showman and kept her guests diverted.

The voices grew louder the nearer she was to the floor. Many of the visitors were from landed gentry whose tenure in America went back a hundred years, and Grace recognized her family's new money was not yet an accepted currency among those whom she and Matthew privately dubbed Virginia royalty. Her suspicions of Thomas Jefferson's flirtations aside, she liked that he shared their cynicism when it came to those who had inherited their status.

It had been her father's singular goal to marry Grace into one of these fine families, and even in those last years, he'd been disappointed about her determination to marry a man with no family connections. The irony was not lost on her that she was now trying to accomplish precisely what her father had dreamed; she'd do everything in her power to maneuver the Millers into the landed and influential families of the Old Dominion.

Grace stepped onto the marble floor of the entry and put on a smile, sweeping her head of her ruminations. A group of women had gathered in the parlor, and she headed straight to them, saying, "Good evening, ladies," as they welcomed her into their circle. There was only one newcomer among them, and Grace chanced that this was the Countess of Dunmore. Her smooth skin was only lightly powdered.

She's as bewitching as the rumors say.

"Good evening," Grace said, stepping forward and curtseying. "I presume that you are Lady Murray? I'm Mrs. Matthew Miller." Grace held her hand out. "I am honored that you and the governor could be our guests. Your presence is truly a blessing."

The woman gave her a warm smile. "Thank you, Mrs. Miller," she replied. "The governor and I considered it our charge to attend." She turned to the others and motioned. "Are you all acquainted?"

Grace smiled and nodded. "Mrs. Wythe is a close friend, and I've met everyone else on past occasions." Grace greeted each wife in turn. She'd studied Rebecca's exhaustive guest list and knew each person's position, endeavors, and relationships almost as well as if she'd grown up among them. The women curtsied one by one. Elizabeth Wythe's husband, George Wythe, was a close friend of Thomas Jefferson. The others were married to influential Northerners. Sally Allen, the wife of a lawyer from Pennsylvania; Mary Alsop, the wife of a prosperous merchant from New York; and Grace Galloway, whose husband was Dr. Franklin's friend. Lady Murray, Elizabeth Wythe, and Grace Miller were similar in age, but the others were at least a decade older.

Elizabeth reached for Grace's hand. "Pray tell, where is Mr. Miller this evening?"

"London," Grace replied. "Dr. Franklin has dragged him away on another adventure, I fear."

"Who, then, manages the farm and factory when Mr. Miller is away?"

"The farm has been in our family since I was a little girl," Grace said. "My brothers are in charge even when Mr. Miller is at home. My husband is oft occupied with the manufacture and sale of his medicines, and he has but a single horse that he refuses to part with."

"I do so appreciate his headache tablets," Sally Allen declared.

"Mr. Miller would be pleased," Grace replied with a smile. "I'll tell him you said so."

"I sometimes take them to speed my slumber."

"I've heard others say the same!" Grace said. "We should change the instructions to reflect this use."

"I am aware that Dr. Franklin has a stake in these tablets," Lady Murray said. "Were they from his experiments?"

"My husband invented them before he met Dr. Franklin," Grace explained, "but Dr. Franklin was vital to their marketing and manufacture. He supplied crucial capital when my husband was highly leveraged."

"To have a mentor such as Dr. Franklin must be a true blessing."

"Yes, indeed," Grace replied. "Until he requires my husband to become estranged from his wife and take on the perils of the sea."

There was an uncomfortable laugh. "I jest," Grace said, smiling. "Dr. Franklin is like a father to Matthew. I cannot fancy our lives without him."

The women relaxed, and Grace was grateful for the white lie. She knew how Matthew treasured his relationship with Ben, but she was uncomfortable sometimes with the role the old man had assumed in their lives. He incited action from her husband at the risk of all sensibility. The last thing Virginia needed was another tempest in the teapot.

"'Tis oft thus with fathers," Lady Murray confided. "They push their sons to the limits. Much of a young man's quest for independence comes at the behest of a strong father."

This one is smarter than she looks.

Grace was suddenly determined to befriend the royal governor's wife.

CHAPTER 21.

DINNER AT MILLER GRANGE

The dinner bell summoned everyone to the formal dining room. They'd expanded the table to accommodate thirty-eight guests. A grand dining hall had been a necessity to Thomas Taylor, whereas Matthew could only roll his eyes when he wandered through the formal-looking chamber. Rebecca had set place cards above each setting, and she stood at the entrance directing guests to their seats.

Much consideration had gone into the seating arrangements. The governor and his wife would have the head of the table. Will sat at the foot as the eldest member of the Taylor-Miller family. Grace placed herself across from Lady Murray. Once they'd taken their seats, the four members of the governor's guard took up positions at the two entrances. More soldiers stood sentry outside the room.

Grace was anxious to know whether her favorable assessment of Lady Murray would hold. Grace gravitated to confident and intelligent women and hoped to cultivate a friendship, rather than just another acquaintance. Servants flitted from the kitchen to the table, and Grace was pleased to see her staff fill the governor and his wife's glasses first. When most of the food was on the table, Will stood. They all knew the script for these formal meals, so the table went quiet as soon as he took his feet.

"Welcome, everyone," Will said, "and especially Governor and Lady Murray. Having you here tonight to discuss the future of a prosperous Virginia is a blessing. Before we ask the governor to lead us in a toast, I welcome my sister, the lady of this fine house, to say a few words in her husband's stead."

Grace stood, nodding gratefully to her brother. "As many of you know, my husband is in London attending business, but he sent his blessings. As a member of the House, he supports this incumbent gathering of the Virginia Economic Congress." Grace took care with the next part. "We are pleased to have an audience with Governor and Lady Murray, and hope this is only the first of many efforts to improve relations between the royal government and Virginia businessmen." Her gaze fell on the governor and his wife for a long moment. The governor was on the wrong side of average in regard to physical attractiveness, and it was especially evident when he sat next to his beautiful wife. Grace emptied her head, hoping not to communicate her thoughts in her manner. She motioned again to Governor Murray, and resumed her seat.

The governor stood. "Thanks to our lovely hostess, Mrs. Miller, for this occasion to dine with all of you. Lady Murray and I look forward to a long residence in Virginia. While there are still bridges to be built, this is a first step in forming a stronger bond between England and her colonies." He raised his glass and motioned for the table to stand. "To King George!" he roared. Thirty-seven people followed suit.

Grace watched the people at the table. Tensions were high enough now for some to show greater enthusiasm than others when toasting the king. Her youngest brother, Jonathan, put the glass to his lips but did not drink. She was thankful that he knew enough to fake his support. Jonathan's thoughts about the English concerned her to the point that she asked him to retire when soldiers came to the farm. Jonathan was attending Freemasons' gatherings in Richmond, and the rumor was that they often conspired against the English. She wanted to forbid him from participating, but she had little sway over her younger brother. She did insist that he not endanger the family by expressing his opinions aloud. It was bad enough that so many were jealous of their prosperity.

Grace looked for Thomas Jefferson, to see if he'd use the toast to broadcast his thoughts. Jefferson caught her eye and returned her inspection with an enthusiastic double gulp and a wink. She smiled and then made an effort to outdo him. Jefferson, she thought, often had a woman's instincts when it came to banquet-table diplomacy. With most men, one never knew what gestures they'd make or what words could come spewing from their mouths, especially after a few glasses of wine.

Grace needed no toast to know where some of the families stood. Joseph Galloway, Dr. Franklin's friend, was an adamant supporter of the king. Grace suspected that Ben shared his opinions. Everyone knew of Ben's preference for London over his home of Philadelphia. Grace's brother

Will was in the same camp, but she suspected he might change his mind if he spent more time on the farm and had to quarter English soldiers.

The guests dug heartily into their meals as servants bustled around keeping plates and glasses filled. Content to remain quiet for now, Grace listened to the debates around the table. She glanced at Governor Murray's guard and noticed that they were also listening carefully. It wasn't apparent whether they were trying to ascertain a threat or were genuinely interested in Virginia affairs. Eventually Grace's attention turned to Edmund Pendleton, whose voice rose over the others.

"The birthright of the first son is dictated by the Lord God himself," he said to Thomas Jefferson. "How else can a man who has worked so hard to build his estate perpetuate his family name and his bloodline? An estate must remain intact, in the possession of a single heir."

"I am aware that the concept is in the Bible," Jefferson replied, "but it is not a commandment. That entails result in a land locked in perpetuity, oft unimproved for generations, is counter to Providence. Did not God command Noah to be fruitful, and multiply, and replenish the earth, and did not Noah fulfill his instructions by becoming a farmer and husbandman?"

"Mr. Jefferson," Pendleton cried. "The very custom of naming the firstborn son after his father manifests entails in our time. Would you force families to have fewer children?"

"Nonsense," Jefferson said, smiling. "Entails or no, I

strongly doubt that men would avoid their wives to protect their fortunes."

"And what of illegitimate heirs?" Pendleton countered. "Would they, too, take an equal share of the family's estate?"

Jefferson pondered this for a moment. "The birthrights of illegitimate children are something else entire."

"I only wish to place the fortunes of Virginia on solid ground," Pendleton added.

"Then debt should be your first concern," said Patrick Douglas, one of the Scottish bankers, who had been listening carefully to the exchange.

George Galloway spoke up. "Dr. Franklin has mentioned in our correspondence that the Scots are under pressure from speculation in the tobacco market." He looked at the other Scottish banker, David McClure.

"I'd hardly call it speculation," McClure replied. "Tobacco shipments to England last year were the largest ever. Virginia planters have reaped the reward." He motioned with his arms to the high ceiling of the fine dining room. "'Tis not speculation for the Ayr Bank to want these debts repaid."

"What about you, Mr. Jefferson?" Galloway asked. "Shouldn't Virginia pay its debts?"

"Tobacco is grown in many colonies," Jefferson replied, "and I do not think only planters revel in this prosperity." He looked at McClure. "Many bankers, too, enjoy the treasure that tobacco has brought."

"Still," Galloway said. "This perpetual debt is contrary to the values of many of those in America—those in the

North, anyway. Most of this debt is south of Pennsylvania."

"Nonetheless," Jefferson insisted, "this debt has held for over a decade. There is more than tobacco at the heart of it." He started to say something else, then stopped himself and sat back, waiting for a reply.

"Who owns this debt, if not Virginia?" Patrick Douglas said, scowling.

"Follow the gold," Jefferson said. "'Tis the British government, and they are placing pressure on more than Virginia."

Governor Murray finally spoke. "Britain has incurred an immense expense defending your western frontier these last few years. It is right to demand repayment."

"And yet the war ended a decade ago," Jefferson retorted.

Grace gave Jefferson a cautioning glance. He met her eyes and calmed himself. She tried to steer the conversation to safer ground.

"My husband oft says that much disagreement would end if the colonies were represented appropriately in Parliament. He believes Americans would gladly share the burden of their own defense."

"Madam, with all due respect," Governor Murray replied, "to say that the colonies are not represented is a misstatement."

"If you speak of this *virtual* representation," Jefferson exclaimed, "'tis the most contemptible conceit ever to have entered into the head of a man." He shook his head in disgust and frowned into his food. Grace had never seen Jefferson this angry.

"And yet Virginia, and I say specifically Virginia," retorted David McClure, "cared little about representation until its debt came due."

It was Jefferson's turn to scowl. "Representation has less to do with debt and everything to do with what is right. We should have a say in how many soldiers remain on our soil for our *defense*. Surely our safety is not the only reason for these soldiers to remain."

"What are the others?" asked Governor Murray.

"Many soldiers are from accomplished families. They'd return to England with a threat of military coup."

The entire table was listening now. Even the guards at the door were following the exchange. Grace didn't know what to say; there was nothing to do but watch it play out. Governor Murray finally ended the silence.

"Madam," he said to Grace. "I now understand the perspective of Virginia's businessmen." He looked pointedly at Jefferson. "What do her families believe about the soldiers' role?"

Grace, wishing she had remained silent from the very beginning, weighed her reply. "I cannot speak for everyone. I am sure there are many different opinions."

"You oft quarter soldiers at your estate," the governor said. "Do you believe 'tis your charge?"

"'Tis English law."

"But if 'twas not, what then?"

"We'd still open our farm to these young men."

"Do you believe they are essential to the defense of this colony?"

"I do not know, Governor."

It was true. When Grace was a little girl, soldiers often returned from the frontier wounded. She couldn't remember the last time she had seen an injured soldier.

"We must not be doing enough to demonstrate the role these soldiers play in Virginia's security," the governor replied.

"My husband does not oft involve me in such discussions, Governor." Disappointment surged through Grace at having to dodge the question like this, but she hoped the governor took it at face value.

Grace saw she'd not escape so easily, though, when Lady Murray spoke up. She corralled Grace with piercing eyes. "I'm sure you have some thoughts on the subject, Mrs. Miller. Are the soldiers necessary for the defense of Virginia?"

Grace met the countess's intelligent gaze. Her sense of kinship for the astute young woman was slowly changing to animosity. "Our colony should be given a choice to defend its frontier with its own militia," she said.

"And you believe that the colony would be better served if the soldiers returned to England?"

"I believe they could be used constructively elsewhere," Grace replied.

The table went silent.

CHAPTER 22.

BLOOD

Servants began to clear away dinner plates and serve dessert. Lady Murray, having made her point, steered the conversation away from statecraft. They were soon discussing the challenges of raising children, and the table's humor turned from heavy to light. Though the topics were often personal, they were safe. It was about eight o'clock when all the guests simultaneously seemed to grow weary and some to allow that they'd drank too much wine. Governor Murray stood and the rest followed his lead. Those staying at the farm went to their rooms and the others took carriages back to Richmond.

Grace supervised the proper cleaning and storing of the china before beginning her evening rounds. She always walked the barns to make sure the horses were housed and fenced appropriately for the night. Grace thought about changing her clothes, but there were still guests walking about and she knew that once she had her gown off, she'd want to melt immediately into bed. Instead, she held her skirts high as she walked through the stables.

Satisfied that all was in order, she patted Silver Star's head and turned toward the house, but before she could complete her rotation, an enormous hand covered her mouth and a red-sleeved arm wrapped around her chest, pulling her off her feet and dragging her through the dirt. Grace's scream trapped in her throat as a low bark. She could scarcely breathe through the tiny space that remained between her nose and his palm, but she sucked in air when she could. The fear, contortions, and violence required more breath than Grace was able to muster and after a few terrifying moments, her mind started slipping away.

No! Awake!

She thrust her head to the side and drew a deep breath, but he covered her mouth again before she could yell.

"This way!" a young man said. She recognized him: one of the governor's guards. Grace's eyes darted around the stables as she struggled against her captor, whipping her limbs in a wild attempt to break free. The churning in her head made it impossible to fix her eyes on anything. She wrenched her arm free and thrust an elbow into her assailant's gut.

"Bitch!" he said. "You wait."

She twisted again, but his arm was a vise around her. He thrust his hand past her lips to press it painfully against her teeth and her mouth filled with acrid tobacco ash. His skin was old, and it matched the rasp of his voice. When she tried to bite, he gripped her jaw mercilessly and cupped his palm, staying out of her reach. The understanding that this man had done this before chilled her soul.

Grace panicked, whipping hard again, hoping someone would hear the tumult, but she was already too far from the house. She could only just hear the voices of the few people who remained. Her dress also conspired against her to muffle her contortions as it wrapped its folds around her legs.

"Better for you if you don't fight," her captor said.

Grace forced herself to go still, trying to regain her composure for one hard attempt at escape.

"There's a fine lass." Her massive attacker relaxed, too, as he dragged her easily between the two main stables. She fought the temptation to fight; she knew she couldn't overpower him. Animals tossed their heads and clomped their hooves in agitation. Grace met their eyes as she was dragged past and it pained her. Horses recognized cruelty, and she chafed at their having to see humanity at its worst.

Matthew's stallion, Thunder, strained against his gate and whinnied loudly. He kicked hard at his stall and bellowed, then suddenly went quiet to watch Grace as she tumbled past. His deep brown eyes were full of helplessness. As they pulled her away, Thunder started to whinny loudly, bellow, and scream.

"Hither!" the sentry said. He was little older than a boy. "Take her away from these animals."

Grace heard a door slide open behind her. They dragged her across the polished wooden floor of the hay barn and the young soldier slid the door shut.

"This should do," her captor said. He loosened his grip on her face. She used the space to inhale deeply and try to scream, but the scream was slapped away by the gloved hand of the young soldier. "You squeak again, we'll kill you," the older guard said into her ear. "And we'll come back and burn this farm to the ground with your little bastards inside." He squeezed the breath from her chest with his massive arm and smacked her again.

"Don't bruise her," the young soldier said. "You should have gloves."

"Shewing her what is," the older man replied. He dropped Grace to the ground, and she tumbled forward onto her hands and knees, crumpled in her dress and petticoat. She turned back and looked into the face of the older soldier. "You mind your manners and it'll be between us. No one will ever know. Not your husband, not the governor, none of your fancy ladies."

"I'm with child," Grace pleaded.

"Good for you," the young soldier replied. "Then there won't be a bastard to explain."

"If you go, I'll pretend nothing has happened—"

"Just like that?" the older man said, laughing. "You ungrateful whore. You'll take what's coming."

"Why are you doing this?"

"My mates died so you could gripe about living on your fine estate." He gestured to the young man. "Pull her dress off and let's see."

The younger soldier dived onto Grace, trying to pin her to the ground, but she rolled away in the folds of her gown and was somehow able to take her feet.

When the young soldier rushed at her, Grace thrust her fist into his face, shouting "Hi-yah!"

He staggered back, blood streaming from his mouth. The larger soldier charged forward and shoved her against the wall, knocking the breath from her lungs. He charged again and lifted her against the wall. She brought her knee up hard, but her skirt stifled the impact of the blow.

"Take this damned dress off," he commanded.

The younger man held her as he ripped her gown open. The older man tore it away from her legs, leaving her in her white undergarments. Grace struggled, pretending to want to keep the dress on, but once her legs were free, she thrust her knee up into his face. She heard the crunch of knee against bone. He staggered back, surprised, and Grace pushed herself off the wall and into the center of her practice floor.

The younger man met his partner's eyes as the older man regained his feet. "Too much woman for you?" he said with a mad laugh. "I like it when they fight." He had a grin like a frenzied predator as he approached Grace. He was deliriously pale.

Grace was free now, standing in the center of the hay barn in bare feet, silk corset, and pantaloons. She knew she was fighting for her life, and she felt like she had a chance. She would die before she'd let them touch her again.

The young soldier walked toward her as she gathered her composure. She executed a perfect spinning kick and hit him squarely in the temple, then stepped back to watch him wobble and collapse.

"Bitch!" the older man yelled, charging.

Her shout was loud and her sidekick was hard, but she was too light to match him, and he reached out and wrapped his arms around her legs and pulled her down to the wooden floor. She struggled and rolled away, but he was on top of her again, and as she felt her strength ebb, she yelled as loud as she could.

The barn door crashed open with a bang and Jonathan burst in, wielding the pick he'd used to smash the lock, ahead of a stream of men, including Governor Murray. Jonathan flew to Grace's side and thrust the pick into the old guard's stomach as the man struggled to his feet. The massive soldier crumbled to the floor.

"Fucking Redcoat," Jonathan spat.

Grace stood up cautiously as the men surrounded her. Their concern was palpable as they tried to assess the situation.

"I fought them," she informed them staunchly. "I'd not let them violate me."

Stand up straight! You're a Daughter of Virginia!

The room was suddenly silent. Everyone was staring at her. Grace felt naked in her white undergarments, and it took a moment for her to realize that their eyes focused on her legs. She followed their eyes and saw that her pantaloons were turning red with blood. Not long after, despite her best effort to stand, Grace collapsed onto the floor, whispering, "Matthew."

She opened her eyes one last time to see a piece of hay float from the rafters to join her on the polished wood floor.

PART II.

VIRGINIAN

"Where there is only a choice between cowardice and violence, I'd advise violence." ~ Mahatma Gandhi

CHAPTER 23.

LAND

Matt walked down the plank followed by David Sutton. Merchants, traders, and seamen crowded the dock. A vagabond in tattered clothes blocked their progress to the wooden platform, perusing the *Norfolk* with a smile.

"Pray, pardon me, sir," Matt said. "Could you move?"

The old man gazed up at the ship's sails. "That an American vessel?"

"It's the *Norfolk*," David said. "Finest ship in the colonies."

"You don't say," the vagrant replied. He moved unruly black hair out of his face, which was cleaner than Matt expected for the way he was dressed. Looking over Matt's shoulder at the young sailor, he said, "You Americans?"

"Mr. David Sutton and Mr. Matthew Miller of Virginia," David replied.

"Virginians proud, are they?"

David started to answer, but Matt stopped him.

"It's been a long journey, sir," Matt said. "May we pass?"

The man smiled and moved aside, and they stepped from the ramp onto the dock. He watched until they were on the platform, then he walked away, all the while watching the ships.

"Odd bird," David said.

"I'd be careful of telling strangers our names," Matt replied, trying to adjust to solid ground. He stepped away from the plank to let a stream of sailors pass. The dock was dark with rain and worn smooth from footsteps and carts. Matt strode wide to avoid a puddle and turned toward the vessel that had been his home for six weeks.

"Takes time to get your land legs," David said as he exaggerated his standing on his two feet while looking down at the wooden dock.

"I'll miss her," Matt said, still gazing at the ship. He smiled at his urge to walk back up the plank and pat the ship goodbye.

"I'm in high spirits to be off her," David replied, rubbing the spot where the bullet had entered his arm. "I've got relations here."

"We have much to do in the next few months," Matt declared.

"I'm most happy to help, Mr. Miller," David said. He dropped the hand from his arm.

Matt was looking forward to being a mentor to the young man. He'd hoped to convince the ship's surgeon to take David as his apprentice, but Callaway had plans to retire to his family farm and spend time with his grandchildren. Matt offered to take David as his secretary until they found a situation that matched his intellect. He knew he could trust David and suspected he'd need allies in the days to come.

"Let's go find Benjamin Franklin," Matt declared as he made another effort to stop swaying.

He surveyed the docks to get his bearings and filled his lungs with morning sea air. It was fresh, with only a hint of the fishy decay that would be overwhelming at midday. Matt scanned the line of structures that littered the dock and then set out to hail a coach. He turned to the *Norfolk* one last time, hoping its crew could be trusted to deliver his three chests. David's footsteps beside him reminded him that these problems were now the purview of his new secretary.

****

Everything around Matt and David made it hard not to be impressed as they made their way to the street, dodging traffic, men, and crates. London was one of the busiest ports in the world, and it was something to see. Once they were on the cobblestones, Matt looked for evidence of the transformed city Ben described in his last letter. He'd alluded to new machines but was not specific.

Matt detected oil and smoke in the air, and he looked up at the sky, but the buildings obscured the skyline and he could not tell whether the sky was overcast or if the grey was industrial smoke. Ben's letters made him suspect it was a little of both. Matt waved down the first hackney coach he saw. It had brand-new leather seats and plenty of windows for gazing out at the city. It took Matt a few blocks to realize that something, indeed, was not quite right. He could have sworn that a bicycle had just passed.

"I'm going to see if I can ride up top," Matt said to David, but the young man had already fallen asleep against the side of the hackney. Matt reached his head out of the coach. "Driver, can I ride up there with you? I want a better view of the city."

The driver steered the two horses to the curb and halted abruptly. Matt opened the door and climbed up next to him.

"Finest city in the world," the coach driver said. His head was shiny on top, with a thick rim of grey hair that extended to his shoulders. The lines around his eyes weathered his face and fascinated Matt almost to silence. The driver waited for Matt to situate himself, then he slapped the reins and the carriage jerked forward.

"A man was riding on something . . . just now."

The driver gave Matt a puzzled expression.

Matt motioned with his arms. "He was holding a handlebar, like this."

"A Ferguson Two-Wheeler?"

"A Ferguson Two-Wheeler?" Matt repeated.

"Don't like them much, myself," the man replied. "Hard enough to drive a carriage around London without young folk on Fergusons jumping about the streets and scaring the horses."

"How long have these Fergusons been around?"

"Few years."

"Has the city changed recently?"

The driver nodded. "Even I've been to an electricity shew."

"What occurs at these electricity shews?"

"Magic, certainly," the man replied. "Never expected to see such in my lifetime. Still not sure if it's natural for a man to control the lightning."

Matt looked back at him expectantly.

"You've never been?" the man asked.

"I've just arrived from America."

"I only seen the modest ones. They say the one at Ferguson Manor is the spectacle."

Matt was not regretting his decision to move up front. "Know much about the inventor of this Ferguson?"

"He's sitting pretty, but ain't one o' them chaps that was born to it. Makes a commoner proud to see one of your own shew them flashy fops."

"He discover gold or something?" Matt asked, to keep the driver talking.

"Got factories in London. Makes brilliant machines, and lots of them, too."

"What kind of machines?"

The driver looked at Matt suspiciously. "Are you joking?"

"We're years behind the times where I'm from," Matt replied as another bicycle passed.

The driver pointed down to his left at a diecast metal insignia on the carriage with a stylized letter "F" integrated into the image of a lion. "Ferguson Industries," he said.

"This carriage?"

"Makes them with something called mass production. Still, there's a waitin' list."

"Interesting."

Matt had thought something was different about the carriage. The cobblestone roads were rough, but the noise of the wheels was muffled and the ride was smooth. He leaned over the side to inspect the wheels and suspension while the driver watched him curiously. The wheels were the conventional spoked wood, but they rested on a coiled-spring suspension. Coiled springs weren't supposed to be on carriages yet.

"What else do they make at this Ferguson factory?" Matt asked.

"I don't know all the machines. Most are on display at the manor. I've never gotten an invitation to the citizens' ball." They watched another bicycle pass. "He makes clocks, too. Like masterpieces, they are." He was excited to have remembered something new. "And the manor—the manor, they say, is lit by stars."

"Candles?"

"Something else entire. No smoke. Imported from America. I am surprised you're not familiar."

"I have some idea," Matt said. Ferguson Manor had to be lit by electric lights. They drove in silence until they found themselves in front of a four-story brick row-home a few blocks from the Thames.

"This is it," the driver said.

Matt shook his hand, paid, and climbed down to the cobblestone street. He opened the coach and looked in on David.

"Hey. Time to wake up."

David sat up in haste, looking lost. "Oh."

Matt reached in for his bag and slung it over his shoulder. David grabbed his own bag by the handle and hopped down to the street. Matt knocked on the side of the carriage and gave the driver a thumbs-up. They stood there across the street from Ben's house and watched the carriage drive away.

CHAPTER 24.

REUNION

Craven Street was crowded with well-dressed Englishmen rushing about on foot and in speeding carriages, and of course, on Ferguson Two-Wheelers. Matt and David jogged through the traffic and stepped up to Ben Franklin's white door. They tapped three times with the cast iron gargoyle knocker and a woman in her early thirties opened the door.

"Yes, sir?"

"Matt Miller to see Dr. Franklin." Matt motioned to David. "This is my secretary, David Sutton."

"Mr. Miller and Mr. Sutton?" she said, surprised. "I'm Polly Stevenson, daughter of Margaret, the owner of this house. Dr. Franklin was not expecting you for another week."

"Pleased to meet you, Polly. He's mentioned you often in his letters," Matt said. "He here?"

"He's in a poor temper," she replied. "Something about throwing himself into the Thames. He's distracted as of late."

Matt laughed. "He can throw himself into the river after we've had a few drinks."

She waved them in, and they followed her into a spacious, bright apartment with expansive windows, then onto a porch and down several steps into a shaded garden where Ben sat at a weathered wooden desk facing the yard. It reminded Matt of his fraternity brothers moving the living room furniture outside for parties.

"You're too young to be working on your last will and testament," Matt called. "Or is it some scheme to change your portion?"

Ben motioned to acknowledge Matt's presence, looked sideways at David, and continued writing. "I must finish these last few paragraphs. You're betimes, anyway."

Matt glanced at David and rolled his eyes. After a few minutes, David tapped Matt on the shoulder. "Mr. Miller, I have relations down by the docks. If it's fine with you, I'll come back in a few days. You can settle yourself."

Matt shrugged. "That's fine. Make sure you check back. I'll ask Dr. Franklin about employment."

David shook Matt's hand and let himself out of the garden gate that led to the alley. Ben glared up at the slam of the gate but returned to his writing. Matt wandered around the garden in silence while the older man completed his paragraphs and signed the letter.

Eventually, Ben sat back and gave Matt a frown. "With all the long-winded nonsense you felt license to speak during our time in Philadelphia, could you not have mentioned a banking disaster such as the civilized world has never seen?"

Matt cocked his head, puzzled, then connected the dots. "It's the debt, isn't it?"

"Isn't it still?"

"I mean the colonies. Virginia and the Carolinas. Debt is practically their business model. How do they even keep track of all the creditors? It would drive me nuts." He contemplated Ben for a moment. "You didn't get caught up in it, did you?"

"Ah!" Ben sighed. "A few hastily made investments."

"I can lend you the money," Matt said, smiling. He wasn't joking, but he knew Ben's moods. It was extremely doubtful that the man had lost his *entire* fortune.

Ben chirped and waved his hand in the air. "I got out before most. It's going to sting . . . for a while."

"I thought you needed the internet to create a bubble."

"Still speaking nonsense?" Ben said. He stood and reached for Matt's hand, clasping it hard, then pulled him close in a bear hug, patting him heartily. He stepped away to inspect Matt's face. "*Now* what befell you?"

"Pirates," Matt said.

"Did you fight?"

Matt pointed to his head. "We outsmarted them."

"Doesn't look like it."

"What news do you have? My driver could do nothing but talk about the magical inventions of a man called Ferguson."

"I wanted you here earlier," Ben explained. "Since I contacted you last, Sir William Maynard, one of Parliament's strongest opponents of American representation, has disappeared. Many believe it to be foul play committed by pro-American groups either here or abroad."

"It's a powder keg in the colonies. Do they suspect anyone specific?"

"They point fingers at anyone who has a stake in America, which is about half of London, including Ferguson. Seems like he came from nowhere. One day I heard his name from some coachman and the next I knew, he's speaking in front of Parliament. He's been knighted."

"He did kind of come from nowhere," Matt replied. "Can you buy a knighthood?"

"These days? You can buy whatsoever you like."

"Have you met him?"

"No, but that will change."

Matt waited for an explanation.

Ben shrugged. "I've been invited to a party." He motioned for Matt to follow him inside and they wound up in the study on the second floor, where Ben retrieved a packet from a large secretary desk before he sat in a padded chair opposite Matt on the sofa. He set the packet on the marble table between them beside a decorative vase of daisies and wildflowers, then held up a folded note.

"This is my invitation," he said, and he tossed a second parchment note. Matt followed it with his eyes as it slapped onto the table and slid toward him. "And that, my good fellow, is yours."

"Mine?" Matt said, leaning forward to pick it up. In calligraphy across the front, it said "Mr. Matthew Miller." Wax sealed the back. "I thought we agreed to keep my visit between us."

"I told no one," Ben replied.

"Only my family and business associates knew," Matt said, "and then in the strictest confidence, and only right before I left."

"How, then, did he know you were coming to London?"

Matt flicked up the wax seal with his fingernail and opened the letter. "A masquerade party?"

"Seems."

"I guess we're going, then?"

"There are some reputable costume shops in town."

"I have an aversion to costume parties."

"Londoners love them."

"The only way Ferguson could have predicted that I was coming was with a network of spies or by having the information already in his head."

"He has enough gold to hire anyone he wants for anything he chooses," Ben said. "A network of spies is probable. Only you can decide whether he has additional abilities."

"Let's assume he does."

CHAPTER 25.

MASQUERADE

The driver stopped the carriage in the portico of a majestic mansion along the River Thames. Ben got out first and waited for Matt, who tripped as he stepped from the vehicle, half-blinded by his mask.

"Careful," Ben said, sticking his arm out to brace him.

Matt adjusted his mask and smoothed his silver cape back over his shoulders. He wondered if he looked anything like a superhero. The mask covered his face from his forehead almost to his nose. It was made of black felt, adorned with metallic decorations that matched the cape, and was attractive as far as masks went. Matt wished now, though, that he had gone with Ben to select the costumes. "I can't see a damn thing in this," he complained.

"It's a fine-looking mask, though," Ben said.

"You want to trade?"

"You won't even notice it after a while."

"Do we wear them the whole time?" Matt held his mask by the nose as he and Ben took in the socialites stepping out of cabs behind them and making excited noises as they passed between the gigantic columns and started up the carpeted stairway.

"He built this?" Matt asked. The marble looked new.

"It was finished a few years ago by some East India fellow," Ben said. "It takes a long time to complete a structure like this, even with all the resources of London at your disposal—longer than Ferguson's been here, at any rate."

"Can't imagine what this cost," Matt said, now inspecting the whole façade.

"Ferguson's aroused some envy, even among the old families."

"Affluence is hard to imagine until you see it."

"These people may be insulted by your pretense," Ben cautioned. "Some here will know that you're no beggar."

"My brother-in-law," Matt replied.

"The breeder of kings?"

"Will started that. I had nothing to do with it."

"Don't expect to hide in a corner."

Their conversation ended as they reached the door, where two men in long velvet evening coats, one a dark red, the other a rich royal blue, greeted guests. A third dressed in green crossed names off a list from behind a desk. The attendants recognized Ben before he lifted his mask.

"Welcome, Dr. Franklin!" There was an exchange of nods and smiles. "Mr. Miller, I presume?"

Matt lifted his mask with one hand and reached out to shake with the other. "Mr. Matthew Miller," he confirmed.

Another attendant stepped in beside them, touched Matt's back, and guided him along a red-carpeted walkway past paintings and statues whose splendor was overwhelming.

Ben was correct in his assessment of Matt's reception

at the masquerade ball. The Millers' Thoroughbred horses and apothecary supplies had made the family known throughout the colonies, and Matt's brother-in-law, Will Taylor, furthered their fame with his import-export business, Martin Enterprises. Will nurtured high demand for Taylor-Miller horses among his partners, and people on both sides of the Atlantic were on a waiting list for their animals. The richer ones paid exorbitant sums to jump to the top of the list. Small chests of gold coins frequently arrived at the farm and Jonathan, the youngest Taylor, secreted them away to a vault in one of the barns. No one but Jonathan and Matt knew how much gold they had, but it was more than the family could spend in a lifetime.

If the art in Ferguson Manor was any indication, success had a new definition in London, where buying luxuries could become a full-time pursuit. Ben pushed Matt along again, responding to an attendant at the end of the hallway who was urging them into the great hall. Matt swallowed a gasp when they entered. The room was brilliantly lit by the evening sun streaming through windows that reached from the arched ceiling to the floor.

Shining gold chandeliers hung the length of the room over tables spread with elaborately embossed white tablecloths and purple-and-white bouquets interspersed with thick candles. A massive unlit fireplace was visible beyond the crowd that had gathered among the tables. The smell of bayberry permeated the air and Matt could feel a light breeze moving through the room. Even Ben seemed humbled by the opulence. Matt tilted his head to inspect the statue of Hercules at the center of the room. Hercules was about fifteen feet tall; his stone arms were outspread and held two glistening metal swords.

"Seems you are not alone in your industry," Ben said, following Matt's gaze.

"Guess not," Matt replied. He stopped himself midway through a comparison of his and Patrick Ferguson's success. Like Matt, the owner of this brilliant mansion had achieved his status using his knowledge of the future. Comparing their abilities to game the system hardly seemed legitimate, but seeing this opulence did make Matt curious as to exactly how Patrick had built his fortune. Patrick would fill his story with half-truths if his explanation was anything like Matt's, but Matt thought he could piece it together. Money like this didn't come from making bikes and carriages.

Sarah Morris had painted Patrick Ferguson in the worst possible light, but it was hard for Matt not to share some kinship with a man who had found himself in a similar circumstance and managed to prosper. Matt considered the challenges that Patrick overcame once he crossed the sea and took up residence in London. He had heard only favorable things about the man since his ship had landed in London.

Ben edged Matt forward again, between the tables and then into the crowd of powdered wigs. Matt reached up and gave his own wig a casual twist to relieve his itchy scalp. He was able to move about this fine English hall with some degree of comfort, but he still needed to put on his game face and remind himself to smile and be affable. Ben, as a contrast, fed off the crowd and his energy increased with every interaction.

"Benjamin!" a man called out, waving. He was standing with a younger woman. Ben responded in kind and Matt followed him over to greet the couple.

"How does it, old fellow?" Ben said, shaking the man's hand.

"Quite well," the man replied. "And you?"

"No city in the world like London. I cherish each day."

"How you flatter us," the man exclaimed. "There's no question why your popularity abounds in my city."

Ben turned toward Matt. "This is Mr. Matthew Miller of the Virginia Colony."

"Mr. Miller, welcome to our fine city," the man said. "I'm George Wellington, and this is my daughter, Elisabeth." The young woman held out her hand to Matt, who raised it higher.

"Pleased to meet you, Miss Wellington," he said.

"The pleasure is mine, Mr. Miller," she replied, staring deep into his eyes through his mask. Matt looked away when it seemed appropriate. "I do love your bubbling tablets. My father keeps a supply at our convenience."

"It pleases me that you should enjoy them," Matt said. "I sometimes forget that Dr. Franklin created a market for our products in England."

"An astute businessman before he was a partisan," George Wellington proclaimed. "I've seen your tablets as far away as New Castle."

Matt glanced at Ben and Ben shrugged. The satisfaction Matt felt promptly melted with the thought that perhaps

Patrick Ferguson was also a consumer of Miller Head and Stomach Tablets. This could result in some probing questions later.

George Wellington turned to Ben. "Any success in the back rooms?"

"I pray I have swayed one or two," Ben replied. "Americans want only the rights shared by every Englishman."

"You know I agree. I'll do what I can and so will Sir Patrick."

"*Sir* Patrick?" The words came out of Matt's mouth unbidden.

"Recent, but quite deserved," Wellington said. "He's done much for the city and England. His efforts alone have filled the coffers some ten percent this year. His enterprise may rival even yours, Mr. Miller."

"I thought knighthood was gained through battle," Matt said.

"Not necessarily," Wellington replied, "but Sir Patrick has served as an adjunct to the royal army for the last couple of years."

"Adjunct to the army?"

"He has military training."

Matt glanced at Ben, who returned his concerned grin. "I had not heard this of Sir Patrick," Matt replied, looking to Wellington for more information.

"I know little of the specifics," Wellington said. "I am aware, though, that he is an expert in something called the martial arts, and swordplay. They pretend he can disarm and kill a man with his bare hands."

The concern on Matt's face was mistaken for disbelief.

"I understand your scruple," Wellington said. "The days of jousting are history, but I'd not bet against Sir Patrick in a proof of human combat. His parts are beyond reproach."

Matt gave Ben a half-satisfied smile and then turned back to Wellington. "I want to meet this fine man at some point."

Wellington turned and scanned the crowd. "In short order," he proclaimed. He waved Ben and Matt forward. "Come!"

CHAPTER 26.

COURTESANS

Sarah grabbed her husband's hand as he assisted her from the carriage. Thomas had wanted her to wear her light-blue gown, but she wore the grey-velvet dress trimmed in white that she had recently purchased in London. Sarah fancied that the color and the modest hoop might assist her in her clandestine mission to steal back her books. Even so, the long skirt snagged on the carriage door, and she fell into her husband's arms. They giggled uncontrollably as he set her on the ground. The comic relief dissipated some of the tension that had grown between them since they had left their hotel.

"I wish we had no intent tonight save to be introduced to as many people as possible," Thomas said, "and for them to envy the beauty of my wife."

"Husband," she proclaimed. "We shall have a pleasant evening and let all other intent come as it may."

"There is nothing I can say to convince you?" Thomas asked. "Even if the Lord Himself put those words into my mouth?"

"Tonight, we should both seek His guidance."

Thomas responded with a look of frustration, then disappointment. He gave her a soft and resigned smile, shook his head, and reached for her hand. Sarah knew that once her husband's hand came out, he'd argue no more. His support filled her with strength and she felt the spring return to her step.

Sarah looked around, wondering whether Patrick Ferguson's spies were already announcing her arrival. Thus far, it seemed they hadn't attracted scrutiny. She dreaded the moment when they were recognized and she hoped there would be time for her to move freely through the party as she figured out how to break into Patrick's office to search for her missing books. Somehow she knew they would be there.

They paused in front of Ferguson Manor, taking in the enormous red ribbons and bright decorations that dazzled over the marble columns, brilliant despite the shadows thrown by the evening sun. Sarah had scouted the perimeter repeatedly, but the deep, glistening reflection of the Italian marble still astounded her.

Sarah had spent hours on her phone paging through her photos of the mansion. She had scrutinized every window and ledge for a weakness that would allow her into Patrick's office. She saw him on his balcony on three separate occasions and had photos of him gazing out over his courtyard. Her phone's facial recognition app grouped these pictures with the ones she took a decade ago when Patrick lived with her and her mother above their first bakery.

Thomas walked beside Sarah, looking up at the enormous red bows that wrapped the columns and were decorated with extravagant black-and-silver masquerade masks.

They talked as they walked up the red-carpeted stairway. "Your fellow does know how to make an impression," Thomas said. "There's no doubt."

"He's not *my* fellow, and money buys a lot of ribbons," Sarah replied.

Tom looked ahead to the three attendants who were greeting guests.

"Good evening," the first attendant said. "Welcome to the home of Sir Patrick and Lady Celia Ferguson."

The second attendant looked at Sarah, then stepped back and said, "Madam, a handsome gown."

Sarah curtsied. "Thank you, sir." She took Thomas's arm as he showed their invitation.

The man behind the table checked his list. "Thomas Mifflin and guest," he said as he crossed out their names with a black-tipped quill. "Mrs. Mifflin, I presume," the man said as he gave them a mischievous smile.

"Most correct, my good fellow," Thomas said, chuckling until he saw Sarah wrinkle her nose at the attendant's attempt at bawdy humor.

"Sir Patrick sends his regards," the attendant said to Thomas. "He has invited you to speak with his secretary, Mr. Trent, concerning an increase in cotton imports."

"I'd be happy to discuss this," Thomas replied.

"Enjoy your evening," the man said. He pointed in the direction of the entryway.

When Sarah didn't respond to the prompt, Thomas led her by the arm toward the hallway. She was going through a checklist in her mind, looking for some clue that allowed her to prepare for her eventual confrontation with Patrick.

Patrick had wanted her here for a reason; she had only to figure out what it was. Was there something more to the meeting between Patrick's secretary and her husband? Was Patrick separating him from her?

Sarah and Thomas walked in relative solitude down the hallway and to the magnificent expanse of the great hall. Sarah scanned the crowd as they arrived, hoping to catch someone observing them too closely.

"Where could Mr. Trent be?" Thomas said.

"The fewer people we speak to, the better," Sarah quipped.

A man stepped in front of them. "Mr. and Mrs. Mifflin?"

"That's us," Thomas replied. Sarah squeezed his hand.

The man lifted his mask and said, "Sir, if you please, my name is Nathan Trent."

Thomas nodded and extended his hand. "I was told Sir Patrick wanted me to speak with you," he said. "I did not think I'd receive an audience so expeditiously."

"My secretary informed me of your arrival," Nathan replied. "I prefer to conduct business betimes at these affairs." Nathan turned to Sarah. "Mrs. Mifflin, forgive me for being impertinent." He reached for her hand. "I'll introduce you to some ladies while your husband and I discuss terms, terms that should be quite favorable to the Mifflin family." He pointed to a group of women near the towering windows along the north wall.

"Certainly, sir," Sarah replied as she tried to sort through the man's intentions. It was strangely satisfying that her prediction that they'd separate her from her husband was correct. Nathan looked at Thomas for permission, then escorted her to the women and eased her into their discussion. Sarah had expected an elaborate charade, but the introductions were conventional. She watched Nathan out of the corner of her eye as she and the ladies exchanged pleasantries. Nathan put his arm on her husband's shoulder and escorted him from the room.

CHAPTER 27.

OPPONENT

Ben and Matt shared casual glances as Wellington guided them through the crowd. Matt wasn't sure whether to be anxious or excited. He searched his memory for some recollection of this moment, but nothing came. There was only that useless feeling of déjà vu. His head injury on the *Norfolk* had brought back the visions, but he was having trouble navigating them. There were too many missing pieces.

Wellington led them up toward a man in a black mask and a cape who was standing alone and looking into the crowd. Matt saw the caped man reach up and rub his temples in the same way Matt did during a migraine. Wellington tapped the man on the shoulder and whispered something in his ear, and the man turned. Even behind the mask, Sir Patrick Ferguson was handsome. He was tall and fit, with a smile full of white teeth. Patrick shook Wellington's hand. "Wellington, dear fellow. To what do I owe the pleasure?"

"My costume did not fool you," replied Wellington with mock disappointment. "I'd like to introduce you to a few extraordinary gentlemen."

Patrick raised his hand. "It's a masquerade, after all." He

turned his gaze to Ben, who was smiling. "I'm in the presence of a true celebrity," Patrick declared. "Hidden behind this mask is a scientist, inventor, author, and politician; he is a truly admirable man. This is Dr. Benjamin Franklin. Am I correct, sir?"

"You are," Ben declared.

Patrick held out his hand. "I am honored by your presence."

"The honor, of course, is mine." Ben shook his hand.

Matt watched quietly as they traded pleasantries, guessing at the etiquette of introductions to masked strangers. How long would he wait until he offered up his identity if the man wanted to play the guessing game?

Patrick turned to Matt, his face filling with a satisfied grin. "I'm Patrick Ferguson," he said simply.

"Matthew Miller," Matt replied. He felt like he should say something else, like thank Patrick or wish him good health, but the words stuck in his mouth, tangled somewhere in the web of intrigue that swirled in his head.

"If memory serves, you are a man of parts," Patrick proclaimed. The grin returned to his face. "Scientist, inventor, politician, breeder of fine horses, and swordsman. Like Dr. Franklin, your fame proceeds you."

Matt was at a loss for words as he looked into the man's eyes. Of all the ways he had envisioned their first meeting, none had included Patrick regarding him with delight. Matt realized he had not done his homework. Could Patrick control the visions? Or had he learned about Matt through conventional spying?

Ben recognized Matt's distracted silence and chimed in.

"Mr. Miller oft doesn't realize he has affected many in the colonies and across the sea."

"My apologies," Matt finally said. He smiled, trying to replace his pensive expression with one that was jovial. "I concern myself mainly with my business in America and forget the efforts others are making on my behalf." He motioned to Ben and smiled, hoping the bottom half of his face was no longer giving him away as a man who cared.

"These headache tablets are such a contribution to the world," Patrick said. "I suffer from chronic headaches and could not live without them." He looked at Matt with some expectation, maybe waiting for confirmation that Matt had the headaches, too.

Matt kept his poker face. He strained to think of how to leave the man guessing at his abilities, and perhaps even his intentions, which even Matt had not yet defined. "I am glad they provide you relief."

"They are much like a remedy once prepared in my hometown," Patrick replied. "I no longer have access to it, and your invention was a welcome addition to my medicine cabinet."

"Again, Sir Patrick," Matt said. "I can only express my satisfaction that you have experienced Miller Headache Tablets and that you are satisfied with their effect."

"We have a connection you may not be aware of," Patrick announced. "I have added two of your Thoroughbreds to my stables. My stable-master pretends they are the finest horses he has ever handled. Their genetic line will be a significant contribution."

Matt looked at him questioningly, considering the proper

reaction to the use of a term that wouldn't exist for at least a hundred years.

"The Taylor-Miller farm breeds the finest horses in Virginia," Ben said.

"And maybe in all of America," Patrick replied with a hint of suspicion. He was about to say something, but an assistant approached and whispered something in his ear. "I believe my guests have recognized Dr. Franklin," he said. He motioned to a group of women near a fountain. "The tall woman in the blue gown is my wife, Lady Celia. She and the others endeavor to hear about adventures from the American frontier." Patrick placed his hand on Ben's shoulder. "Would you be so kind, sir? Debutantes are shameless around celebrities, though I allow that *my* lady accommodates them too much. I assure you that your stories will be the talk of the town."

Ben bowed happily. "I could attend to some ladies."

"I'd enjoy a discussion with Mr. Miller without these masks on." Patrick motioned toward the staircase. "I'll bring him back to you before you have exhausted the ladies' attention." He motioned to the man beside them. "Mr. Trent will introduce you."

Ben patted Matt on the shoulder. "Come save me when you're done."

Matt's head filled with the image of his being caught in a web with the spider fast approaching. His instinct told him to resist the urge to struggle so he could look around a bit. He and Patrick watched Ben follow Nathan to the women.

"I'm looking forward to speaking with you," Patrick said to Matt. "We have much in common."

CHAPTER 28.

PIGEONS

Sarah was irritated that Nathan Trent had been able to separate her from her husband so easily, and that Thomas had allowed it to happen.

"Let him go, dear," someone said to Sarah. "They like to run off together. They'll be smoking cigars and drinking whisky soon."

Sarah turned toward the voice. A woman in an ornate mask who was perhaps three inches taller than Sarah had spoken. Although her face was concealed, she broadcast beauty and confidence as she held her hand out. "How do you do. I'm Lady Celia Ferguson."

"Celia who?" slipped out of Sarah's mouth.

"Celia Ferguson," she repeated. "Lady of the house."

Sarah was dumbfounded. She had not anticipated meeting Patrick's wife. It took a moment to compose an intelligible reply. "I'm Sarah Mifflin, wife of Thomas, of Mifflin Enterprises." Sarah was immediately disappointed. She had hoped to come up with some reply that seemed confident, or at least intelligent.

"You're an American," Celia observed with pleasure.

"Yes, m'lady," Sarah replied. "From Philadelphia."

"I fancy that the Mifflins are importers," Celia said. "My

husband is so very interested in raw materials. Our factories work day and night."

Sarah smiled and nodded, relaxing. The threats, either real or imagined, were dissipating. Whatever Patrick Ferguson had planned for her this evening, it seemed he was going to take his time. She resolved to beat him at his game. "Ferguson Industries is in manufacturing?"

Celia nodded. "Manufacturers are the new nobility in England, though I fancy such a concept might be foreign to an American."

Sarah found it hard to interpret Celia's tone.

"Your husband's intercourse should be lucrative for you and your family. Trent rarely spirits a man away unless big events are underfoot."

"Intriguing," Sarah replied. "Could you direct me to the powder room? It was a long trip through London, and I desire to freshen up."

"Certainly," Celia replied. She pointed to a staircase that split the center of the house. "I hope we have a chance to talk again, dear."

"Very pleased to meet you, m'lady," Sarah replied with a sincere bow. Against all her suspicions, she liked Celia Ferguson, but she was relieved when she was finally able to walk away. Sarah looked back over her shoulder to catch Celia watching her, but she was already speaking with someone else. She'd seemed to take no interest in Sarah at all.

****

Sarah hiked up her dress as she climbed the stairs. A woman coming down was waving to friends, but took no notice of Sarah. Sarah intended to cross the marble landing to the double doors of Patrick's office in the very center of the manor. At the top of the steps, though, an attendant greeted her.

"Can I help you, madam?"

"Could you guide me to the powder room?" Sarah grimaced and touched her stomach. "The lady's curse is upon me."

The man's eyes widened in alarm and he motioned to a door two rooms to the right of the double doors that Sarah knew led to the office. The man caught her looking at the double doors, but he mistook the frown on her face for discomfort. The attendant put his arm out to escort her. "It's the grey door, madam," he said. "Over here."

The doors along this level were out of sight of the great hall below; the noise of the party was muffled as Sarah moved closer to the doors. At the door to the powder room, the attendant motioned politely. Sarah grimaced again, back in character. "Thank you, sir. I fear I may be in here for a while."

The man blanched. "I understand, madam." He walked about six strides away and stopped to watch additional guests making their way up the steps.

Sarah had been tempted to wander through the office doors as they passed, or to bend over in pain and grab the knob to check the lock. She needed to distract him somehow. "Ah!" she said. "Better to fix this out here in the light." She stood in front of the powder room playing with the folds of her gown, hoping the man would wander off, but he remained to stand sentry at his new post.

So much for Plan A!

Walking through the office doors in an unsupervised hallway had been her optimistic first plan. Plan B was to locate a side door into the office and sneak through unseen. Georgian-era rooms usually had connecting doorways with simple warded locks. Sarah had a locksmith on their payroll in Philadelphia and had become adept at opening locks with a few simple tools; tools that she had in a leather case under her bodice.

Sarah stepped into the powder room and let the door close behind her. She moved through an anteroom that contained three mirrors and a narrow daybed and into the main powder room. There were basins here and stalls that she assumed enclosed toilets. It was unlike any other bathroom from the era save the one she had designed for her own home in Philadelphia. She scanned the room for a connecting door and found none.

So much for Plan B.

Sarah stepped to an open window and stuck her head out. She pulled her head back at the sound of flutter and feathers from startled pigeons scrambling in all directions. She stuck her head out again. This was Plan C. Dried pigeon droppings littered the marble ledge that extended past the powder room windows to the next room and then to a balcony less than twenty yards away. The ledge was wide enough to walk on, and there were plenty of outcroppings to grab along the way.

CHAPTER 29.

PLAN C

Sarah latched the powder room door and sprang into action, removing her shoes and most of her clothing. She had matched her undergarments to the exact grey of the marble of Ferguson Manor. The sun was low enough that she would melt into the wall. Leather slippers and leather gloves went on in place of her dress, and she was ready to make her way across the ledge. Stepping along the brick divider and letting herself into the office from the balcony door had been an option she had prepared for since her first day in London, but she had to stand at the window and gather her courage.

Sarah pushed her fears away and peered out the window to scan the yard. A few heads were bobbing here and there in the distance, but no one was directly below her. The sun was setting on the far side of Ferguson Manor and the building threw a long, dark shadow on the lawn. She checked that her phone and the tools in the pack around her chest were secure, then crawled out along the third-story ledge. She looked down once, panicked, and resigned not to look down again. Three stories was higher than she'd imagined.

Sarah gathered herself and shuffled one foot to the other

and developed a rhythm. At the balcony, she straddled the railing and plopped onto the stone floor. She kept her head low as she duck-walked to the windowed doors, and then adjusted her head to look between the blue velvet curtains into the office. The dim light of the early evening filtered through other windows and she could see the entire room. The office was empty.

Sarah tried the latch; the door was locked. She removed the pack from her chest and took out the credit card she'd carried with her from the twenty-first century. It was perfect for jimmying eighteenth-century doors. She read the name of the sixteen-year-old girl who once owned the card, and the expiration date. The fact that the card was valid for another two hundred and fifty years made her smile. She slipped it between the doors and eased one open. Sarah crept into the room and quietly shut the door behind her, tucking the card back into her pack.

Sarah stood up to look around. There was no safe or lockbox, but there were five large pictures and three closets. The first closet had clothing and the second contained office supplies and what looked to be rejected mechanical inventions. The third closet yielded a solid iron lockbox, but her excitement immediately turned to dismay. "Crap!" she whispered. She could open any number of key-based eighteenth-century locks, but no tool in her pack would help her with a seven-digit combination.

She pulled a chair in front of the safe and sat to ponder the seven dials, each numbered zero to nine. The room had dimmed, so she stood up, opened some of the curtains, and returned to peruse the lock. She wasn't going to give up without trying. She had spent enough time with Patrick Ferguson to know that his seven-number combination wouldn't be random.

Seven numbers? A telephone number!

Sarah unbuttoned her pack and pulled her phone out. She had brought it for the flashlight, but now she was hoping it could provide clues. She pressed the ready button and the security display flashed on. She touched her thumb to the button to unlock the phone and paged through her contacts for Patrick's Tennessee number. They'd exchanged numbers in Philadelphia when they were testing whether messaging and texting worked without cell towers. Patrick was on his phone constantly back then, hoping to find more time travelers.

Sarah turned the dials to Patrick's phone number, tried the latch, entered it again, then backward, but the safe remained locked. She entered her phone number and then her mother's, and still nothing. She sat up in the chair to look closely. The fading light told her she had already been too long. She used her thumbprint to bring back the screen.

Wait!

Patrick had burned his thumb in an accident, and his thumbprint had never worked to unlock his phone. She looked at the twelve icons on the security screen, trying to remember his swiping pattern. *Damn it, I'm not getting anywhere!* Sarah looked at the clock in the corner. Ten minutes had passed since she entered the powder room. How long before the attendant checked?

She looked down again at the security screen. Seven numbers were three swipes on the pad. She dialed 1, 2, 3,

6, 9, 8, 7 into the safe—nothing. Her fingers were starting to shake. She tried 3, 6, 9, 8, 7, 4, 1—nothing. *I have to go.* She stood up, desperate to leave, then sat down again, trying to remember the motion of his fingers when he sat in their bakery. 3, 5, 7, 8, 9, 6, 3—there were noises in the hall. *I have to go!*

Sarah pulled the lever at the same time that she was standing to leave. Thunk! The swinging lever sounded like a gunshot. *Crap!* She froze, listening for a commotion outside, but none came. She leaned closer to the safe and eased the door open. The top shelf held the red backpack she had carried with her from the twenty-first century. Tears welled up in her eyes. Patrick's quantum phone and its kinetic charger were on the second shelf next to pieces of his bike, including an LED flashlight. The bottom shelf had four bound record books with Ferguson Industries labels.

Sarah slid the backpack to the conference table at the center of the office. Her fingers were shaking hard from adrenaline, and she almost knocked over one of the chairs surrounding the table as she set the heavy pack down. She moved two chairs out of the way and stepped back to the table to unzip the pack. All four Advanced Placement textbooks—*The American Experiment*, *Biology*, *Chemistry*, and *Calculus*—were there. The chemistry and history books were smudged and worn. Her copy of *Twilight* brought a smile to her face. It still looked new, so it was evident that Patrick wasn't a *Twilight* fan. Sarah was anxious to reread it.

Conscious of time, Sarah zipped the backpack, pushed it to the center of the table, and walked back to close the door of the safe. She planned to drop the backpack off the balcony into the hedges and retrieve it when it was dark. As Sarah reached for the door, a ledger labeled "American Payments" caught her eye. Wondering whether it had anything to do with her husband's business, she pulled it from the shelf.

The bound ledger was relatively new, and most of its pages were blank. The first section, "Priority One," showed ten pages of projected payments from British companies. Each company had a subsection listing the debts of American merchants and growers. A ten-page section labeled "Priority Two" appeared to be a list of British citizens, their addresses, positions, payments, and due dates. Some of the payments were already complete, and others were six months to a year into the future.

"Priority Three" caught Sarah's attention. It read like a who's who of the United States' Founding Fathers: important American colonists, their last known addresses, and the individuals responsible for contacting them. Thomas Jefferson and Benjamin Franklin were numbers one and two. Her husband was number seventeen. Their Philadelphia home and current London address were listed.

Sarah thought first to steal the ledger, then reconsidered and began taking pictures with her phone. It took her five frantic and precious minutes to lay the ledger on the table and photograph the pages. She scrambled to return it to the safe.

Sarah looked at the shadow of her backpack on the table. After traveling thousands of miles to retrieve it, could she possibly decide to lock it back in the safe? *Twilight?* Was she willing to risk all the names in that American history textbook to investigate the names in the ledger? The tattered books were clearly consulted often; Patrick would miss them almost immediately. Voices sounded outside the door and she made her decision.

She jumped to the table and picked up the pack, taking care not to hit another chair, then hurried to the safe and gently slid the pack back onto its shelf. She closed the door, spun the dials randomly, and walked to the table to replace the chairs she had moved. Now she heard activity at the door, like the ringing of keys. She took only a second to check that everything else was in place, then hurried onto the balcony, easing the door shut behind her just in time.

Candlelight seeped through the drapes as someone entered the office. Sarah climbed softly over the rail and hurried along the ledge to the powder room, where someone was pounding on the door.

"Madam!" the attendant called through the door. "Are you ill?"

Sarah poked her head into the room from the ledge. "One moment," she called.

"Others are waiting, madam," the attendant scolded. "If you are ill, go to the physician."

"Oh! How my new dress is stained!" Sarah cried as she tumbled through the window. "I want a moment to clean it." Sarah's glance into the glass caught her smeared makeup. It would be hard for the attendant to doubt her poor condition when he saw her again.

****

Sarah unlocked the door to the powder room to the

scrutiny of a dozen irritated ladies. Two lifted their masks to show exactly how angry they were, but Sarah kept hers down. She descended the staircase as casually as she could. Thomas was talking to another man but turned to her as she approached.

"Husband," she said. "We must go. I am ill."

"I have business with Mr. Harrington." He gestured to the man who was standing in front of him.

"The curse is upon me, and I fear I have ruined my gown. I've cleaned the stains for now, but it would be embarrassing should others take their place."

Harrington immediately squirmed. "I can visit your apartments later in the week," he said.

Thomas looked at his wife, irritated. He shook his head and turned back to Harrington. "Wives," Thomas said with a smile. They exchanged pleasantries and shook hands.

As Harrington receded into the crowd, Thomas said, "I believe at times that you do not want my business to succeed."

Sarah saw the gleam in his eye that meant he was only humorously angry. "Husband, your business is already successful." She lifted her mask, gave him a flirtatious smile, and kissed him.

"Was it there?" he asked.

"Yes."

"Dropped where we planned?"

"I left it in his office." She could see the questioning look on his face even through the mask. "This situation is complicated," she explained. "I must show you something and tell you a secret I have kept for many years."

CHAPTER 30.

THE PROPOSAL

Pigeons fluttered outside Patrick Ferguson's office window as a servant moved around to light oil lamps. They soon filled the room with a warm glow and Matt settled into a padded leather chair; Patrick took his seat behind a large mahogany desk that held a few precise stacks of papers, two ledgers, a blotter, inkwell, and quills. It occurred to Matt that Patrick, a mechanical engineer, could have designed a better pen. Matt inspected the only other items on the desk: bronze models of a carriage and a bicycle. They sat on oak bases, and their metal had a rich brown patina.

"You've sold a few of those," Matt said, hoping to start the conversation. When Patrick did not reply, Matt turned to follow his gaze over Matt's left shoulder.

"Odd, that," Patrick said. He stood and crossed the room to the conference table in front of the glass-paned French doors that led onto the balcony. Patrick straightened the chairs, then stepped back, evaluated them another time, and readjusted them. He leaned away to take in their full perspective and then moved over to see that the balcony doors and nearby windows were locked.

"They look straight now," Matt said.

"The maids know," Patrick replied. "I must speak to them." He gestured casually, as if to remind himself of more pressing issues, and retook his chair. His back was straight, and he looked directly at Matt. His posture along with his choppy vocal pattern reminded Matt that Patrick had military training.

"What's your background?" Matt asked. "Education and such."

Patrick looked at Matt suspiciously, trying to size him up. "A master's in mechanical engineering from the Imperial College, and then Sandhurst."

"Sandhurst?"

"The Royal Military Academy. The equivalent to your West Point. And you?"

"I have an undergraduate degree from the Philadelphia College of Science and a Ph. D. in chemistry from Kansas."

"Science geek," Patrick said with no hint of humor in his voice.

Matt had spent too much time among ranchers and horseman not to know when he was being probed for weakness. "I try to think my way out of problems," he said. "If another approach is required, then so be it."

"And genetics?"

Matt thought a moment and then shook his head. "I know the basics. I woke up on a farm after the reactor accident and chose to stay and learn the horse business."

"Reactor accident?"

"They never contacted you?"

Patrick looked back with squinted eyes and a crease in his brow.

"That's why we're here," Matt explained. "There was a reactor accident, whatever that means. It pushed us through a wormhole. The scientists, maybe the ones who caused the accident, figured out a way to text me on my phone. They offered to take me back to the twenty-first century if I was willing to risk the wormhole again. I chose to stay."

"You could have returned?"

Matt nodded.

"How many others?"

"Only the ones you know—me, you, Sarah, and her mother."

"The Morris women," Patrick said. "I often wonder what became of them."

"How'd you know about me?"

"I've developed my abilities."

"You saw me in a vision?"

"No," Patrick replied firmly, but then he seemed to regret his answer. "Dr. Franklin's efforts to market your tablets made me curious about their inventor. Imagine my surprise to learn this *inventor* was one of most prosperous men in Virginia and a member of its House of Burgesses. We share similar aspirations, you and I."

"I've as much as I need," Matt said, hoping not to sound arrogant. He glanced at the Rolex on his wrist. It had been his most noted lapse in frugality as a young man. He'd once spent an entire signing bonus on that watch and a new car. He sometimes guessed at what had become of the car. He hoped his dad had sold it. He no longer obsessed about having enough money, though. Grace took full charge of the business after learning accounting under Robert and

Graine Martin, and Matt only half-listened when she gave him financial summaries. He was proud of the numbers—mostly because she was—but the care that consumed him now was protecting the future of his wife and children.

Patrick's voice pulled Matt from his thoughts. "I allow that my wife has a greater concern with our financial status than I. I wish to command."

"I didn't have a chance to meet your wife," Matt said. "I hear she is from a distinguished family."

"Our wives married down, perhaps?" Patrick's grin was warm. "Celia has been patient in our attempt to be accepted by the nobility."

Matt shrugged.

Patrick fixed on Matt's face, waved his hand casually, and shook his head. "Modern Americans like to act like they have little concept of birthright. They bow instead to their celebrities, their wealthy. There is nothing worse than a lie we choose to accept . . . and live by."

Matt shrugged. "Gotta love the media."

"People want leaders from an elite lineage," Patrick explained. "Even your John Adams will want to refer to the president of the United States as Your Majesty. A little-known fact about your government is that some years after it's formed, a considerable contingent will lobby to replace the president with a monarch from one of the European royal families. Even Americans don't believe that the *vulgar man* is qualified to lead."

Matt gave Patrick a knowing smile. "You have me at a

disadvantage," he said. "I don't have a college textbook on American history."

Patrick answered with a face that was a combination of satisfaction and amusement.

"What about you?" Matt asked. "Do you have the pedigree to lead?"

"Mine was a renowned family that was bombed out of existence during the second world war. My father was orphaned and never recovered."

"You've done much, then, to reestablish the Fergusons' prominence." Matt gestured at the richly decorated office.

"My father died a broken man trying to regain all that had been destroyed. Would it not have been better to deter such suffering altogether?"

Matt found himself leaning back, shaking his head, and clenching the arms of his chair. Catching himself, he raised his head and looked directly into Patrick's eyes. "The devil's in the details."

"I'd like your help in changing the course of history," Patrick announced.

Matt looked back at Patrick with a blank face, waiting for more of an explanation. Patrick took it as either disinterest or disagreement.

"You'd risk your farm and family in a revolution?"

"I'm hardly in a position to stand in your way," Matt replied.

"Why did you come across the sea?"

"Franklin asked me to join him."

Patrick frowned. "I'd like to believe that we are serious men."

"Why did you take the textbooks?"

"They've contributed little to my success."

"Yet you've never returned them."

"They made cupcakes," Patrick replied. "They were doing quite well when I left. How are they?"

"Successful."

"What shall happen to the Morris women when British soldiers occupy Philadelphia?"

"And you'd prevent that?"

"The American Revolution will waste financial and human capital. The damage done to the British Empire and the world will not be realized for another hundred and fifty years. It's our moral duty to prevent it."

"You can trace every fucked-up thing that's ever happened in the world back to someone's concept of *moral duty*," Matt said. "There's going to be a cost if you try to change history."

Patrick did not attempt to hide his pained and disappointed expression.

"We can debate whether you have the *right* to change the future," Matt continued, "but I'm certain you don't have the ability." He smiled mildly.

"Almost eighty million people are going to die in two world wars because the Americans and the Brits can't get their act together," Patrick explained. "This city will be decimated in the Blitz. Thirty thousand people will die . . . right here."

"You think you can avoid two world wars?"

Patrick gave Matt a knowing smile. "You wouldn't have

come all this way if you didn't believe I had some capability. Franklin knows?"

"I do believe you could make a mess of things. And yes, Franklin knows."

"You've been perfectly happy to enrich yourself."

Matt waved him off with a casual sweep of his fingers. "I sleep fine."

Patrick looked sternly back. "My children have been treated with a new vaccine for smallpox. It comes from cows. William Jenner was not supposed to publish these discoveries until the end of this century, yet there they are." Patrick scrutinized Matt to gauge his reaction. "You sell a medicine to treat wounded soldiers. Is it an antibiotic? Are you not worried that your cures may save the next Joseph Stalin or Pol Pot?"

"The antibiotic is penicillin or at least some form of it," Matt replied. "And yes, I'm behind the publication of the smallpox cure. I'm glad your family has been vaccinated."

After witnessing a smallpox outbreak in Philadelphia, Matt had convinced Ben to publish a home remedy in every major newspaper in the colonies. The remedy consisted of substituting cowpox for smallpox during variolation, which was a crude eighteenth-century form of vaccination. It had taken a few years to break down skepticism, but now the procedure was widely available. Farmers were propagating cowpox in their animals, collecting the pustules that resulted, drying them, and selling them to local doctors.

Cowpox was a mild variant of the smallpox virus passed from cows to humans. It produced few facial pustules and was rarely fatal. The immunity of milkmaids to smallpox had been part of local lore for some time, although no one recognized the connection to cowpox. The expressions "pretty as a milkmaid" and "milky smooth" skin spoke to the fact that milkmaids were unscarred by smallpox because their exposure to cowpox had made them immune. Now, due to Matt's intervention, almost anyone could be immune.

Fine! Ferguson had it right. If Matt was indeed worried about changing the future, he wasn't acting like it.

CHAPTER 31.

WESTERN MAN

An hour later, Patrick had not gotten to anything that resembled a proposal. Matt's head was swimming, and he didn't want his concept of possible futures to interfere with Patrick's explanation of his plan.

"Cut to it," Matt finally said. "What do you want?"

"If you're not going to help, at least stand aside," Patrick said. "I've initiated a ten-year plan to strengthen the British Empire. England is the world's best hope. No one will challenge western civilization for a thousand years."

"No one could challenge western civilization in our time," Matt said.

"Call it God, call it karma, call it whatever you want," Patrick said. "We've been sent back to the eighteenth century for a reason. I believe it is to abate human suffering."

"Strengthening the British Empire will abate suffering?" It came out of Matt's mouth as more cynical than he intended.

"British common law created the most successful countries the world has ever seen. Wouldn't you like to be the one responsible for ending slavery in the United States a century early?"

"We'd be messing with things we can't control."

"I feel fortunate that I was never given a chance to return to my old time. I can make a difference. Here. Now."

"Say that in theory, I agree. Say that I'm even willing to help you. What's your plan?"

Patrick looked hard at Matt with a silence that was longer than was comfortable. His first expression was one of doubt, then it went to quiet contemplation, and ultimately, a kind of "what-the-hell, why-not" acceptance. Patrick pulled some pages from the leather portfolio on his desk and pushed them across to Matt, then spent the next half hour systematically listing the details of his plan.

CHAPTER 32.

BROTHERS IN ARMS

After their conversation was finished, Matt followed Patrick across the second floor of Ferguson Manor. The noise of the crowd became louder as they neared the staircase. Patrick motioned for Matt to stop and then continued to the edge of the balcony. There was no longer any light streaming through the expansive windows, so the illumination came from eight massive oil chandeliers They rode on pulleys that were bolted to the ceiling and could be raised or lowered from the ground floor using chains. Matt inspected the rigging, thinking the chains must be strong to support the massive lamps, especially when they were full of oil at the beginning of the evening.

Patrick signaled to the attendant who had been watching the stair. The attendant crossed to the opposite side of the railing, putting on a pair of white gloves, and struck a chest-sized copper-plated bell three times with a padded mallet. The tones echoed through the hall. He waited to let the sound take its effect on the crowd. Voices were still loud, so he took three additional swings. This time, the floor went silent. He looked at Patrick and Patrick signaled that he could step away.

The crowd turned toward Patrick as the closest chandelier was being lowered to bathe him in brilliant light. The other chandeliers began to descend from the ceiling and Patrick's black velvet mask and red-trimmed cape shimmered brightly in the lamplight.

"Welcome!" he shouted, raising his arms. "Welcome to the masquerade!" He scanned the crowd and strode along the rail to look out over the great hall. He put his hand up to shield his eyes from the lanterns. "Are you all having fun?" he shouted.

"Yes!" was the reply, then roaring applause.

"Capital, capital!" Patrick shouted back. When they settled down, he continued. "We've done many experiments since the last ball. Do you want to see an electricity shew?"

The chandeliers were low now, casting light in seven distinct circles over the people below them. Applause met the lowered lamps and people stepped back to let them touch the ground. Patrick remained quiet until the seven chandeliers were resting on the floor. Six chandeliers lit the great hall; the seventh was at the base of the stairs. Servants circled each brightly glowing oil lamp and when Patrick pointed at the seventh chandelier, they extinguished its flames simultaneously. The steps went completely dark.

Now all eyes were on the bright marble hall. Patrick waved to the farthest end; two chandeliers went dark. He motioned to the middle of the room, and the light from two more vanished. A woman cried out.

"Do not fear, madam," Patrick called. "The dusk still precedes the dawn." He waved again and the light from the next two fixtures went out. Only the chandelier closest to Patrick remained. The attendant who rang the bell began dimming its lamps one by one until Patrick faded from view. Now the manor was completely dark. Another woman cried out in fear and then came the shout of a man. Patrick waited until the crowd went still before he began to speak.

"And so it was, when the Earth was created, God said, 'Let there be light,' and there was light." Electric bulbs high on poles lit up where the chandeliers had been burning, then went dark abruptly. "And God said that the light should be divided from the dark." A group of bulbs in the farthest corner lit, and then the next, until all the bulbs around the perimeter were shining, then were extinguished in the same order until the room was dark again.

The crowd stood hushed, waiting for the next light. A horn sounded and the bulbs in the farthest corner flashed on and off. Another horn sounded in a different tone; the opposite corner flashed. This repeated across the great hall, trumpets and flashes jumping from place to place. The pitch of the tones rose as the lights began to move in a counterclockwise pattern. Matt snickered, thinking of *Close Encounters of the Third Kind*.

The lighting reversed, moving clockwise, and the sounding horns sped up with the racing lights. When it went dark, the hall filled with applause. Gradually, as the applause faded, the sculpture of Hercules at the center of the hall was illuminated. First his legs were visible, then slowly his midsection, then his chest, and finally his arms and the long metal swords he held high above his head. There was buzzing, then a mechanical sound, like an electric train engine. A spark snapped from one of Hercules' hands to the other. There was another snap, and an arc of electricity formed between the two swords.

The arc snapped and disappeared, and another took its place. It crackled up the sword, then snapped and was gone. Twenty times the arcs repeated, each traveling farther than the last before disappearing. The crowd shouted in awe with every small thunderbolt. The servants began to light the oil lamps and the perimeter of the room took on the warm hue of burning oil as the chandeliers rose again.

The final snap of electricity coincided with the chandeliers reaching their apex. The crowd was ecstatic as Patrick bowed three times. When the applause died down, he shouted, "Should we have a display of swords?"

People barked, "Yes!" with a roar of applause.

Patrick waited for quiet. "Usually I ask for a volunteer from the crowd, but tonight, we have a special guest, Mr. Matthew Miller from Virginia, a man of parts who most recently helped fight pirates on the Atlantic Ocean."

Patrick motioned Matt forward, and Matt obliged, wondering what Patrick had in mind and how he knew about the pirates.

"Mr. Miller," Patrick shouted into the crowd. "Do you agree to be a partner in a display of swords?" Matt looked out at the masked masses, unsure what he was volunteering for. A cheer went up as Patrick put his arm on Matt's shoulder and waved. Patrick leaned into Matt. "Agree, please. There's no mortal threat to your person."

Matt faced the crowd and shouted, "I agree!"

As the crowd applauded, Patrick leaned back into Matt. "I cannot guarantee your pride, though."

CHAPTER 33.

FREIGHT TRAIN

Matt waved his acceptance to the people below, and he and Patrick made their way down the stairs. Servants were scrambling around the long banquet tables. In a flurry, they transferred the food to the perimeter of the great hall and pulled off the tablecloths to reveal a wooden platform the size of three boxing rings stacked end to end. There were steps on each side. More servants moved through the crowd with a velvet-topped cart laden with shimmering weapons.

Matt was relieved to find only swords, daggers, and fighting cloaks on the velvet-covered cart. Patrick had an odd eccentricity about him, so Matt had half-expected shields, spiked flails, or Thor hammers. Patrick guided Matt through the crowd to select the weapons. Ben stood a couple of rows away from the platform. The older American gave Matt a disappointed headshake when their eyes met. Matt put his hands up in a "What can I do?" gesture.

At the cart, Patrick put his hand on Matt's shoulder. "One or two," he said. The swords were all practice rapiers with rounded sides and tips. This also was a relief. Matt had practiced with real swords, but that wasn't something you did with a man you'd only just met and mostly didn't trust.

"They are the finest blades from Spain," Patrick said. "I insist on them, even in practice."

Matt was eyeing a rapier with an elaborate handguard. He hefted it. The handle was comfortable and well balanced. Matt studied Patrick's face, wondering at the need for two weapons. The practice daggers were more like short swords than knives. Fighting with two weapons was not Matt's preference, but he could always drop the dagger, so he grabbed one and put his two blades aside.

"Excellent choice," Patrick said for the crowd. "He's chosen a sword of Spanish steel and a short blade from the finest swordsmith in London. Mr. Miller must know a thing or two about blades."

Matt waited for Patrick to select his weapons, hoping he wouldn't pick two daggers. The last thing Matt wanted was to fend off some kind of crazy kung fu fighting style, but Patrick also selected a dagger and a rapier.

Two manservants approached and Patrick gave them his cape and mask. Matt did the same. He looked toward Ben, whose disappointed frown had not changed. Matt understood his concern. The feeling Matt had in his stomach was like sitting in a twenty-first-century roller-coaster, ready for it to start. He was prepared for the ride, but didn't know what to expect, and he hated roller-coasters.

When the servants stepped away, Patrick collected his blades in one hand and motioned for Matt to climb the stairs to the platform. Matt grabbed his weapons and went to the center of the ring. Patrick began talking as he reached the top of the steps. "It is our tradition to have a demonstration of skill before combat," he shouted.

Matt's apprehension peaked, but he met Patrick's eyes with a show of boredom.

"Mr. Miller," Patrick called. "Do you agree to four or five displays of skill?"

Matt was examining his blade. The blunt edges and point gave him some confidence that he would survive the evening. He delivered his response to his sword. "Perhaps three," he called out. "Your guests are anxious for combat, as am I."

Applause went up. Patrick gave Matt a sly smile. Matt recognized his opponent's eagerness to have the crowd on his side and assumed he'd not concede their applause so readily. "Americans!" Patrick shouted. "We know how impatient they are . . . bating when their taxes should be paid." The crowd laughed.

Matt readied a witty criticism of Britain, but Ben, who had stepped closer, put his hand up in a subtle gesture. He should take the high road. Matt executed an elegant and generous bow. "A display of attacks high and low as our first?" Matt called. Ben's instinct to leave the insult unanswered had been correct; the audience cheered. Matt set his dagger to the side.

Patrick returned Matt's bow. "So it shall be," he called. He dropped his short blade and the men faced each other. "Much of the sword is automatic," Patrick announced. "Actions are instantaneous. The body knows whether to defend or attack before the mind can command. On guard, Mr. Miller."

Matt raised his blade.

"An attack to the face," Patrick said, "may not be fatal, but even a glancing blow brings much blood and pain. Some can come from high—" He thrust toward Matt's face and swept the sword to Matt's left. Matt met the blade in an upward motion with a sharp clink and swept it out and away. Thrusts to the face were a favorite of his sword-master, Henry Duncan, in Richmond.

"A perfect counter," Patrick called. "Now the low!" Patrick thrust low. Matt circled his sword around Patrick's to push the blade out and down. Patrick repeated the attack, this time stronger and faster, and it took all Matt's skill to deflect the second thrust.

"Now a high attack by Mr. Miller," Patrick said, inviting Matt to take the offensive. Matt held his blade parallel to the ground, his elbow bent. He was not going to broadcast whether his attack would come from high or low. He snapped forward and up at Patrick's face. Patrick countered easily, pushing Matt's sword while stepping away. Matt did not pause but attacked from above. Patrick circled his blade from under Matt's and defended again. This time he sliced at Matt's face and Matt reacted just in time. Matt reset his stance and reminded himself that even a demonstration could become deadly.

"Now an attack to the middle," Patrick said, holding his blade up nonthreateningly. "There are two places. The gut is an easy target, but the blow is rarely fatal until the battle is finished. Such a wound makes an opponent reckless and unpredictable. I prefer chest strikes, which oft end the battle abruptly. If not fatal, such an injury may persuade an opponent to yield. On guard, Mr. Miller." Patrick leveled his sword at Matt and circled it.

Matt aimed at Patrick's torso. Patrick began another rotation of his blade but surprised Matt with a forward thrust that slashed diagonally across his chest. The edge ripped through Matt's silk shirt. It would have been fatal with an actual sword. Henry had drilled the defense against this lunge into Matt, but his recognition had come too late.

"A well-scored tip cut," Patrick called. He backed away and swatted his sword in the air three times. "I hope Mr. Miller brought his tailor!" The crowd laughed and applauded. Matt bowed.

"On guard, Sir Patrick," Matt called. He waited for Patrick to be ready and then walked forward.

Patrick thrust against Matt's forward motion. Patrick's blade was high, so Matt flicked hard to take his point, then jumped forward and thrust into Patrick's solar plexus, then leaped back before his opponent could counter. His speed surprised Patrick, who reached up to rub his chest where Matt had bruised him, then put his blade in the air to speak.

"Seems Americans are not as helpless in their defense as they claim. Perhaps His Majesty's soldiers should come home and save the expense."

Matt glanced at Ben, whose instructions had not changed: Matt should not insult the crowd. "Perhaps now a full parry," Matt called.

"A fine plan," Patrick answered. "The parry requires all a swordsman's parts and speed. While it rarely wins the duel, it teaches one much about his opponent." He attacked in a flurry at the last consonant.

The surprise put Matt on his heels and it took all his concentration to keep up with Patrick's slashing blade. Patrick pushed him back so swiftly that he nearly fell off the platform. Matt met his blade low on his sword and let it slide close. He reached out and pushed Patrick with a closed fist.

Patrick glared at Matt, but it was no foul in Matt's mind. He hammered Patrick steadily to the center of the platform, where Patrick regained his composure and mounted his defense to put them in a stalemate.

"A fine parry," Patrick said eventually. He raised his sword in a gesture of neutrality. "Are you ready for combat, Mr. Miller?"

"I am, Sir Patrick."

The crowd applauded.

"Two judges to referee the match," Patrick announced. "Nathan Trent and Benjamin Franklin, would you come forward?" Ben and Nathan climbed the middle steps to the platform. "Mr. Trent," Patrick said. "Could you explain the rules of the contest?"

Nathan faced the crowd. "The competitors will be allowed a rapier and a dagger. They will begin when this cravat hits the ground." Nathan waved a bright silver necktie for all to see. "Should a man start before, he is the loser. Once begun, the contest continues until a winner manifests or someone yields. If none yields, the winner is decided in conference between Dr. Franklin and myself and I will shout out 'Winner.' A man who continues to fight after the winner is called—he is the loser. Should a man be compelled from the platform or step from it, he is the loser." Nathan paused. "Questions?"

"None," Matt and Ben said in unison.

"Take your positions."

Matt retrieved his dagger and Patrick did the same. Matt hefted it with a traditional grip, pointing the dull blade toward his opponent. He'd use it only to deflect Patrick's sword. Even in combat with a razor-sharp blade, it was rare to land a blow with a short blade when facing a rapier.

Matt adjusted his stance from his usual right-foot-forward to one where his left foot was closer to the front. The stance gave him a better chance at binding Patrick's rapier with the small blade and making rapier strikes of his own.

The men faced off with more than a sword's length between them. Nathan pointed to the steps for Ben, who turned and gave Matt a thumbs-up signal. The gesture was something that Matt had used quite often during their time together in Philadelphia. Ben accompanied it with a wide grin. He looked less worried now than he had when Matt first stepped up onto the platform. Maybe the demonstration had proven that Matt was competent enough to put on a good show.

When Nathan had reached the ground, he turned to face the two men.

Patrick said, "Mr. Miller, take care to defend yourself. One can never afford to relax, even with dull blades."

"I fret for your good fortune, Sir Patrick," Matt called. "The host should be healthy enough at the end of the game to call for sweets and cognac."

There was roaring laughter, and Patrick gave Matt a respectful nod. "Healthy, indeed," he called.

"On guard," Nathan said. He raised the bright necktie

above his head and let it fall to the ground. Patrick was on Matt like a freight train.

CHAPTER 34.

PARLEY

Matt retreated under the pressure of Patrick's onslaught. His dagger hand went numb after he deflected three successive cutting blows. Teetering on the end of the platform, he edged Patrick to the left. Now they both backed up to the platform's narrow end, and then, somehow, Patrick made the mistake of continuing in the rotation so his back was to the short end. Matt controlled most of the platform.

Realizing that he had been outsmarted, Patrick tried to coerce Matt into making a similar turn, but Matt refused to yield. Patrick advanced hard with his leading foot, circling his blade. The combination came with enough strength and speed to make Matt retreat. Matt stumbled backward and turned slightly to regain his balance. The motion put him low enough for Patrick to slash at his face; Matt felt a searing pain as the dull blade took off a chunk of his cheek. Matt countered as Patrick's blade passed from his face. He thrust hard into Patrick's belly as Patrick retreated. A sharp tip would have given a lingering and fatal injury, and the blow made Patrick grunt loudly.

Both men backed away to take stock. Patrick reset his stance, placing his right foot forward for maximum reach with his rapier. It minimized his ability to use the dagger.

Matt adjusted his stance but was unwilling to match Patrick exactly. He'd concede rapier reach to protect his left side with the short blade.

When Patrick advanced with his lead foot, Matt slashed at his face. The opening had been there, but Patrick countered with a sweep of his rapier. Matt thrust with his dagger to tie up Patrick's sword and slashed hard across Patrick's chest, tearing his shirt and drawing blood. Patrick jumped forward and slashed. He came fast at Matt trying to overwhelm him, and Matt could only parry and back away. Suddenly, Matt was losing.

Patrick made a downward slash as Matt thrust his sword up. Patrick's blade smacked the elaborate handguard on Matt's rapier. Matt twisted his wrist and pushed upward. Their swords flew from their hands and went sailing into the crowd. The men faced each other with daggers, circling.

"Winner," Ben shouted. Nathan glared at him, but Ben repeated, "Winner!" and rushed onto the platform. "I'll not let you bludgeon one another to death," Ben whispered. He stepped between the fighters and shouted, "These men have given us an excellent display of swordsmanship. British citizens from both sides of the Atlantic have demonstrated their parts and courage!" The crowd applauded loudly until the men left the platform.

Patrick moved close to Matt and said, "You were bested."

Matt turned to Patrick and winked.

CHAPTER 35.

WHITE CASTLE

Matt shook Patrick's hand after the party. His face had stopped bleeding and the event ended in seeming goodwill and relative camaraderie. Ben refused to talk about the fight or his decision to end the duel, but Matt had been fine with his stepping in. He'd been prepared to fight Patrick to the end, but Ben was right. Both men were looking forward to bruises and hangovers that neither needed.

Ben was boisterous as they walked home along London streets still packed with revelers. "So many singular women in one place," he said. "London truly is the greatest city in the world. I find myself in tearing good spirits."

"You're drunk as Davey's sow," Matt replied.

"Wine is constant proof that God loves us," Ben replied, chuckling. "I'm happy to meet Davey's fine animal."

"I wish I was drunk."

Ben became serious. "No fault but your own." It made Matt think he might be wrong about the man's state of intoxication.

"We weren't there to flirt," Matt said.

"We certainly weren't there to fight."

"If the host asks you to demonstrate your swordplay,

there's not much you can say besides yes. I had a long discussion with Ferguson in his office."

"You learnt only what you were meant to learn."

"I spoke with many important men. You should have been around to back me up."

"You're spouting nonsense," Ben declared. "Lady Celia told me she has four children. She's a delightful woman and very protective of her family, including her husband. She speaks highly of him."

"So?"

"She worries about his health."

"Headaches?"

"Bruises on his face."

"Why bruises?"

"I have a theory . . . I suspect they are a source of his success."

"The bruises?" Matt asked. "You're too drunk to be coherent."

"Suit yourself. There's nothing we can do about *Sir Patrick* now, anyway."

"He has a convincing plan."

"To change what you believe must occur?"

"Who's to say what must occur?"

"You're making excuses for a questionable course of action."

"I'm not at the excuses stage yet."

"To change the future?"

"To make a better future."

"To play God."

"To save one hundred and sixty million lives."

"And Ferguson will remain an anonymous benefactor?" Ben asked.

"Does it matter when the lives of so many are involved? You've spent your time in London trying to change the future."

Ben scowled. "Any blockhead can see relations between the colonies and the Crown are worse than ever. I'd be here whether I'd met you or not."

"I've told you the future, and you're trying to change it."

Ben brushed Matt off with a wave. "What does Ferguson stand to gain?"

"He has ambitions in the British government."

"So there is a price for providing this peace?"

"What's it matter as long as lives are saved?"

"How many lives will he trade?"

"It didn't involve any."

They had reached Ben's home. Ben glanced at Matt and smiled. "You're right," he said as he turned the key in the lock. "I'm weary and a bit drunk."

CHAPTER 36.

LONDON SLEEPS

It was almost ten thirty by the glowing dial on Matt's Rolex as he lay in bed listening to Ben's snores echo through the thin walls. Matt wanted to blame Ben for his insomnia, or his aching face where Patrick had slashed him, but he expected his mind would be racing regardless. Ben had kept Matt awake before with his wheezing and snorting, but tonight the old man's noise was nothing compared to everything else that filled Matt's head. If anything, it was a comforting reminder that the Leonardo da Vinci of the eighteenth century was sleeping a snore-shot away.

Matt sat up in bed. The bright moon in the cloudless sky lit the floor through the windowpane. Matt scanned the partial white orb through the sparkling new glass, thinking maybe its clarity was responsible for his restlessness, but he knew that was another convenient excuse. While pondering his host's new windowpanes, which had none of the yellow cloudiness of their predecessors, it occurred to Matt that it might be bright enough outside to go for a walk. He pulled back the covers and dressed quietly by the light of the moon, then eased himself down the creaking steps. He grabbed Ben's walking stick from the foyer and slipped out onto Craven Street.

The street was moderately crowded, and Matt knew that it would stay that way for a few more hours, so he could walk around in relative anonymity. Nonetheless, he hefted Ben's stick a couple of times, aware that it would deter someone from trying to take his purse.

St. Paul's Cathedral, London, England

Matt struggled to lock the door behind him but then was on his way. He could see the dome of St. Paul's Cathedral silhouetted against the light of the moon. Lamps shone in its topmost windows and it seemed a reasonable destination for a man with nowhere in particular to go. He set off with the singular mission of touching its wall.

Matt's path took him along the Thames, past rowhouses and a pub district where drunken patrons spilled out onto the street to block his path, but no one seemed to notice him as he threaded his way through the revelers. St. Paul's columns loomed as Matt drew near; the dome that dominated its profile from a distance gradually disappeared. The white marble of the west façade reflected the moonlight and made the plaza glow.

Matt could hear faint organ music coming from the

cathedral. He soon found himself at the edge of the court-yard, then moving up the stairs to the landing and through the columns. Matt reached out to push himself off the enormous wooden door and begin his journey back home, but to his surprise, the fifteen-foot-tall door pivoted away from his touch, bathing him in the warm radiance of lantern light and organ music.

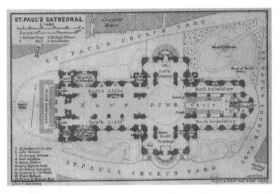

Floorplan of St. Paul's Cathedral, London, England

Matt chuckled at the thought that angels were inviting him inside. He poked his head through the door. Eight standing lanterns were burning along the length of the nave and he could almost see the center dome. Matt eased himself inside and pushed the door closed, thinking he would sit down in a pew and listen to the music. There were no seats in the nave, so he continued toward the dome. His soft footsteps were hardly discernible above the organ, but the music went silent and his last step echoed through the cathedral.

"You're not allowed in here," a man called. His echo lingered deep in the corners of the building.

"I'm sorry," Matt replied. "I can go."

"What brings you here?" echoed the voice. The acoustics of the space made it impossible to tell where the speaker stood. Matt smiled, thinking he might be speaking directly to one of the angels he had imagined. Maybe it was God.

"I couldn't sleep," he replied.

"You're not from London," the voice said.

"America. Richmond, Virginia."

"Was it your intention to end up in God's house this night?" Before Matt could answer, he heard shuffling, hinges, footsteps. Suddenly he was face to face with a prematurely greying priest who had already reached for his hand. "I'm Father Vincent."

"Matt Miller."

"Why did the Lord guide you here?"

Matt thought for a moment, willing to take the bait. "Because I must choose between two different paths."

The priest motioned for Matt to follow him under the dome. "I like the Word close by when seeking the Lord's guidance," he said with Matt trailing behind by two steps. "The Scripture is nothing less than breathtaking." The priest thought for a moment and said, "Did you know 'twas a man from this very church who planned William Tyndale's arrest in Antwerp? We're not very proud of that."

"I'm sorry, Father, but you're going to have to tell me who that is," Matt said. "I didn't grow up in the church."

"William Tyndale was executed a century ago for translating the New Testament into English and smuggling copies into England. Church leaders were so furious that they burned his Bibles in the plaza. Tyndale said the book burners were evil and that they did it to keep the world still in darkness, and to exalt their own honor."

The priest reached down to open a Bible that was nearly two feet tall. It took his full effort, and it finally fell open with a thump. "I come here sometimes to read," he said. "Scripture seems to take on its full meaning when surrounded by God's splendor." He gazed up into the dome. Matt's eyes followed. The soaring ceiling merged lantern-yellow with the blue-white shadows of the moon. "Magnificent even in the dark," the priest said. "I often wonder if I am wrong to insist on maintaining this splendor."

"These old churches *are* inspiring," Matt said.

The older man peered upward again. "If we are in awe, we are more likely to open our hearts to the Lord. The prophet needed only a boat floating offshore to reach thousands."

"He was a capable orator, from what I hear."

"So they say," the priest replied slyly.

"Would you rather preach from a boat?"

Father Vincent shook his head, resigned. "Probably not. I must trust that the Lord put me in the midst of all this grandeur for a reason." He paged through the Bible. "Do you know the story of Abraham?"

"Father of Israel," Matt replied.

"He repaired to a strange land to do the Lord's bidding. He was tried greatly before he was rewarded."

Matt laughed. "Sounds about right."

"What answers do you seek in this new place, Mr. Miller?"

"I want to know how to save my wife's life."

"Is she ill?"

"Someone will kill her five years from now."

The priest scrutinized Matt's face, then squinted into a frown. "Is it God's will that she be saved?"

"I don't know."

Father Vincent pointed to the Bible. "The answers are there, and on your knees."

"I've been both places. Nothing is obvious."

"Only the beginning of your path will be manifest. How you reach its end is up to you."

"How do I know if I'm even walking the right way?"

"Honor, verity, and duty will nourish your soul. They are the very presence of God."

"Is it honorable to let someone you love die?"

Matt looked down the long stretch of the nave, waiting for an answer that did not come. He turned back expectantly, but the priest had slipped silently away. Unnerved and alone, Matt lifted the Bible's cover with both hands and shut it with a resounding thump. He listened to the silent cathedral, then meandered to the door and let himself out.

Matt made his decision. He'd offer to help Patrick and see where the path led.

CHAPTER 37.

7 CRAVEN STREET

As Sarah and Thomas walked silently across the Westminster Bridge, she took note of how the morning dew gathered differently on the stone, wood, and iron surfaces of the structure. Even something as simple as dew on a wooden railing became interesting in the space created by a morbidly quiet husband. They'd had a sleepless night after rushing home from the masquerade early to inspect the images on Sarah's quantum phone.

"How do you know he's going to be there?" Thomas asked, breaking the silence. His voice brought Sarah an overwhelming sense of relief.

"I don't know," she replied. "Mother knows from their correspondence that he spends the early morning writing. We should be able to catch him."

"And he knows of all this?"

"He knows that Patrick Ferguson is a time traveler."

"What concern will Ferguson be to Dr. Franklin?"

"He'll be interested in learning that he is the second name on the list," Sarah replied. "Dr. Franklin is oft interested in intrigue long before others."

"He has seen this *phone* before?"

"Many times, husband."

"And yet this is my first?"

Sarah grabbed his hand and stopped him, forcing the man behind them on the walkway to an abrupt halt. They nodded an apology and leaned against the rail to let him pass. Even this early, the Thames was thick with vessels floating people and supplies from one side of the river to the other.

"I hoped never to show anyone that phone again."

"Still."

"I will spend my life making it up to you," she said. "But for now, we should concentrate on the immediate task."

Thomas frowned. "Do not act like this is some distraction on my part," he said. "'Tis exceedingly rare that a husband learns his wife is from the future."

"And don't you dare expect me to have all the answers," she replied. "I was sixteen years old when I was brought here against my will." Sarah pulled him forward by his hand. "We can argue later."

Thomas skip-stepped to catch up to her side. "There was a time when I believed you were a witch. Do you know that?"

"That's funny." She smiled. "I'd make a good witch." Thomas looked down at her, shocked.

"I'm only joking," she cried. "Sometimes I forget when and where I am. I'm not a witch, in any case." She thought for a moment. "I trust you will not throw me in the river to see if I'll float."

"Why would I do that?"

"Something I read when I was a young girl." She

warmed to the sound of his voice, glad to have him back on her side.

"Maybe my name was in this ledger for legitimate reasons," Thomas said. "The traffic Trent proposed will benefit Mifflin Enterprises beyond my greatest ambitions."

"Not every man on that list is a merchant," Sarah replied. "Most are successful."

"Patrick has another plan. I can feel it. Every name has something to do with the American Revolution. You included."

"Do not speak of such things!" Thomas scolded, scanning their surroundings to see if anyone was within earshot.

"No one can hear."

"Do not speak openly of treason!"

"Fine," Sarah moaned, knowing he was right. England in 1772 was not ready to accept many things, and among these were casual references to witchcraft, American independence, and maybe, vampires. Ever since she saw her copy of *Twilight* in Patrick's office, she had wondered if it would be safe for anyone to see her reading it.

They were now stepping off the bridge. The Westminster buildings filled the horizon to their left. Sarah checked the map the hotel porter had drawn and pointed at a staircase to their right. Thomas let go of her hand and guided her down to a cobblestone sidewalk along the bank of the Thames.

The morning sun glistened on the river, and recent rains made the waters smell uncharacteristically fresh. It was as pretty a riverwalk as she had ever seen, but instinct told her time was short, so she yanked at her husband's hand and practically pulled him up the Northumberland stairs, down Northumberland Avenue, and onto Craven Street. Looking up at the street sign, she said, "It's seven."

They walked to Ben Franklin's residence, a four-story brick rowhouse sandwiched between two similar structures. The houses were built at different times, but an attempt had been made to match their colors and proportions and the ground floor of each was plastered stone, so they seemed almost like the same building. Ben's house had a decorative cast iron fence and a red-brown door. The Mifflins stood at the door, motionless, as if neither wanted to fall deeper into intrigue. Eventually, Sarah reached up to the tarnished gargoyle knocker and let it fall twice.

After a couple of minutes, the dead silence convinced them that no one was home, but Thomas slapped the knocker three more times. They heard it echo through the glass windows.

"I'm coming," said a man angrily above their heads.

A moment later the door opened to reveal a disheveled but mildly handsome man who was not Dr. Franklin. He squinted wearily at their silhouettes from the foyer.

"What is it?"

"Mr. Miller?" Sarah said, surprised.

CHAPTER 38.

THE HANGOVER

Ben refreshed his quill and wrote down the names as Sarah read from the photo on her phone:

1. Thomas Jefferson
2. Benjamin Franklin
3. John Adams
4. George Washington
5. Thomas Paine
6. Marquis de Lafayette
7. John Paul Jones
8. Nathan Hale
9. Ethan Allen
10. Thomas Hutchinson
11. Alexander Hamilton
12. James Madison
13. Paul Revere
14. Aaron Burr
15. John Hancock
16. Patrick Henry
17. Thomas Mifflin
18. James Monroe
19. Hugh Mercer

20. Nathaniel Greene
21. Henry Knox
22. Horatio Gates
23. Friedrich Wilhelm von Steuben
24. Daniel Morgan
25. John Sullivan
26. Louis Duportail
27. Matthew Miller

"I don't know whether to be insulted or relieved," Ben said, leaning back in his chair. "Mr. Jefferson seems to have nicked the first spot and Matthew has made the last. I can only hope Sir Patrick intends to distribute bribes according to our ranking."

"Unless it's an assassination list," Matt quipped.

Ben looked over the top of his glasses. "Let us consider sophisticated alternatives before assuming that Sir Patrick is an habitual assassin."

Matt shrugged. "The road to hell is paved with good intentions."

Sarah weighed the phone in her hand and glanced at Matt. "There's something different about your name." She handed him the phone.

"The ink or quill wasn't the same, as if my name was added later," Matt said. "Would it be higher after my meeting with Ferguson last night or dropped from the list entirely?"

"What did you talk to Patrick about?" Sarah asked.

"He discussed the first and second lists," Matt said, "but not the third."

"How will he use them?"

"He'll pay incentives at home and abroad," Matt explained, "and assume debt until Britain approves of American representation."

"He wants to delay the American Revolution?" Sarah asked. She looked at her husband to make sure he was still with them. Thomas rolled his eyes.

"Prevent it," Matt replied. "There's a strong sentiment in London that Americans mostly seek independence from their creditors and that the demand for 'no taxation without representation' is a ruse."

"List two?" Thomas asked.

"British businessmen and bureaucrats," Matt said. "It's an insurance policy. He's rich, but his funds aren't unlimited. He mentioned some of these men."

"He'll bribe them?"

"Not outright, as he sees it," Matt replied. "He described it as making sure their interests are in line with American representation. It sounded like he wants to build relationships."

"What's in it for him?" Thomas asked. Sarah faced him and smiled. It had taken her husband very little time to adjust to this new state of affairs. His question was a confident one.

"He grew up poor," Matt replied. "His father was orphaned in the second world war." Thomas looked at him questioningly. "It was a war that engulfed almost the whole globe starting in 1939," Matt explained. "Almost seventy million people died. London was in ruins."

Matt saw the look on Ben's face at the prospect.

"And he'd want to avert this war?" Thomas asked.

"His family lost everything," Matt explained. "Ferguson said his father was a broken man."

"He wants to change his family's place in history?" Ben asked.

"He wasn't sure it would work," Matt answered. "He wants to try."

"And if he changes the fate of his family in some unexpected way . . ." Ben began.

"Does he disappear?" Sarah asked.

"I don't know," Matt said. "He thinks it's worth the gamble to restore the Fergusons to their rightful place, and it's hard to argue against keeping all those people from dying."

"Ambitious men," Ben said quietly, perusing the list. He raised his head. "It's as steady as the sun rising each day."

"He convinced me," Matt said.

"Why did the third list remain secret?" Ben asked.

"I could have another meeting," Matt replied. "I'll ask him if there are other plans."

"Too blatant," Ben answered.

"I know many of these men," Thomas said. "They'd not be easily bought."

"Something can be learned from the ones Ferguson has chosen as his representatives. The ones that are assigned."

"We could ask around," Thomas said. "Maybe one or two would tell their story."

"I'm uncommon sure Ferguson employs many men who'd report back on Americans asking questions."

"What about Sutton?" Matt asked. He'd been trying to

keep David Sutton busy since they arrived in London. Matt saw the blank look in Sarah's eyes. "He's a young man who sailed with me on the *Norfolk*," he explained. "He lives down near the docks. If he were caught asking questions, he'd be tough to trace back to us."

"Do you trust him?" Thomas asked.

Matt nodded. "I saved his arm from amputation on the ship and he's counting on me to be his benefactor. Smart kid, but a little rough around the edges."

"Have Sutton come," Ben instructed. "He's no agent provocateur, but I think we might manifest the need for subtlety in the young hemp's investigation."

"Anyway, he owes me," Matt said.

CHAPTER 39.

DAVID SUTTON

David Sutton knocked on the door at 7 Craven Street, looking up at its four-story façade. He could count the times he'd been there on one hand. He'd hoped Dr. Franklin would offer him accommodations and keep him close, but Ben found a position for him at the dock. It paid well and was minimally interesting, but he knew his infrequent visits to Ben's house were no substitute for being around all day.

Matt answered the door. It had been almost a week since he'd come down to visit David at the shipper. "Young Sutton!" he said, reaching out to shake his hand heartily and lay a gentle palm on David's shoulder in the way that men sometimes embrace each other during a handshake. It was the same arm where they had removed the musket ball. "Fully healed?"

"Yes, sir."

Matt pulled him into the entryway. "Let's see it, then." David unbuttoned his cuff and rolled the sleeve up. The scar was still puffy where they had sewn the flesh, but the redness was nearly gone.

"It's healed perfectly," Matt said with pride.

David allowed that he was very thankful. A shudder

went up his spine as he thought of the surgeon the day after the battle, standing there holding his saw as Matt pleaded with him to extract the ball and sew the wound. Gangrene was almost certain, and once it set in, a man had two weeks before they tucked him into bed with a spade. "I am in your debt, sir," David confessed.

Matt nodded happily. "Your continued health and success are all you owe," he said, shuffling David into the house. "We have a new affair that pays well. Franklin may offer you a prize too, should your intelligence be sound."

Matt led David to Ben's sitting room at the back of the house, where Ben was at his desk writing frantically. Ben put his finger in the air in that way David had seen him do on the first day they met. Matt rolled his eyes at David and made a twisting motion in the air with his index finger. David had spent enough time with Ben to know he was a stiff rump. Growing up, he and his boys would have fleeced a fat cull like him.

They waited while Ben finished the last sentence and dumped fine sand on the parchment to absorb the ink, then cupped the letter to pour the brackish powder back into its box. He set it all aside and smiled at them. "Mr. Sutton! How does it with you, young fellow?"

"Well, Dr. Franklin," David replied. "And you?"

"Well, my lad, also well. Take a seat so we can explain your task." Ben pointed to a sofa and some chairs around a coffee table. Ben plucked a note off the table and handed it to David, indicating that he should unfold it. Six names were listed.

1. Joshua Tucker
2. Samuel Pepys
3. John Newcomb
4. John Rann
5. George Smith
6. William Bell

"We'd like to know a thing or two about these gentlemen," Matt said. "They may have booked passage to America. Ask around at the dock."

"Square toes?"

"They could be your age," Ben said. "We don't want them to know we're looking for them. Not a squeak to even your most trusted mates about myself or Mr. Miller."

"They'll stand buff," David said, "but 'twill take some silver."

Ben pulled a cloth purse with a drawstring from his coat pocket and hefted its weight. "This should loosen a few tongues. None for your own pocket. You'll be well paid when your task is complete."

"What about my place at the docks? I'll want more time than the Sabbath to daub the proper scabs."

"I've already spoken to Mr. Longfellow," Ben replied. "Your labor at the dock will resume when you've located these men. I'm paying double your salary. You'll receive an extra prize should you spy the cloven foot." He gave the purse to David with a look of unbridled optimism.

"Anything else?" David asked.

"These men may be in the employ of Sir Patrick Ferguson," Matt replied. "Be careful whom you speak to."

"Sir Patrick?" David asked, surprised. "He's a fat cull, no doubt. Controls the dock, he does."

"We're aware," Ben replied.

"Twice my salary is beggar's pay," David reply. "Should anyone catch me standing budge, they'll put me to bed."

"Triple your salary, then."

David shook his head.

"I saved your arm," Matt said.

"And fiddler's pay for that, sir," David said. "Arm's no use if I'm stone dead."

"Four times," Matt said. "But that's as high as we'll go."

David nodded and stuffed the purse full of bribes into his pocket. "Anything else, good sirs?"

"Report back to us on the week to let us know what you've found," Matt said.

David nodded.

"I'll walk you out," Matt said. When they were at the door, Matt reminded David, "Remember, total secrecy."

David put his finger to his lips. "Strictly on the lob, sir."

David heard the door click shut behind him as he took his first step down Craven Street. He felt the coins in his pocket and thought of his new salary. It was a dead set if he planted the books right. He pulled out his watch to check the time. He'd have to run if he didn't want to be late for his interview with Mr. Trent.

CHAPTER 40.

DECEPTION

It was just after noon and the midday sun was streaming through the windows into Patrick Ferguson's office. Four days had passed since the masquerade party and London was still abuzz. Patrick smiled as he thought of his wife's demeanor since the party. Many of her old friends, even the London aristocrats, had attended, in dramatic contrast to their conspicuous and intentional absences from previous parties at Ferguson Manor.

Patrick had had other reasons for putting people in masks, but he hadn't considered that a minute degree of anonymity was enough to excuse the curiosity of the London elite. His visions were still muddled, but he suspected they'd taken the first step toward regaining the prestige that Celia craved and his plans required.

Patrick reached up and massaged his temples. The pain had diminished throughout the week, as usual, but his visions had vanished quickly. He suspected this had something to do with the empty spaces created by interacting so intimately with Matthew Miller, but there was something — somebody else — obscuring his vision, a blot he couldn't see past. Was there another traveler?

"It's fine," he said to himself. He had tried lately to wean himself from the need to predict every detail. When he allowed the obsession to take root and blossom in Philadelphia, it resulted in his complete mental breakdown. He knew enough now to push it away when it began to take a firm hold on his mind. He'd already set the gears in motion, so he wouldn't need another treatment any time soon.

There was a knock on the door. "Come in," Patrick said, knowing it was Nathan. Even without treatments, he had learned very early after his arrival in the colonies that he could predict the immediate future easily and with few side effects. Unexpectedly, though, Nathan was accompanied by a young man. The thorough surprise was both exhilarating and disconcerting.

Is he connected to this shadow, or is he the shadow? Patrick searched his mind for some clue, but the empty blot obscured almost everything.

"Sir," Nathan said, seeing the look of contemplation on Patrick's face. "This is David Sutton."

Patrick stepped around his desk and shook David's hand. "Pleased to meet you." He tried to guess the man's occupation—his hand was rough and calloused—then caught himself and backed away from searching his memory rather than asking simple questions. Patrick glanced at Nathan.

"Mr. Sutton works for you," Nathan said. "He was a crewman on the *Norfolk*, the American frigate that brought Matthew Miller to London."

"Explains many things," Patrick said. The men looked back at him, puzzled. "What is it that you have for me, Mr. Sutton?"

Nathan began to answer, but Patrick waved him off, preferring to hear it directly. Nathan nodded at David, whose hesitation to speak went a long way toward convincing Patrick of his sincerity.

His interaction with Miller is the reason this man is a mystery!

"Sir Patrick," David said. He waited for permission to continue. Patrick nodded. "Sir Patrick," he repeated. "Mr. Trent hired me to watch the doings of Mr. Miller on his journey to London. I kept an eye on him, I did."

"And what did you learn?"

"He's a skilled fighter, sir. Stopped them from taking my arm."

"Speak of what has befallen since, Mr. Sutton," Nathan said, annoyed.

The young man gathered himself again, pulled a folded piece of parchment from his pocket, and handed it to Patrick.

Patrick read it sedately. "How did you come by this?"

"Dr. Franklin gave it to me," David replied. "It was him and Mr. Miller."

"And how did *they* come by this list?"

"Neither spoke of it, sir," David replied. "I'm in their employ to reveal the whereabouts of these men and their intent in some scrap."

"And did they give you a clue to this *scrap?*"

"No, sir, but they believe these men have nefarious intent."

"And you gathered this how?"

"They asked me to investigate these names down at docks and learn whether they'd booked passage to America. Go gingerly, they said, because you'd be tweaked to learn that someone was asking questions."

"To what end do they believe these men sought passage to America?" Patrick demanded.

"Nefarious intent, sir," David repeated.

The room went silent for a very long time. Patrick looked David up and down. "Can you tell me anything else about Mr. Miller?"

"Ain't no loggerhead, sir. Bit fancy—maybe a swell that don't know the struggle of—" David went quiet. He looked up, then at Patrick, then at the opulent office.

"Of the what, Sutton?" Patrick asked.

"The poorer types," David replied simply.

"He's a fat cull in Virginia."

"Good in a fight," David added. "Saved our ship from pirates, and my arm."

Nathan, who had been struggling to remain silent, finally spoke. "Mr. Sutton, I think that's all we want for now." Nathan reached into his pocket for a purse and gave it to David. The young man took it without note. His manner dispelled any questions Patrick had as to his loyalty; it went to the highest bidder. Nathan looked directly at the young man. "You are not to make any inquiries at the docks."

"They'll expect something from me," David replied.

"Come back tomorrow morning, and you'll have your cock-and-bull story." Nathan nodded with finality.

"Thank you, good sirs," David said. "Tomorrow morning, then. Good day." He gave a slight bow and was gone.

Patrick waited until the door was closed. "How the hell did they get this list?"

"I know not," Nathan answered. "Some connection has been made between these names and the grander scheme."

"It was stolen from your records somehow."

"I never transcribed it from the ledger."

"They were locked in my safe," Patrick replied, "and never left this room." He searched his memory for some clue as to who was involved, but nothing—nothing at all was visible. "There is someone else," he said. "Someone significant, somewhere, who is working against us."

Nathan waited for him to explain, but Patrick remained quiet. Nathan knew that his boss had an unexplained ability to sense people and events in a way that others could not. Finally, Nathan said, "Sir, I should assure you that I was not responsible. I alone have spoken to the men on this list. I could understand one name, but all of them?"

"I do not believe you are responsible."

"Then whom?"

"Did anyone gain access to the office within the last week?"

"Many as we prepared for the party, but you are the only one who can open the strongbox."

"Our servants are well compensated and loyal. I do not see them easily turned. Any suspicious activity?"

Nathan gave Patrick a look of revelation. "The drunk lady."

"Drunk lady?"

"The wife of Thomas Mifflin. Mr. Weatherly griped about a woman in the powder room. He believed her to be drunk. She locked herself inside, supposedly suffering from lady's sickness, and wouldn't come out."

"Thomas Mifflin is the cotton exporter," Patrick said, thinking aloud.

"A modest merchant from Philadelphia," Nathan explained.

"And the name of his wife?"

"They signed as Mr. and Mrs. Mifflin." Nathan saw that Patrick wasn't listening. His eyes were darting around the room.

Patrick unlocked the balcony door and stepped onto the balcony. Nathan followed close behind. Patrick pointed at the footprints in the dust and pigeon waste that coated the ledge. "She stepped out onto the ledge from the powder room, made her way along the side of the building, procured access to my office, and somehow opened my safe," Patrick said.

"What kind of lady would crawl out onto the ledge of a building?"

"Mrs. Mifflin, I believe."

"She did this to retrieve a list that no one knew about?"

"She may have been here to take something else."

"And she knew the combination of your safe?"

"She may have had a way to open it."

"A lady?"

"Someone was in here the night of the party," Patrick said. "The chairs were arranged incorrectly when I came in with Miller."

"You think he had something to do with it?"

"He delayed our conversation so the theft could take place. Of course he had something to do with it."

"What was she here to take?"

"It doesn't matter," Patrick replied. "Her full name is perhaps Sarah Morris Mifflin. She is a woman of ill repute known to me from Philadelphia. She came here as a burglar and by some unfortunate accident found our ledger. She wrote the names down."

"And she knew enough to take our plans to Dr. Franklin?"

"She is most certainly operating as an agent for Dr. Franklin," Patrick said. "We must assume that Sarah and Thomas Mifflin are working with Franklin and Miller to some end. How much longer until we have everyone safely away?"

"The first ship doesn't lift anchor until next week," Nathan replied. "The last sets sail in three weeks."

"Then you must expedite their passage."

"It's not that easy," Nathan said. "We spent weeks planning these voyages."

"Bribe them."

"These ships must be crewed and provisioned."

"Pay them."

"We've already spent a fortune," Nathan said. "I'll see what can be done, but even you cannot afford to send half a dozen merchant vessels across the ocean with no cargo."

"Do your best," Patrick said. "In the meantime, we must plan a diversion for Mr. Miller and his colleagues. They must not learn the whereabouts or the aspirations of our men, especially before all have sailed safely from the harbor."

CHAPTER 41.

BRIAN PALMER

"Good day to you, Mr. Palmer," Digby said. "Where are you off to, then?"

Brian Palmer stood still to massage his temples. He had gotten used to Londoners asking questions about the simplest of details. Sometimes it was trivial, like where he was going, whom he was visiting, or where he was eating. Other times it was personal, like whether he was leaving the house with enough money or the last time he'd been to church. When they weren't asking, they were watching.

Brian looked into the crinkled eyes of the landlord, who had stopped sweeping to wait for an answer. "I'm going to visit Mrs. Palmer," Brian replied. That was, at least, the truth. The key to an alibi was simplicity, and this was a perfect one. Mrs. Palmer, the story went, spent most of her time taking care of her elderly mother. The explanation had been adequate for both Digby and the maid who came to the rowhouse daily to clean and make Brian's evening meals. Digby's memory was steadfast, and Brian joked that the old crank had a chart somewhere with the hourly location of all his tenants as they ambled about the city.

The real story of Scarlett Palmer, aka Rachel LaPorte, aka Catherine Dunmeade, was so much better. She was brilliant and beautiful, and had no compunction whatsoever when it came to reaping the rewards she felt she deserved. Every man in London was attracted to her—until they learned what she was, and then even sometimes after that. Something in Scarlett's past compelled her to believe the world owed her a massive debt. In the six months Brian had spent with Scarlett, she'd never volunteered an explanation, and he'd never cared enough to ask, although he was curious on occasion about precisely what it was that motivated her.

Brain had met "Mrs. Palmer" on his second trip to London, when he arrived with a pocket full of synthetic diamonds he wanted to convert to cash. Selling even one had proven difficult. His accent had immediately sown distrust among the jewelers, and his diamonds were so perfectly clear and cut that they'd been rejected outright. During one particularly boisterous negotiation, Brian watched an attractive woman in a low-cut dress casually slip a ruby ring down the front of her bodice. She looked smoothly back at him, smiled to acknowledge his complicity, adjusted her bosom, thanked the jeweler, and walked out of the store.

Brian could almost see the energy field that bewitched everyone around her. He spent days looking for this magical redhead. Their six months together hadn't been without incident, but that was to be expected when you're cheating people. Incident was the crux of their relationship, as far as Brian could tell, and it kept them busy.

Brian had come a long way since he was run out of Oak Ridge Laboratories for lighting up NORAD monitors across the continent by opening up a hole in space-time to pull Matt Miller back to the twenty-first century. He'd rolled the dice, like all pioneering men in science should, and he'd lost. Those government bastards even considered trying him for treason and manslaughter. In the end, there were too many secrets in play to risk going public, and they gave him an offer he couldn't refuse. Brian took a generous severance to sign a nondisclosure agreement stating that he'd never work on Chernenko-Einstein particles again.

Unbeknownst to Brian, his signature represented a trial and a conviction that made it impossible to pass a federal background check. It wasn't until his third job offer was rescinded that a hiring manager thought to tell him they didn't hire convicted felons. Brian's wife, a successful lawyer in the State Department, soon received her own severance. In addition to the grim prospect of being married to an unemployable man, she realized that her continued association with a convicted felon would keep her from ever getting a security clearance. She moved out one morning while he was at another unsuccessful interview. She took the furniture, the cat, and eventually half of his money.

Sitting on a folding chair in his empty condominium one night, Brian made a decision. He packed a duffle bag, drove that ridiculous Prius his wife had convinced him to buy to the Toyota dealer, dropped the keys into the mail slot, and took a taxi to the train station. Brian rode the train from city to city, taking odd jobs only long enough to refill his wallet. He was tending bar in St. Louis when it finally occurred to him that Dr. Brian Palmer was dead. He was no longer a man who wanted to chase after the next major scientific discovery or change the world for the better.

Brian left St. Louis and didn't stop until the continent ended. Americans who had run until there was nowhere else to go filled Los Cabos, a city that was surprisingly receptive of an outsider from Tennessee. He laughed when he thought about how screwed up everyone in the Cabos was and how perfectly he fit in. He got in with a group of friends that he affectionately called the End of the World Gang. There were plenty of women among them, and they, too, were receptive after he had a little practice in the art of seduction.

Brian had an advantage, in that he could not have cared whether the women of Cabos were interested or not, and more than a few responded readily to a man who had other things on his mind. He stayed in Cabos for three years, shacking up with various women, working and partying, and he almost forgot his past. One night, though, while drinking tequila and high on mescaline, the secret to harnessing Chernenko-Einstein laid itself out perfectly in his mind. He saw a way to use the particles without detection, and he knew how to travel across time.

Brian was living with Alejandra at the time, a Latin goddess, ethereal, sweet, and sexy, and she should have been enough for him to forget his obsession with making Matt Miller pay. His old ambition jacked him up, though, day by day until his head was too high to breathe. He took all the money he had, found the right yacht off the coast of Cabos, and was soon on a ship to Taiwan, where a fully equipped laboratory awaited him. The Taiwanese were interested in harnessing a nearly limitless energy supply and weaponizing it against the mainland.

Brian was able to construct a working reactor soon after arriving in his new country, and it wasn't much longer before he could scan the timeline. The most recent quantum signal was from 1771. He hoped that Matt Miller had achieved success beyond his wildest dreams. Brian slept little for the two months it took for him to construct the portal and the mechanism that could bring him home. When he left, he expected to transport to the colonies. He woke up in a London alley.

Brian had never imagined he'd find Patrick Ferguson. The fact that Ferguson had survived his trip through the wormhole made Brian seethe even more. Matt Miller had refused to come back and prove that time travel was possible, so instead of receiving the Nobel Prize, Brian had been pushed from the herd. Matt Miller had ruined his life, and he was going to pay.

Brian's first visit to London lasted four weeks. He had programmed the reactor to return him home by opening a wormhole at the location of the transmitter he carried. Brian supported himself during that first trip by selling tools he brought in his pack. He explored London and learned as much as he could about Patrick Ferguson, hoping he could help locate Matt Miller. On his last day in London, Brian was sitting in a tavern drinking enough to cushion his trip home through the wormhole when he saw a display for Miller Head and Stomach Tablets. He transported back knowing he'd found his clue.

Scarlett was the one who identified Ben Franklin as the

English distributor for the medicine, and discovered that he had a house in London. Ben Franklin, as intelligent as Brian considered him to be, was no match for a fetching woman in a low-cut dress with funds for a large purchase. It hadn't taken long for Ben to brag that he knew the inventor of these fantastic tablets: Matt Miller was traveling on a ship called the *Norfolk* and was expected in London by early summer.

CHAPTER 42.

NIGHT AT THE OPERA, PART I

A knock at the door woke Matt up an hour after sunrise. It was a week since they'd hired David Sutton to investigate Ferguson's list, and Matt, expecting David, was anxious to learn whether he'd found anything. Matt hopped from bed and bounded down the steps in his robe, knowing that no one else was able to answer the door. Polly and Margaret were in North London visiting family, and Ben, who woke sometime before the sun, would already be at his desk on the second floor. Ben usually sat in some form of undress with the windows open, based on what he believed were the healthy effects of the fresh air. He called them *air baths*.

Matt continued down the next flight to undo the night chain that served as a second lock. He swung the door wide. "Wake you, did I, Mr. Miller?" Mrs. Milton said. Her smiling face warmed him. Matt made a concentrated effort to hide his disappointment that she wasn't David. She handed him a steaming basket of bread. "Fresh out of the oven," she said. "Mrs. Stevenson let me know she and Polly would be gone."

Matt grabbed a purse from the table by the front door and dropped a shilling and a few pennies into her palm, saying, "Thank you kindly." Mrs. Milton curtsied and stepped away. Matt closed the door when she reached the street and called, "Breakfast's here!" He liked to give Ben plenty of time to dress. He could convince the older man of very little, but he insisted Ben be fully clothed in his presence.

Matt set the steaming basket on the dining room table and grabbed a pewter plate from the cabinet, unwrapped a loaf, pulled it in half, and put a piece on his plate. He rewrapped the loaf and returned it to the basket next to jars of butter, peach jam, and a cold sausage. "Ben," he called again.

"Getting dressed," Ben replied. "Though it should not be necessary."

"It's necessary," Matt called back. Matt went to take a bite of the warm bread but heard the knocker on the door again.

"Damn it," he whispered to his meal. He set the bread down on the pewter plate and walked down the hallway to the door. He undid the latch and found a teenage boy holding a wax-sealed packet.

"Yes?" Matt said, irritated.

"Delivery for Dr. Franklin," the boy announced. He looked past Matt to the staircase, hoping to catch a glimpse of Ben, who had become a celebrity in London.

"I'll take it," Matt said, reaching out.

"I'm only supposed to give it to the doctor," the boy said.

"He's getting dressed," Matt replied as he held his hand out again, this time with intent.

The teenage boy gave him a disappointed glare, looked past him, and reluctantly released the letter. Matt reached again for the purse, grabbed a few pennies, and dropped them into the boy's open palm.

"Thank you, sir." The boy looked at the staircase one last time, turned, and left. Matt closed the door and redid the latch, determined to eat his bread while it was still warm. He tossed the note on the dining room table and sat back down at his plate.

Ben finally walked in. "Who was that?"

"You got a letter."

"I wasn't expecting anything," Ben said.

Matt's mouth was now full, so he pointed at the packet. "I was hoping we'd hear from Sutton today," he mumbled through his food. "We should be doing something else in the matter."

"I'd expect to give this young man, Sutton, another day or two before going off half-cocked," Ben replied. "You said he was beyond reproach."

"He's the one person in the city that I trust." Matt heard the pride in his own voice. Ben opened the letter and began to read, still standing. Matt pulled another chunk of bread from the basket and reached for the knife. "Better get some before I eat it all."

Ben set the letter down, pulled out a chair and reached for the food. "Sir Patrick has invited us to opening night at the opera," he said as he rummaged through the towels for the second loaf. "Four seats in a luxury box. You, me, Sarah, and Thomas."

Matt's vision went haywire. He shook off a memory and

looked back at Ben. He had trouble explaining to his friend exactly how he could perceive the future but not predict specific events. "He knows we have the list."

"Perhaps."

"We're not going," Matt said. "Something bad is going to happen. I can feel it. We'd be walking right into the wolf's lair."

Ben rolled his eyes. "We've been through this. I know you have more than an academic understanding of future events, but malice lurks everywhere in London. In the end, it should not deter us from leaving our apartments."

"Something bad is going to happen," Matt repeated.

"Tell me."

"Everything having to do with Ferguson is cloudy."

"The house will be packed," Ben said. "The seats are the best in the building, and there is nothing inherently perilous in our attending. The Burlington House Theatre is hardly the wolf's lair, but take a dagger if you like."

"We should be making our own plans rather than playing into his," Matt said. "The fate of the western world lies in the balance, and we're going to the opera?" ·

"Do citizens of the United States—those in your time—oft put the normal course of human events in such context?"

Matt shrugged.

"You've seen no famine, no plague, and no smallpox. You told me that you didn't even fret about bombs that could destroy your whole city. Neither one of us has lived through a time when the world was *in the balance*."

Matt gave Ben a dirty look.

"The Burlington is only a short walk from here," Ben said.

Matt recognized the determination on Ben's face. "Can we involve the authorities somehow?" he asked.

"To solve what crime? Would you build a case with the list of unknown colonists that you wrote with your own hand? Or would you shew them a picture of the original list on a magical device that no one has ever seen?"

Matt fell silent. Ben was right. One missing anti-American member of the British Parliament, whose disappearance was still unexplained, was hardly a reason to mobilize Scotland Yard. Matt wondered if there even was a Scotland Yard yet.

"Constables are investigating the disappearance of Sir William Maynard," Ben said. "A handwritten list of names wouldn't have any effect on them. Even so, we've no evidence that Sir Patrick had anything to do with Maynard's desertion. He's not on any of the lists."

"I'm sure Ferguson's involved."

"That and half a shilling will purchase a tankard of ale."

"Fine," Matt replied, resigned. "What time?"

"Three o'clock. Wear your best suit. Where will Sir Patrick be sitting? Maybe in the same box?"

CHAPTER 43.

NIGHT AT THE OPERA, PART II

It was opening night at the opera and Patrick and Celia Ferguson were sitting across from each other at an elaborate Jacobean table in the most expensive carriage built by Ferguson Industries. The benches on each side of the table were a plush black leather, framed by glossy smooth wood. The outside of the carriage was painted a rich burgundy cherry and decorated with gold paisley trim. The two drivers, trained as bodyguards, were dressed in clothes appropriate for sitting atop Ferguson Industries' most expensive carriage. They controlled four stallions that pulled the heavy vehicle through London's cobblestone streets.

Celia was a boisterous and religious attendee of the opera, while Patrick was anything but. Nathan and a few escorts usually accompanied her, but she had convinced Patrick at the last minute to come. Patrick had avoided Burlington House since it started offering half-price tickets to the footman's gallery. These cheaper tickets attracted a different station, and these new fans had no problem heckling performers or rioting when a performance didn't end as they hoped. They also had the bizarre ritual of banging on cowbells, which made Patrick's headaches worse.

But tonight Celia had convinced Patrick that it was the

perfect time for London to see them again after the masquerade. She insisted they dress in their finest and take their best carriage. Patrick was wearing a light-blue suit with a brilliant white cravat to play the part of a London aristocrat, but it was nothing compared to Celia's deep-blue gown. Around her bare neck glistened sapphires that sparkled whenever the sun caught them through the open windows of the carriage.

Patrick didn't like playing the "gentry game," as he called it, mostly because he wasn't very good at it, but he did it anyway. He appreciated its potential for political sway and his wife insisted. Celia was a juggernaut when it came to social status, but power games aside, his wife was the most elegant and captivating woman he had ever seen. He admired her from across the carriage. Her blue eyes shone with a brilliance that challenged the glow of the jewels around her neck.

Catching him watching her, she smiled. He looked slowly from her eyes down to her full lips and white teeth as she opened her mouth to speak.

"What is it?" she asked softly.

Looking into her eyes again, he said, "You look radiant tonight, my dear. You may be the most enchanting woman in all of London."

"I do not know if this is true, husband," she replied, "but I am at once becoming the most fulfilled."

"You like the opera that much?" Patrick replied, joking.

She looked back seductively and smiled. "I like what we have become, you and I, and I like the future that is being made for our children. There is much to be thankful for."

"All it took was one successful party?"

She squinted and shook her head. "We have struggled to take our place among the noble families for many years. I did not think it was possible to rewrite expectations steeped in hundreds of years of tradition. I believe my father was a man of much foresight."

"So 'twas your father that made all this possible?" Patrick ran his fingers across the rich black leather seat. He did it to emphasize his point and for the smooth and soft feeling of the hide against his skin.

"I did not readily accept our marriage," Celia said.

"And now?"

"My father had much wit. I look forward to all that our children will accomplish for our family and England."

Patrick reached across the table and took her fingers in his. Hers was an arranged marriage to a man willing to bid a very high price. Early on, she had done her duty to fulfill the deal her father had made. Patrick had made it his goal to win her over, especially after she had their first child. He knew he was a good-looking man, but it was vital for him to seduce her mind. Through hard work and sheer will, he had finally gotten her to look at him with love in her eyes.

Patrick's thoughts of Celia were almost enough for him to put the vision of John Newcomb's corpse out of his mind, but they weren't enough to make him forget the man responsible for his murder. Newcomb was the third person on the list of six that Matthew Miller had given to David Sutton. Patrick worried now that his other five men were in danger. When they arrived at Burlington House Theatre, though, Patrick did his best to cast Matthew Miller from his head. For tonight, he vowed to leave his concerns behind and enjoy the opera with the alluring woman who faced him. He looked forward to watching her mingle and her smiles as she bathed in her newfound popularity.

Patrick stepped from the carriage and then reached up to help Celia to the ground. She was breathtakingly elegant. They entered the opera house hand in hand, enthusiastically greeting London socialites, a few of whom, Patrick thought, were fine people. He let Celia take the lead, but many of the men came forward to chat and he tried his best to play to his wife's satisfaction. He knew the path to power would pass through the minefield of the noble families even beyond the Industrial Revolution.

All the niceties had exhausted Patrick by the time they took their seats in the box to the far right of the stage. His drivers stood guard outside the door. They sat there for a while, talking about the people below, until a commotion caught their notice and Celia pointed. "There. It's Dr. Franklin. I recognize the young lady beside him. She was at the masquerade. A delightful girl, but somewhat distracted."

Even after a decade, Patrick recognized her, too. "Her name is Sarah Morris Mifflin," Patrick replied. "Her husband is a cotton merchant." He had to look twice to believe his eyes: Benjamin Franklin, Matthew Miller, Sarah Morris, and Thomas Mifflin were ascending the stairs to the box directly across from them. Patrick seared with anger and he blinked away the jittering in his mind that spoke of something ominous.

The people he considered among the most deadly in

London had come to taunt him on the one night he wanted to escape the world. It felt as if he had, only now, revealed the serpent, and it was already standing before him and hissing. His desire to confront them directly was overwhelming.

"I should go and give my regards to Dr. Franklin," he said, trying to sound unexcited.

"Should I come?" Celia asked.

"No. I may be required to speak plainly."

"As you wish, my husband." Celia smiled knowingly. "I'll keep an eye out, should the plain-speaking become threatening."

Patrick nodded and stepped from the box. One of his guards followed him down the steps and to Matt Miller's box on the opposite side of the theatre. It was unguarded, and everyone was watching the stage. Patrick leaned down and tapped Matt's shoulder.

Matt looked up in surprise.

"You came here to antagonize me?" Patrick asked coldly.

"What are you talking about? I thought you were coming to welcome us." Matt stood, now aware of the anger on Patrick's face, and backed away. He looked relieved when Patrick chose not to close the distance.

"You came here to antagonize me," Patrick repeated.

"We came at your invitation."

Patrick leaned closer to Matt. "I did three tours of the Middle East. I know what a modern gunshot wound looks like. I'll make you pay."

"Modern gunshot wound? I've never used my weapon."

Patrick glowered at him. "It's the last man of mine you'll murder."

Matt began to reply, but a shockwave shoved the words back into his mouth as the opposite wall of the opera house disintegrated. The blast pushed both men off their feet and slammed them against the back wall of the box and to the floor.

Patrick's ears were ringing, his mind stuttering from the concussion. There was rubble everywhere. He grabbed the back of a chair to pull himself to his feet and see where the blast had originated. He looked across the opera house to where his wife had been sitting and saw only a gaping hole in the wall. Matt pulled himself to his feet, staggering and shocked. He had taken the full brunt of the explosion in the face.

"You son of a bitch," Patrick yelled. He dived for Matt's throat.

CHAPTER 44.

RED WIRE

Matt was riding fast on his motorcycle, rocketing into a pitch-black horizon. He looked at the mayhem that chased him and guessed at whether he could stay in front of the maelstrom. He twisted the throttle and felt the motorcycle leap faster into the future than he had ever gone, but time sped up behind him, matching his speed and closing the distance.

Matt became desperate to outrace his destiny.

Time was close enough now to see. Events lapped out with tendrils, trying to trap him, snapping around him like bullwhips as he stayed barely out of reach. Men lay dead in his pastures, horses screamed and stampeded from burning stables, a factory exploded. He fired the Walther as fast as he could pull the trigger until cannon balls overwhelmed him. At the very end, Grace was there, buried under the grand oak next to her mother and father.

He knew then that speed wouldn't be enough. He'd need skill and cunning. Matt turned the motorcycle hard to the right, hoping to escape the snapping bullwhips, but he was going too fast to make the turn, and the bike flipped. Pain seared through him as he rolled side over side and finally scraped to a halt on the pavement. He had a single moment of absolute solitude before everything he had tried to out-race smashed into him like a wrecking ball. Hot shrapnel pelted his face until it tore the flesh from his skull.

****

"Matthew, wake up!"

Matt opened his eyes to Ben Franklin. He was in his bed in Ben's house on Craven Street. "What happened?" Matt asked groggily. Words came from his throat as a whisper. Moving his jaw felt like cracking plaster. He reached to brush the stiffness away, but Ben grabbed his wrist and pressed it to the bed.

"They've only just scabbed," he said. "They'll scar if you tear at them."

"What happened?" Matt repeated in a scraggly whisper.

"'Twas a bomb in the opera house," Ben explained. "Celia Ferguson and her guard are dead."

"Patrick Ferguson?" Matt replied. He was having trouble controlling his mind. Visions of the future were still peppering his face.

"He's fine," Ben said. "His wife and a guard were killed."

Matt was finally able to put Ben's words together without them being diluted by jittering visions. "Accident?"

"A bomb planted where they sat."

"Who lit?" Matt whispered.

"Sarah said 'twas something called a time bomb." Ben showed him a piece of charred grey plastic connected to two charred insulated wires. Under the grey plastic, the red and black insulation was still intact. "I found this," Ben said.

Matt's thoughts swam through his throbbing head. "From the future," he whispered.

"Sarah said it," Ben replied.

"Future," Matt repeated.

"Do you remember that Ferguson tried to kill you?"

"Why?"

"He thinks you planted the bomb. He tried to strangle you. Thomas Mifflin punched him to pull him off."

"Why I can't talk?"

"Yes," Ben replied. "You didn't plant the bomb?"

Matt closed his eyes and shook his head. The fact that Ben had asked cut him to his soul.

"I've seen explosions, cannon fire, mortars, and the like," Ben explained. "There was no smoke or smell."

"Who?" Matt whispered, but then his world went black and he slipped into the shadows.

CHAPTER 45.

MUSE

Brian Palmer's coach was almost at Scarlett's London house when the distraction of passing wagons pulled him out of his visions and then to the ambition that sustained him. He would never have predicted how much making one man suffer could give him so much purpose. He admitted too that his growing fascination with Scarlett was affecting him in ways that he had not expected. Even he was not immune to Scarlett's charisma. Her presence had made it easier to extend his stay for six months this time, and to think about visiting again.

Brian reached up to massage his temples. The headaches were still severe, but as on his last two trips, they were starting to subside. Brian had submitted himself to a full battery of physical and mental tests before and after each trip. There didn't look to be any lasting physical effects except for some striking changes in his brain. MRI scans documented a three-percent increase in neuron density after his first trip and an additional two percent after the second. It was not surprising that headaches were a side effect of the wormhole; the capillaries that fed these growing neurons with oxygen lagged far behind the neuronal growth rate. His new brain cells were starving for oxygen.

Hypoxic stress aside, Brian's increased brain volume had manifested in a seventeen-point rise in his already high IQ. His intelligence and memory had developed astoundingly. He could now play chess against himself in his mind. Another interesting side effect of the wormhole was an ability to predict events before they happened.

His prescience was minimal after the first trip and mostly came in the form of dreams. They increased dramatically after the second journey. Since his third, he could dream at will. When he allowed himself to look down that hallway in his mind, he could see time as a separate dimension.

There was some danger in not keeping his distance from the visions. They were like walking along the slippery bank of a rushing river. You could easily lose your balance, slide in, and be swept away. He had learned to pull himself out of the river on those occasions when he did fall, but it was getting harder as his premonitions became more vivid.

His prescience made him aware of two futures that were diverging, although the four-dimensional map of time wasn't always so easy to read. Understanding time was like communicating in a foreign language that you barely spoke; you caught words here and there and tried to read body language and facial expression. Brian's visions of the future gave him two probable outcomes: one presented as static and "normal," and the other as a purposeful manipulation.

Nothing in his mind told him whether one future was better than the other, but it was certain that Matthew Miller was driving toward the manipulated timeline. Despite

Brian's growing skills, forecasting the actions of either Patrick Ferguson or Matt Miller was difficult. Brian could only make inferences about the empty holes that engulfed the events around them like explosions along the flight path of a bomber. Some holes connected to the normal future, some led to the manipulation, and they were often too entwined to sort out.

Brian had spent days in the dark playing and replaying sequences of events in his mind until the conclusion was unmistakable: Miller and Ferguson were in an alliance to change the future and had already caused the death of one anti-American member of Parliament. They were willing to kill to accomplish their goals, and Brian saw no reason not to match their fervor. He understood where they were coming from. If they shared even a small amount of his ability to see time, they too recognized that biological life was trivial compared to the energy that composed the universe.

The carriage slowed abruptly and the driver turned. "Eighty-five, Strand." Brian hopped out. His head throbbed at the concussion of his feet against the ground. He steadied himself against the carriage.

"You all right, sir?" the driver asked.

Brian wasn't sure how long he'd been standing there in pain when he acknowledged the concerned face of the cabbie. "I'm good," he said finally. He reached into his pocket and handed over the fare.

"Thank you, sir," the driver said as Brian stepped back.

Brian watched the coach through blurred vision as it disappeared into the night. He turned to Scarlett's row-home. Light from the transom helped him see the lock. He jiggled the skeleton key until the deadbolt receded from the jamb. The solid oak door clicked and swung open. He closed it quietly behind him, thinking he would surprise her, despite the fact that there was some risk in startling Scarlett; she had a propensity for keeping a pistol nearby.

Brian walked through the hall and past the steps to the upstairs bedroom, looking toward the darkened stairway with some anticipation. Maybe he could convince Scarlett to go up there tonight. She was in the parlor at an oak workbench, surrounded by bright oil lamps, fixing a fake diamond into a gold setting. She had become a capable jeweler in the last six months. The image of her starting a jewelry shop and earning money in some legitimate enterprise made him laugh loud enough for her to hear.

"I'm busy," she said without looking up from her work.

"I know better than to disturb you," he replied.

"Was it you?" she asked, still looking down at the ring.

"What?"

"The *Gazette*."

He looked around for the newspaper.

CHAPTER 46.

SCARLETT

Scarlett glanced up from her jewels and waited for Brian to finish the article. She suspected as soon as she read it that he had been involved. She set everything down on the table, looked him up and down, and reconsidered why she stayed. Her affection had been for hire for so long, it was hard to remember what kind of man she preferred. Was this new ruthlessness physically alluring, or was it just another kind of currency? Scarlett trafficked in fame and fame was essential in London. Men's reputations were tangible, like gold or land. If you controlled them, you set their value and could exchange them for other assets.

Scarlett had become an affluent woman by hiring herself out to men of extreme wealth. These men were brutal when it came to managing money, companies, and people, and she was brutal when it came to controlling their good name. They entered her life with wealth and family, and in the end, they were willing to trade their assets for hers. She was not unwilling to compromise, and many negotiated hard to leave their fame unscathed. Like any skilled nego-tiator, she took the time to understand the person sitting across the table. She never asked for more than they could afford. Many shrugged their shoulders at the cost. A few had been willing to sit at the table a second time, and some a third.

Scarlett did not know what to think of Brian Palmer when he first tracked her down and presented a handful of fake jewels that were the best she'd ever seen. She only knew they were fake because he had an endless supply. He'd left one with her, told her where she could find him, and walked away. She remembered turning the brilliant in her fingers, 'round and 'round. It was heavier and colder than a real diamond. She remembered breathing on it to shine it against her dress. It fogged easily, which surprised her. Scarlett knew immediately why no one bought them as loose stones; they needed a story. It took time to learn to set them, but she was a natural at coming up with a narrative.

Her tales were even easier to believe when they came with a tight bodice and a bosom that testified on her behalf. She liked to profile the jewelers as her sham played out. Some doubted her story from the beginning, but greed brought them around. Others fell for the tearful, impoverished mistress forced to sell a ring her ex-lover had given her after using her indiscriminately. Some, she knew, would sympathize with the scorned wife who was vying for revenge against an adulterous husband. Even those who pitied her only offered half what the brilliant was worth; their complicity in the ruse was certain. Even if they believed the stone was fake, they'd have no qualms about passing it on as real at a discount price.

Brian dropped the newspaper on the table and feigned dismay. "Wasn't me," he said.

Scarlett knew that was what he had to say. "It doesn't surprise me that 'twas someone."

"Wasn't me," he repeated.

"People like Ferguson make many enemies in the course of business. 'Twas only a matter of time before someone had enough."

He tapped the newspaper with his forefinger. "So there. It could have been anyone in London."

CHAPTER 47.

GOODBYE

Patrick stood dumbfounded and numb as the procession of people walked from St. Paul's Cathedral. He had never been a fan of long funerals, so had asked the priest to take no more than an hour. Patrick's eldest daughter, Catherine, was his only child to stand by his side. At seven years old, she already demonstrated her mother's poise as she accepted condolences. She smiled politely at comments that ranged from compassionate to amazingly tone-deaf and inappropriate.

Mary, Patrick's two-year-old, huddled in the arms of her governess while Celia's two sisters held the hands of the twins, Marcus and Margaret, who were almost five. Celia's sisters had been surprisingly helpful during the time leading up to the funeral. Neither had ever shown any affection for Patrick, presumably for the same reason that most of London had shunned him, but now that Celia was dead, they came to his aid with extreme kindness.

London was full of children, great and poor, who had lost one or both parents. Almost every prominent family had seen some recent death, and mechanisms were in place to help Patrick's children prosper in the face of the hardship that came from the loss of a mother.

****

The funeral procession from St. Paul's made rapid progress through the streets of London, but it would be an hour before they reached Celia's family plot. Nathan, who sat next to Patrick, had paid people along the route to ease their passage through the crossroads. Patrick sat in silence, listening to the sound of hooves on the cobblestone. He and Nathan looked out at the passing homes from opposite sides of the carriage.

When Nathan finally broke the silence, Patrick welcomed the interruption; he was getting nowhere in his thinking. Rage and grief were each taking a turn at overwhelming any attempt he could make at a coherent plan. He was usually better at controlling these kinds of thoughts.

"Let me say again how sorry I am, sir," Nathan said.

"I appreciate it, Nathan."

"I feel responsible," Nathan confessed. "I should have sent additional guards. Only Deighton was close enough to light that fuse."

"Celia's bodyguard had nothing to do with her murder."

"He's the only possibility, sir."

"And he killed himself by accident?"

"It wouldn't be the first time an assassin died by his own hand." Patrick reached into his pocket and pulled out a piece of plastic. It was a charred grey liquid-crystal display. A clear window had survived the explosion to protect the electronics underneath. Patrick waited for Nathan to examine the burned object.

"It's from America," Patrick explained. "The clock is set

to ignite the bomb at a time of your choosing, or someone could trigger it from afar."

"Who has such a device?"

"Franklin and Miller. It was likely intended for me, but I left to confront Miller. I'm sure of it."

Nathan looked both stunned and confused. "Miller was injured in the explosion."

"I summoned him to his feet," Patrick explained. "He'd have been protected within the confines of his box like Franklin and the others."

"What now, then?"

"Vigilance," Patrick said. "They are revolutionaries, willing to commit murder to accomplish their ends. That they have this device tells me that others may be involved."

"We should bring the sway of the British government against them," Nathan said. "You have many allies."

"No," Patrick replied. "We cannot risk Miller exposing one piece of our strategy. Our countrymen wouldn't understand. I want no connections to William Maynard, unfortunate as it was. None."

"We will accelerate our plans," Nathan said.

Patrick nodded. "Those men must sail for America, whatsoever the cost."

"'Twill take another week," Nathan replied. "The ships want for cargo and provisions."

"You must assume that their lives are threatened by Mr. Miller and his lieutenants."

"His organization remains hidden from us."

"Sutton?"

"Sutton has seen nothing of their people," Nathan

replied. "We've men in our employ who could make Franklin and Miller disappear."

"It would be nearly impossible without an incident," Patrick explained. "Franklin, too, has allies in Parliament. We'll deal with him at some later time."

"And Miller?"

"Lure him away."

"I'll find some men."

"He should come to me," Patrick said with venom. "I'll look into the eyes of the man who murdered the mother of my children. As he takes his last breath, I'll look into his eyes."

CHAPTER 48.

MARGARET AND POLLY

It was early morning, but Ben was already gone. Matt had an open book on his lap but no longer felt like reading. He was sitting in Ben's writing room in front of the multipaned windows that looked out onto Craven Street. His face had healed enough that he no longer felt pain while chewing. Looking up from his book, he watched the coaches that passed in front of the house, and he tried to catch glimpses of the neighbors who lived in the identical row-homes across the street. Most kept their curtains drawn, perhaps in an attempt to protect their eyes from Ben's air baths.

Matt remembered that he needed to finish a letter to Grace so he could send it out on the next ship. He set his book down and sat at Ben's desk. Margaret brought tea on a silver tray as he trimmed a new quill.

"Feeling better, Mr. Miller?" she asked.

"I'm almost ready for a walk."

"Dr. Franklin warned you not to retire from our apartments."

"Why?"

"He fancies your life is in danger."

"Did he say from whom?"

"He said to trust no one."

"Where is he?"

"Investigating your situation."

"Is *his* life in danger?" Matt asked.

"He doesn't believe so, but recommended that you take quiet for a few days until he is certain."

Margaret Stevenson was a handsome woman of about fifty and was so often at Ben's side that most people in London assumed they were married. Polly, her daughter, was a regular visitor to her mother and Ben. She was in her early thirties and married to a well-known surgeon, William Hewson, who was Ben's friend. Polly and William were in negotiations with Ben to take over the house so William could conduct medical classes there. Ben was unwilling to change apartments until Matt left London, so the Stevenson women had a vested but friendly interest in Matt concluding his business in as little time as possible.

"Good morning, Mr. Miller."

Matt turned to see Polly enter the room as Margaret left. Polly sat down next to him and gave him a teasing smile. Polly was a flirt, and Matt did his best to keep her at arm's length. Detachment seemed essential, considering the relationship Polly had with Ben. Married or no, she had been in Ben's life for more than a decade, and she filled the older man with joy. Sometimes Ben talked to her like a father, often like a teacher, and there were times when Matt swore they could have been lovers. Polly was another on a long list of complex relationships Ben maintained with the opposite sex. Matt had long since given up on sorting them out.

"How are you today, Polly?" Matt asked.

"Quite well, Mr. Miller. Your face has almost healed."

"I feel better," Matt replied. He thought for a moment. "I feel well enough to go about my business, if only your mother and Dr. Franklin would allow."

"Mother says there is some peril to your person."

"So it seems."

"Oh," Poly said, reaching into a pocket hidden in the folds of her dress. She pulled out a letter and presented it to Matt. "Someone brought this to the door a moment ago. It's from Virginia."

Matt took the letter. Polly curtsied and left. Matt leaned back in his chair, hoping that it was a long letter, with plenty of good news from his family. He missed them now more than ever. Disappointingly, it was only a single page. He broke the seal. The hand was unmistakably David Taylor's. David had never written Matt before, and the sight of his handwriting caused Matt alarm.

Richmond, Virginia, June 27, 1772

Dear Nephew,

I hope this letter finds you well and you have been successful in the enterprise that entreated you to join Dr. Franklin. There is no other way to apprise you, so I'll make haste. Perhaps a month after you repaired for London, Grace experienced a trauma that caused her to lose her unborn child. She remains extremely ill, though I don't believe her life is in danger. The doctors cannot tell the time it will take her to recover, or if she ever will.

The circumstance of her ordeal should also be disclosed in that it may affect your affairs in London, especially if your intercourse concerns the English government. The events leading to Grace's injury were as follows: We hosted Governor and Lady Murray, and a dozen other delegates after the Virginia Economic Congress. Ten Redcoats accompanied the Governor as part of his personal guard. They were staying in the shacks, some on watch, others sleeping or eating. Two soldiers dragged Grace into a barn while she was putting the farm to bed. She was able to fight them off ere she was violated, but she and her unborn child were injured. The inside of her legs became wet with blood, and she lost the baby soon after. It is hard to know exactly what motivated these men, but Grace believes they were angered by words they overheard whilst standing guard outside the dining hall. Besides their evil constitution, there may have been political motivations.

I am sorry to be the bearer of bad news, but I believed you should be made aware. I cannot understate the urgency of your returning to Virginia.

Your friend and Uncle,

David A. Taylor

****

Matt dropped the letter softly onto the desk and sat stunned. He fought back the urge to rage and kick, then to fall to the floor and sob, and then a moment later, the rage returned. He stood up and faced the doorway.

"Polly!"

Polly came bounding in with a smile that dissolved as soon as she looked into his eyes. "Yes, Mr. Miller?"

"Do you know anyone down by the dock? I'm looking for a gentleman, maybe of a lower station."

"My husband has men he employs for finding cadavers and such," she said hesitantly. "Why do you ask?"

"I need old clothing."

"There are tailors on Strand."

"Used clothing that fits me, like a vagrant would wear. Complete sets," Matt said. "I want an old wig or two, and a bottle . . . the kind a drunk carries. Costume beards, too, like in the theatre."

Polly looked at him, puzzled. "You're willing to pay for these items?"

"I'll pay a fine price if they're here before dark. There should be two of each, my size, maybe a bit larger."

Polly reached cautiously between Matt and the desk to the drawer. Matt slid his chair back so she could pull out a sheet of parchment. Polly assessed his face again, and then set it in front of him. "Write your list."

Matt dipped the quill into the ink. His fingers were shaking with rage.

****

Three hours later, Matt was looking out the window of his third-story bedroom when he heard the doorknocker. He rushed down three flights of steps and jogged through the hall to answer the door. He met Margaret halfway.

"I got it," Matt said.

"A delivery?" she asked.

"Something for my business," Matt muttered. "I got it."

Margaret returned to her room and Matt continued to the door.

"Who is it?" he asked through the door. Ben's warning that his life was in danger was still on his mind.

"Delivery for Mr. Miller."

"What delivery?"

"Old clothes," the man said.

Matt opened the front door and looked into the eyes of a scraggly seaman. He was holding a heavy grey burlap sack and sizing Matt up. "Should fit," he said simply. "One pound, ten shillings. Bottle's half full."

"Too much for old rags." Matt wasn't in the mood to be cheated.

"Lumping pennyworth," the old man replied. "The distance 'twas too far for any price!"

Matt dug down in his pocket, fished out the coins, and kneeled down to do a quick survey of the bag's contents. Satisfied that everything was there, he stood back up and counted the coins out into the man's palm. The old seaman glanced down once more at the sack of clothes in the doorway and then closed his hand. He nodded, turned, and walked away.

Matt picked up the sack, locked the front door, and returned to his bedroom. He closed the door behind him and took stock. He had two pairs of striped sailor pants, spotted and stained as if they'd been flecked with a tar brush. One pair came with a rope belt. There were two dirty white shirts, an old overcoat, some nasty-looking wigs, an old hat, and two balls of fur that turned out to be fake beards. The wigs didn't look lice-free, but that was true with everything you put on your head in the eighteen century. Matt tucked it all back into the bag and slid it under his bed to wait until the house was empty.

****

Matt heard Ben come home around three that afternoon. Margaret had prepared cold meats, cheese, and bread. Matt sat with them and ate until he could excuse himself, saying that he was tired. He made no mention of his news from Virginia. He waited for Ben and Margaret to leave for a party, then put on the sailor's clothes and fitted the wig to his head. He tried a beard but decided against it, since it would require trimming to look right.

When his costume was complete, Matt looked into the mirror, decided that he wasn't sufficiently grubby, coated his hands with soot and ash from the hearth, and worked it into his two weeks of beard growth. He pulled the hat down over the wig and grabbed the bottle. He looked in the mirror one last time, walked down two flights of steps, eased himself out a back second-story window and across the roof, and dropped down into the garden.

CHAPTER 49.

JACK TAR

Having escaped Ben's house unseen, Matt made his way along an alley behind the rowhouse, up to Charing Cross, and to a bench fifty feet from Craven Street. Row-homes packed each side of Craven, so there was no way to watch Ben's residence anywhere near the front of his house without being obvious. Spies would most likely be at the Charing Cross end of Craven where Matt was sitting, or down at the other end by the river. Charing Cross had constant traffic of carriages and pedestrians, so it was the best place to sit. Matt would check the river end if he needed to later.

Matt leaned back on the weathered bench, tilted the bottle up to his mouth, and drank some of the tea he had used to replace the old whisky. It was almost too easy to recognize the men watching his street. They were massive characters dressed in ill-fitting suits, standing around re-reading copies of the *London Gazette*. Matt took another drink and gave an exaggerated cough. He wiped his face on his coarse woolen sleeve, stared at the ground, and coughed again.

Matt closed his eyes for a moment to put his face into the sun. When he looked down again and opened his eyes, three sets of ratty leather shoes were standing in front of him. They belonged to teenage boys who were now blocking his view.

"Move along, kiddies," Matt grumbled in his drunkard's voice. "I ain't sharin'."

"*You* move along, you old soaker," the middle boy said.

Matt scanned their bodies and faces. The middle one was the leader. His face and clenched fists told Matt that he had something to prove.

"Don't want no trouble," Matt said. He saw the boy relax.

"Sit on another bench."

"Yeah, you old cuff," the boy on one side added.

All their faces were dirty. Matt took another drink and made the same exaggerated cough. He wiped his face on his sleeve again and looked hard where he had wiped. He reached up with his thumb and forefinger and played with his sleeve, pretending to pick off boogers. He exaggerated the motion it took to shake them from his hand.

"He's disgusting," declared the middle boy.

"Come on, you old fumbler," said the last boy. He reached out and poked Matt's shoulder. Matt cleared his throat. He wasn't going to leave this bench until he could follow the men who were watching his street. He imagined himself spending the next few days in costume as he investigated the bombing. The boys presented the perfect opportunity to rehearse his old-drunkard persona.

"Too weary to stand up," Matt proclaimed in an old man's voice. "Bunch of natty lads, you are. Anyways, there are plenty of benches. Let an old man be." He waved his empty hand and pointed up and down Charing Cross.

The middle boy asserted himself again. "This is our bench," he declared.

"Why d'you want this bench?" Matt asked. "Ain't movin, no how."

The boys turned to one another, uncertain now of their next move. "He's gonna keep us from getting paid," the boy on the left said. "I want them coppers."

"How many you gettin'?" Matt asked.

"Mind your beeswax," the middle boy said.

"Leave an old man alone to take his nap," Matt declared. "Ah'm so sleepy. The sauce does it to me . . . every time it does." Matt shimmied to the very end of the bench. He waved randomly for them to sit. The bench was just long enough for the three boys. Matt leaned back to show his intention to take a nap. He snorted as if he had already fallen asleep and had re-awoken. "It's my bottle," he gurgled in between snorts. "Young hemps . . . ain't sharin." He let his head fall forward and reached up to tilt his hat to hide his eyes.

"Swallowed a hare," the middle boy said, tilting his head low to try to see Matt's face.

Matt answered with a low snore. He could see their ragged shoes shifting as they argued their plans. He thought he had them pegged; at least two of the boys were not prepared for a physical altercation on a busy London street.

"How 'bout one of them other benches?" one boy asked, pointing. "We could still see."

"Mr. Palmer said it gotta be this bench."

"One o' them others?"

"He said this one."

There was a long silence, and then the bench shifted as the boys sat beside Matt. He felt a sharp elbow in his side. "You awake, you old soaker?"

Matt jerked, snorted, and gave a loud snore.

"Shut him up," the middle boy said.

Matt felt the elbow again. He snorted and went quiet.

"He ain't wakin'," one boy said. "Drunk as a skunk."

The boys shifted around again. Convinced now that Matt was sleeping, their attention went elsewhere. Matt watched from under his hat. "Ah don't write much," the middle boy said. The teen immediately next to Matt accepted a modern-looking pad of paper from the one who had just spoken.

"We're supposed to write when he comes and goes," the middle boy proclaimed. "Mr. Palmer ain't gonna pay less we fill it. Exact times, he said. Kin you see the clock?"

"Ah can," the boy farthest from Matt said. "It's four."

"Write that down."

The boy next to Matt wrote the number 4 on his paper next to a dash. He was using a yellow Number Two pencil. "You know what Ben Franklin looks like?" he asked.

"Old and fat," the middle boy said. "Can't miss him."

"Miller is tall with dark hair. Normally don't wear no wig."

"What time is it now?"

"Still four."

"How much we gettin paid?" asked the farthest boy.

"Two pounds."

"Maybe I should walk down there and see if James is watchin'."

They were silent for a long while until Matt felt the bench shudder as the boy farthest from him got up and walked away.

"He should look in the window to see if anyone's home," the middle boy said. "We could write that down."

"Thought Dr. Franklin was away."

"Carriage took him and his wife," the middle boy said.

"Somebody watching him?"

"Don't matter. Mr. Palmer cares most 'bout this Miller. Stole something."

There was another long silence, and then one boy asked, "Whatcha gonna spend yer silver on?"

"Bread for me and my mummy," the middle boy replied. "Some pudding, too, if there's any left."

"Sweetmeat," the other boy said, "and jerky for my pocket."

"Hope Mrs. Palmer gives it to me," the middle boy replied. "Like an angel she is. Ain't his wife, though. Been givin' money to me and my brother fer a year. Goes by whatsoever suits her. Heard people call her Miss La Porte. This Palmer shows up, and suddenly she's his missus without any nuptials. She's a first-rate, though, puttin' money in our palms whenever she comes from her house. The first time, 'twas two shillings. We turned right 'round and went inta McAllister's for a fresh pigeon pie and that thick ale. They weren't gonna let us sit since they knowed us from begging."

"Ain't beggin' now, though," the other boy declared.

"What time is it?"

"Half four," the middle boy read off the tower clock. "Better write that down with the saying, all clear. Heard a watchman say that . . . down at the dock."

"Why'd you wanna go down there?" the other boy said. "Smells like fish."

"Chasing another fellow," the middle boy declared. "Damn easy to follow, and I didn't hafta write nuthin'. Drove one of them Ferguson carriages."

"He Miller's fellow?"

"Nah," the middle boy replied. "I asked around at the dock hoping I could figure out where he lived. One boy talked about how this fellow was in the company of Sir Patrick Ferguson."

"Sir Patrick?"

"Never seen Ferguson," the middle boy replied. "Name of Trench."

"Odd name, that."

"Fine carriage, though."

The third boy returned and sat back down on the bench with a thud. The bench shuddered, and Matt took the occasion to pretend the movement woke him. He stood up with his bottle to walk down Strand until he was well out of sight of anyone who could be watching. He passed the two men who were still rereading the *Gazette* and found a coach at Carting Lane.

"Cabbie," he called up to the man sitting on the carriage.

"What you want, you old scrub?"

"Ain't no scrub," Matt said. "Just an old sailor, down on his luck. Topping wife, though. I got a question."

"Topping wife?"

"Gives me silver not to come home."

"How much?"

"Enough to pay you."

"What's your question, old man?"

"You ever heard of some place called McAllister's? I'm lookin fer fresh pigeon pie and thick ale. You know the place?"

"I know it. So?"

"How much you want to take me there?"

"Too much."

"Three shillings."

"Lemme see."

Matt reached into his pocket for a handful of coins and showed them to the cabbie. "I can find another who will take my silver."

"Calm down, old man." The driver waved Matt up into the buggy. Matt climbed into the coach and looked to the sky. There was still plenty of light left to search for the Palmers.

CHAPTER 50.

WATHING STREET

Just past St. Paul's churchyard, Matt's carriage crossed Bread Street and pulled to a stop along a stretch of row-homes. The cabbie turned his head and pointed. "This be McAllister's."

"Pigeon pie and thick ale?"

The driver nodded. "Three shillings."

Matt handed the money over and stepped out onto a busy cobblestone street crowded with horse-drawn carriages and people hurrying about on foot. He reviewed his plan as he watched the driver pull away, then looked across the street at McAllister's. It looked like any other English pub, with a dozen full tables on a cobblestone patio. He could already see the pigeon pies.

Row-homes like the ones on Craven lined Matt's side of the street. He sat on one of the benches along the thorough-fare and began his vigil, but the smell of pigeon pie and the thought of a thick ale made his stomach grumble. He smoothed his wig away from his face and crossed the street to McAllister's.

Matt was greeted with disgust as he entered the pub. "You can't come in here," a man proclaimed.

"Why?"

"We don't allow drunks." The man pointed at the bottle dangling from Matt's hand. "Not with that, either."

Matt reached into his pocket for a shilling and used his best King's English. "I have a strong proclivity to sit outside, closest to the street."

The man looked at him twice, then at the shilling.

"Rich wife," Matt explained.

The host looked him up and down, then snapped his fingers a couple of times. "Show me some silver."

Matt reached into his pocket and pulled out his coins.

"Who'd you shake?"

"She pays me to be gone for days." Matt gave the man another shilling, enjoying his increasingly confused grin. "Heard you have a thick ale." Matt smoothed the tattered wig away from his face again. "I pledge to be on my best behavior."

The man stood there, still unable to act.

"Dude," Matt said in a modern American accent. "You want my money or not?"

Now thoroughly disoriented, the man led Matt to a table by the street with an excellent view of all the row-homes. Matt started scheming of ways to draw out dinner for an extended stakeout of Wathing Street. The man left and was replaced by a waitress who had no trouble showing her disapproval of the homeless drunk at one of her most valuable tables.

"Who seated you?" she asked.

"I can pay," Matt replied. "That's all that should matter." He used his modern American accent again. She took a second look at him, glanced across the street, and appeared to contemplate something. Matt handed her a shilling. "I'm waiting for someone to pass by and I'd like to stay here for as long as I can. Let's negotiate a fair price for me to sit, maybe for most of the night."

"Ten shillings."

Now it was Matt's turn to be bewildered. He had expected her to decline or negotiate. "Five shillings up front, five when I go," he replied, giving her the money. "You're not to mention our arrangement to anyone, right?" He added another shilling to the five in her palm.

"Not a word." She smiled.

"I want some of the pigeon pie," Matt said, "and a tankard of the thick ale."

The waitress scrutinized him, puzzled, and scanned the houses across the street.

"Sometime soon," Matt insisted.

"Yes, sir." She left and returned with the ale. "The pie will be here shortly. Anything else?"

"My old fellow Mr. Palmer told me about this place," Matt said. "I'm waiting to surprise him. His wife is a beautiful woman and charitable. Gives to the poor children out front."

"The redhead?" the waitress asked, satisfied to have finally made a connection.

Matt shrugged.

"She's been paying the beggar boys. They never repair. Like stray cats." She gave him a smile that was wicked at best. "No insult intended, of course."

"Of course," Matt repeated. He found himself fascinated

by this waitress. It hadn't taken her long to throw in with his game. Matt nodded to one of the houses. "Red door?"

"I thought you knew this lady and her fellow."

"Maybe not so well as all that." He gave her two more shillings.

"She's a fancy woman," the waitress explained. "Always with topping fellows and wearing the finest clothes. Are you one of her men?" She smirked and searched his face, as if trying to discern what relationship an old fake sailor could have with the redhead across the street.

"What's she been doing lately?" Matt asked.

The waitress put the coins that she had been collecting into a pocket and pointed. "It's the tan brick between the whites. You've missed her. She takes a hackney around noon and comes back at all hours. Seems to be only one fellow now—" She went quiet and dropped her eyes to her empty palm. Matt put two more shillings there. "He came here, too, asking questions. Sat at almost the same table, but didn't have any coins. Want to know how he paid?" She opened her palm once more, and Matt dropped two more shillings. She unbuttoned the top of her blouse and pulled out a sparkling gem on a chain.

"He gave you a diamond for dinner?"

"For information."

"You haven't sold it?"

"Me and my mum are leaving London once we have enough money."

Matt nodded. "Tell me about this man."

"Rubbed his head, like 'twas aching," she explained,

raising her fingertips to her temples. "There's something else." She held her hand out again.

Matt put two more shillings there.

"Same voice as you."

"Voice?"

"Like an Englishman or an American, but like I never heard. I can usually tell where they come from—Cornwall, Suffolk, even Virginia or New England. Couldn't place him, though. Haven't heard it again 'til today."

"If he comes by, will you tell him I was here?"

She shrugged. "He'd pay a fine price to know that some old sea crab was spying on his lady."

Matt gave her a guinea. "Not a word for two weeks and there's another one waiting for you." Matt knew that whatever he paid, he didn't have long until she sold him out. She left for her neglected tables and Matt looked across the street, suddenly wishing he had brought the Walther.

I may have to kill a man.

CHAPTER 51.

DIAMOND RING, MY FRIEND

Map of Eighteenth-Century London

Matt dragged himself out of his bed in Ben's home at sunrise the next morning. He had tossed and turned all night as his mind alternated between rage and sadness, unable to get the vision of Grace bleeding out of his mind. He looked like hell when he checked his face in the mirror and allowed himself a sad smile. The bags under his eyes would help his disguise. Matt pulled the second set of clothing from the burlap bag along with another wig. Today he would look old and disheveled, but presentable.

Matt trimmed the fake beard with a small pair of scissors until it fit properly. The rawhide string went around his ears and tied underneath the beard. When he was done, he looked into the glass again and saw a young Willie Nelson. He walked softly down the steps, trying not to make them creak. He checked the second-story hall and saw that Ben had already shut himself in his writing room,

Matt tiptoed back up to the third story and climbed out the window, down the gutter, into the garden, over a hill, and onto Villiers Street. At Charing Cross, he decided on his direction. The road was already busy. He checked for spies as he walked past Craven Street, but no one was watching it. *Maybe they're not awake yet.* He smiled as he questioned whether the average eighteenth-century mole had a routine work schedule. Did they expect time off for lunch, weekends, and vacation? Not much work-life balance in thuggery, he thought.

Matt walked down Whitehall almost to Westminster Bridge. He took the alley down to Northcroft Carriage and Stables. He'd been there with Ben on two previous occasions when they hired carriages for day trips to East London. Adam Northcroft was Ben's dear friend; Matt knew he could trust him. Matt walked into the office and saw that a new teenage clerk was behind the desk. The boy smirked at Matt's appearance.

"Good day, sir," he said.

Matt stayed in character. "Is the proprietor here?"

"He's out back. He'll not want to be bothered."

"I want to hire a carriage," Matt said. "I know you got five or ten back there."

"How'd you know that?"

"Been here."

Without saying anything, the boy stepped away from the counter and left through a rear door. He returned with Adam Northcroft, who assessed Matt for what seemed like forever. "We'll take you where you want to go. We only hire carriages out to regulars."

"Adam," Matt said, still in character. "Don't you recognize me?"

"Why would I recognize you?"

Matt pulled the beard away from his face. "Matthew Miller, Dr. Franklin's friend. Good day, sir."

"Mr. Miller," Northcroft said. "What foolery is this?"

"Long story." He pulled his beard back up over his cheeks. "Official government business and highly secret, so not a word." He put his fingers to his lips. "I'm required to hire a hackney and two horses."

"Coachman?"

"Me."

"You gotta have a license to drive in London."

Matt gave him a puzzled look.

Northcroft rolled his eyes. "I have a carriage. A constable stops you, I'll know nothing of it."

Matt nodded. "Agreed."

"Fine disguise, but you don't look like no coachman." Northcroft led Matt into a sizable tack room in the back of the building. "I got some clothes in here." Northcroft showed him into a shed made of old grey weathered wood. It looked like the shed was the original structure, and the surrounding barn had been built up later. Northcroft turned to Matt to assess his size, then chose breeches, a shirt, and a coachman's jacket from different stacks of folded clothing. "This should do you. They'll match your beard." He handed the folded garments to Matt. "Ain't easy navigating

London streets, despite what the papers say," Northcroft warned.

"Official government business," Matt repeated. Northcroft shrugged his shoulders and walked out, closing the door behind him.

By the time Matt was dressed in his coachman outfit, Northcroft had a faded red carriage and two horses ready. The back wheels were twice as big as the front wheels which had plenty of space underneath the carriage to navigate the narrow city corners. The coach box, where the driver sat, was out in front near the horses. The single bench inside could seat three people, though it would be tight.

"It ain't one of them fine Fergusons, to be sure," Northcroft said, "but the inside is scoured and sharp. A government gentleman would have no issue." He motioned for Matt to step up onto the carriage. "I know you're a horseman, but take the corners slow, or you'll tumble her. Careful of ruts and watch for citizens. Constables don't take kindly to hackneys running down patrons."

"Got it," Matt said.

"Know where you're going?"

"I've been in London for a couple of weeks now."

Northcroft stepped to a cabinet and pulled out a tattered map of London. "You know how much to charge?"

"I'm only looking for one fare," Matt said. He pointed to the intersection of Wathing and Bread Streets. "Starts here, but I don't know where it'll end."

Northcroft grabbed a thick lead pencil and drew a series of widening circles on the map, then added a price to each ring. "That should do," he said. "We can settle up when you return."

"I'll be back in the afternoon," Matt replied. He climbed up into the coach box and shook the reins, and the horses jumped forward.

****

Matt trembled with expectation as he made his way along Charing Cross. He slowed as he drove by Craven. The Craven Street Irregulars, as he now called the boys in honor of the street waifs Sherlock Holmes employed in his investigations, were on their usual bench. Matt fought the urge to give them a clever jab as he passed. At the least, the boys would tell Palmer about the strange cabbie who had shouted at them. Matt had already been too cavalier with the waitress at McAllister's and had the overwhelming feeling that she'd sell him out as soon as she could.

Matt drove the carriage up Strand to Fleet and past St. Paul's churchyard, then came to a rest at the intersection of Wathing and Bread. The designated hackney stand was a block away on Cheapside Street, but from here he had an unobstructed view of both McAllister's Pub and Mrs. Palmer's house.

Ten minutes later, he was lost in thought when a man climbed into the carriage, saying, "Take me to Westminster Abbey." The man had bushy red hair, and a red mustache and beard. It took Matt a moment to come out of his daze. The thought came to him that it could be Mr. Palmer, but his accent was wrong. Matt hadn't considered that random pedestrians would be interested in hiring a coach.

"Coach's broken," he muttered. "You'll have to go up to the stand."

"Who you waiting for?"

"My horses are lame," Matt lied. "Won't move."

"Both?" the man said incredulously.

"We had a long trip yesterday . . . rough terrain."

"Seems damn odd." The man stepped out of the carriage and then hopped from the footboard to the ground.

Matt pointed down the block to the hackney stand. "One block."

"I know," the man called back, irritated. He gave Matt another dirty look and then proceeded to walk down the street. Matt spent the next hour explaining that the carriage was broken or the horses were lame to almost everyone on Wathing. Eventually, he saw the black door of the tan row-house open and an attractive redhead step into the street. Matt felt his blood pressure rise, hoping that she'd walk to his coach.

"Are you for hire?" she asked up at him.

"Certainly, m'lady," Matt said. "I just dropped off."

"Anyone I know?"

"Gentleman. Red-haired, like yourself."

"Ah, Mr. Barnard. Where did he come from this morning? 'Tis usually the time he retires."

Matt hopped off his perch to open the door and help her into the carriage. "Where you going, then, m'lady?"

"Jewelry district, and then to pick up my husband for the theatre."

Matt closed the door behind her and climbed up into the coach box. He wasn't familiar with the jewelry district, so he grabbed Northcroft's map, but it wasn't labeled. "Streets, m'lady," he said. "I need streets." He turned around to look through the window at her.

She leaned forward. "Haven't been doing this very long?"

"I only recently purchased this carriage and team. Gets me out of the house."

"Hatton Garden and Cross Street." She leaned back again so Matt could no longer see her.

Matt took some time to locate the intersection on the map. "I got it," he said finally, and set the map to the side. It was about two miles northwest, across multiple city blocks; maybe half an hour away. He slapped the reins against the horses' hindquarters and the carriage shuddered forward. Their clacking hooves and the rumble of the wheels on the rough cobblestones echoed between the buildings and made it hard to hear until the street smoothed and widened.

The redhead leaned forward. "I'd become familiar with the jewelry district, certainly. 'Tis one rum cull after another that goes."

"And you?"

Matt hadn't thought about the loaded nature of his question until it came out of his mouth. She was quiet for longer than was comfortable.

"A lady must make her own way in this world. 'Tis best if she is wealthy." She sounded more thoughtful than irritated, and there was an undertone of sadness.

"'Tis *best* if she is doing what she desires, and is around people she loves," Matt corrected. "Gold usually cannot buy those things."

She went quiet again, and Matt entertained that he had struck a nerve, but then she peeked through the window. "Wealth seems to be requisite for a fine lady, at least in London," she replied cynically. "Where're you from, Mr. —"

"Bradshaw," Matt replied. "Virginia. I moved here after my wife passed." He felt strangely guilty in telling his lie.

"So what *can* gold buy?"

Matt stroked his fake beard. "Not saying it isn't necessary, m'lady. An old man I know says gold is like air. You don't appreciate its value until there's none."

"Your old fellow is wise," she said. "I have gold."

"And, of course, you are happily married." Matt was weirdly regretting everything that came out of his mouth, and her long silences reinforced the feeling.

"What is it that you did in America, Mr. Bradshaw?"

"Tobacco farming," Matt replied. "Sold my land for a king's ransom. I don't need so much for the life I have." The story seemed real in his mind, almost like this person he was creating was somewhere inside him. It brought him back to the days when he was trying to convince everyone in Virginia that he was from Pennsylvania, rather than some guy from the future who was sucked into a wormhole.

"Why do you drive a hackney?"

"To meet interesting people like you. And because life is nothing without some useful pursuit."

"I believe still that gold is a requisite for happiness, at least in London."

"Do you have children, m'lady? People pretend that family can fulfill a woman in ways she does not expect." Matt felt a twinge of sadness. In another context, this intriguing woman might make an interesting friend.

"I cannot fancy bringing children into such a cruel world."

"A charming and intelligent woman like yourself should not be so jaded."

"Jaded?"

"Many people say they don't want to bring children into the world, but there is nobility in getting up every day and confronting God's creation, even for children."

"To do what?"

"To make things better, certainly."

"Will you find another wife and begin again?"

"Life has not defeated me."

"You are quite the philosopher," she declared. "What would you have me do then, philosopher?"

"I'll repeat that you are a charming and intelligent lady. I say this as a teacher rather than as a man talking to a woman . . . if you can believe."

"You shew your parts, telling a lady what she wants," she replied doubtfully. "You are trying to seduce me."

"If that lady wants to hear that life is only about responsibility and not about happiness, then my seduction is complete."

"Maybe this lady wants to hear that life *is* about happiness."

"Have you at least imagined your children?"

"Of course I have, like all ladies."

"Would you want your son to be happy? Or would you want him to accomplish great and noble deeds?"

"I've fancied a heroic destiny for my son. Many ladies would adore him for his accomplishments."

"A heroic destiny will be his defense against a cruel world," Matt said. He stopped the carriage. They were at Hatton Garden and Cross Street. The jewelry district was before them, as his passenger had predicted.

CHAPTER 52.

INVEIGLEMENT

Matt waited with his carriage outside the Hatton Garden jeweler, fingering the two shillings the redhead had slipped him before ducking inside to complete her business, which probably had something to do with the fake diamond hanging from the neck of the waitress in the pub. It was a stroke of luck that she had asked him to wait; it saved him the trouble of having to find a plausible reason for driving her to her next destination. None of the justifications he had thought of sounded the least bit sincere.

True to her word, she was outside in under fifteen minutes with a smile on her face. Matt jumped down to help her into the coach. When she turned to speak to him as she stepped up, her foot glanced off the step and Matt caught her in his arms. She looked into his eyes and his body stirred; something told him to beware. He scanned his mind for some stencil of the moment and briefly slipped into a vision, but Scarlett's voice pulled him back to the present.

"Thank you, Mr. Bradshaw," she said, smiling.

Matt helped her again onto the step. This time she made him grab her waist to boost her into the carriage. "You are very welcome, Miss . . ."

"Mrs. . . . Palmer," she said. She winked. "Scarlett Palmer."

He waited until she was settled before closing the door, then returned to the box. "Where to now, m'lady?"

She leaned forward to see him. "Do I look like the wife of a great lord?"

Matt laughed. "I'd be remiss to say anything but yes. All women should be treated as such." Unquestioned chivalry was one of his favorite things about the eighteenth century. The rules were defined and easy to follow.

"So you say," she said doubtfully.

He waved it off. "Where to?"

"To pick up Mr. Palmer. Then to the theatre. Keep track of the fare, though I assume you don't want for the money."

"I always take the money. The church will appreciate it."

"You don't strike me as a religious man."

"How should a religious man strike?"

"He'd not ask such intimate questions of a lady."

"I came late to the church," Matt said jovially. "What streets?"

"Three Dorset Street, down near the river. It's close to St. Bride's. Then we're off to the Theatre Royal. I can show you on your map."

Matt was already tracing the route on his guide. He knew where the church was, and Dorset Street was well marked. His fingers trembled with adrenaline as he touched the destination and thought of meeting Mr. Palmer. He forced himself to relax.

"I know St. Bride's and the Theatre Royal. I've seen

performances there." He tucked the map under the seat, slapped the reins, and they were off. Once they were moving steadily, he said, "What play?"

St. Brides Church

"*The Tempest.* Do you know it?"

"Not so much. I have it in my library, but I much prefer the others."

"*Hamlet,*" she said, disappointed. "It's every man's favorite."

"I allow, though I did learn to appreciate *Henry the Fifth*. It was my father's favorite. And yours?"

"*Much Ado About Nothing*. I was much affected, too, by *King Lear*. My heart filled with such pathos watching the mad king with his daughters."

"Beatrice and Cordelia were resolute," Matt replied. "Do you see yourself in these ladies?"

Scarlett gave him a thoughtful laugh. "Perhaps a little," she replied. "And what of you, Mr. Bradshaw? Is there only tragedy?"

"I like a good comedy," Matt replied, "but it may have something to do with the smiles they bring to the ladies in the audience."

"Smiles are so few these days."

"Most men I know would do anything to see a smile on the face of their lady."

When she fell silent again, Matt's thoughts returned to his inevitable confrontation with a man who, likely as not, was an assassin. He spotted the spire and golden cross of Saint Bride's in the distance and made the next right into Shoe Lane. They still had a ways to go, but now he had a landmark. Shoe Lane was a busy thoroughfare, and it looked like it would take him all the way to Mr. Palmer.

They waited forever to cross Fleet Street, but the traffic never ceased. Matt inched the carriage into the street expecting outbursts and instead got irritated grins from drivers who expected no less. At Dorset, Scarlett peeked up through the window and pointed. "It's number three. The brown brick with the white fence."

Matt stopped in front of a duplex flanked by alleyways.

"Could you knock and let him know we're here?" she asked. "It's the left one."

Matt crossed the yard and let the brass knocker fall twice on the glossy black door. He heard footsteps on stairs, then latches moving. The door opened onto a man in a white shirt and dark-grey breeches. Shadows partially obscured his face. Something about him was oddly familiar. He was Matt's age, with an average height and build.

"Yes?"

"Mr. Palmer?"

"Yes."

"Mrs. Palmer is in the carriage. I'm here to take you to the theatre."

"You're early. Pull in front of the alley. I won't be but a moment."

"Thank you, sir," Matt replied.

The waitress at McAllister's had mentioned Palmer's accent, but he sounded like any other Londoner to Matt. Matt climbed back up to the coach box and leaned down to his passenger. "He'll be a moment, m'lady."

"There you go again," Scarlett laughed.

Brian emerged through the back gate ten minutes later. Matt hopped down to open the carriage door, hoping for a clean look at the man he suspected of killing Patrick Ferguson's wife.

Brian extended his hand. "Thanks, my fine gentleman. Name's Dr. Brian Palmer."

"Adam Bradshaw," Matt replied.

Brian looked squarely in Matt's eyes as they shook. This wasn't Matt's usual sense of déjà vu. He was sure he had seen this man in London somewhere. He was less attractive and shorter than Matt predicted, especially considering the striking beauty of the woman awaiting him in the carriage, but he also radiated a strong and unnerving confidence.

The coach shuddered as Brian climbed up and he and Scarlett rearranged themselves on the single seat. "Theatre Royal," Brian called to Matt.

"Yes, sir." Matt mounted the carriage and slapped the reins. The theatre was ten or so blocks away through evening traffic, but once Matt emerged onto the quieter Fleet Street, he was able to hear their voices. They were talking mostly about the play.

Scarlett called, "Mr. Bradshaw, have you had the chance to see Shakespeare at the Theatre Royal with Mr. Garrick?"

"No, m'lady," he called back. "I'm quite new to London."

"Where are you from?" Brian called.

"America," Matt replied. He'd intended to say very little; Brian might recognize something that would give him away. "I've only been in London for a few months."

"Where in America?" Brian asked.

"Virginia. I farmed tobacco until my wife died."

"I've heard that the American farm country is magnificent."

"It is, sir. But a lonely place for a widowed man."

"Mr. Bradshaw's favorite play is *Hamlet*," Scarlett interjected. "I so do wish Mr. Palmer enjoyed the theatre enough to have a favorite play."

"In time, my dear," Brian replied. "Where do you keep apartments, Mr. Bradshaw?"

Matt's mind raced. Brian already knew where Matt lived. "Salisbury Street, off of Strand. Comfortable enough for a bachelor."

"Will you remarry?" Brian asked.

"Time will tell, sir," Matt replied.

Every sentence risked Brian recognizing him. Matt wished he had been less friendly from the start. It was a relief when they reached the Strand and the rougher cobblestones allowed him to pretend he couldn't hear them anymore.

Matt turned right at Saint Mary-le-Strand Church and headed up Little Drury Lane to Drury Lane, one of the busier roads in London. They were now behind the Theatre Royal. Matt circled the building whose roof and white marble columns looked like a miniature Parthenon and whose arches reminded him of a Roman aqueduct.

Matt halted the carriage in front of the theatre and hopped down to open the door. He helped Scarlett, then Brian, down to the cobblestones. Brian dug a coin from his purse and gave Matt a shiny gold guinea. "This should cover it."

"The fare is half that," Matt replied.

"Keep it. Mrs. Palmer did so enjoy your conversation." Matt accepted the coin and gave him a short bow.

Scarlett stepped closer. "Safe travels, Mr. Bradshaw. I'm almost sorry to end our exchange. I'd like to speak more about confronting this cruel world."

"Noble deeds, m'lady, for you and your children."

Theatre Royal

Matt bowed, and she answered with a curtsy. She put her arm out for Brian and they joined the queue for the theatre. Matt went to close the carriage and saw something sparkle on the black leather cushion. He reached in and picked it up: a solid gold bracelet adorned with three large rubies. He turned it in his fingers to see the engraving inside: *Robert Dunmeade, October 17, 1751*. Matt turned back to the theatre to see that Scarlett and Brian were nearly inside.

"M'lady," Matt called, then louder, "M'lady."

Scarlett turned and Matt waved her to him. The people in line were staring, probably trying to determine what sort of royalty this beautiful redhead was. Scarlett returned to the carriage, clearly uncomfortable under the crowd's scrutiny, while Brian held their place in line.

She was mildly exasperated when she reached Matt. "Mr. Bradshaw. I was quite manifest regarding *lord* and *lady*?"

"Old habits are hard to break, m'lady."

"What is it?" she asked, resigned.

Matt held the bracelet up. "Drop something?"

"My bracelet! I would have been so upset."

Matt set it in her outstretched hand and watched her fasten it on her wrist.

"How much do I owe you?"

Matt rolled his eyes and smiled. "Noble deeds, m'lady ... though I would take the story of the name and date engraved inside."

"My father," she said. "And the day that he died. It was a cold winter."

"I'm sorry for your loss, m'lady, but I'm glad to be able to return something so precious." Scarlett smiled and curtsied.

"Good day, Mr. Bradshaw."

"To you as well, Miss Dunmeade."

Matt watched her walk away. She glanced down at the bracelet before she and Brian disappeared into the theatre.

When Matt turned to leave, a man was climbing into his coach, saying "Bedford Street." Matt glanced at the long line and decided to take the fare. He drove down Bridges until it hit Strand, then turned left.

"It's there, you idiot," his passenger called, pointing.

Matt pulled the horses up short. "Get out," he called. "Find another coach."

"You're going the wrong way."

"This one's broken." Matt opened the door and waited patiently until the man finally climbed out, then regained the coach box, tore the fake beard from his face, and slapped the reins. He would ride as fast as he could to Dorset Street. There was evidence there that proved Brian Palmer had bombed the opera house. Matt was sure of it.

CHAPTER 53.

3 DORSET STREET

The twenty minutes it took Matt to return to Brian's home felt like hours, but eventually Matt arrived and pulled the carriage into the alley where Palmer had met them. The alley had a station to feed the horses. One trough had hay, and there was another with a water pump. Matt worked the handle to fill the trough with water, and the horses settled in to drink and eat. There was enough there to keep them happy for half an hour, which is how long Matt hoped to be in Brian's home.

He left the horses and walked around to the garden behind the house. From outside the fence, it seemed about the size and shape of the yard behind Ben's house on Craven. Matt pushed at the wooden gate and it swung open easily. Inside was a well-maintained collection of trimmed grasses, flowering bushes, and intermittently spaced Roman and Greek statues. Matt latched the gate behind him and scanned the neighboring houses. No one seemed to be watching; a black shutter covered the only window in the home directly behind Brian's house. Matt was mostly satisfied that he could explore unseen.

Matt began looking for a way in. He stepped to the solid oak doors that opened into the backyard. He knew before he touched them that they'd be locked, but he jiggled them anyway. Burglars roamed the London streets at night, so doors and locks tended to be sturdy and people spent an excessive amount of time securing their homes before they left or went to bed. Matt stepped back into the center of the garden and considered the ways he could break in. He had seen Brian lock and check the front door, and Dorset Street was too busy for someone not to notice a man crawling up the front of a house.

Matt opened the wooden gate and went back out into the alley. The windows there were second story or higher, and all looked shut, and the wall on this side was too smooth to climb. There was a ledge, but no easy way to reach it. He'd have to pull the carriage back, stand on it, and hope there were enough footholds to work his way up the side of the building. He decided it was nearly impossible.

Matt returned to the garden. Two of the back windows were accessible from the second-story ledge, but he'd be visible from neighboring yards. He'd have to work fast. The sun was low in the sky now; he could stay hidden in the dark shadows beginning to envelope the back of the house.

Move!

Matt crossed the yard to where the fence ran close to the house. He jumped high enough to grab onto the top and gradually pulled himself up, becoming painfully aware that he had gained some weight while in London. Even so, he was soon balancing on the fence and leaning against the side of the brick house. The horses in the alley were below him as he stepped easily onto the brick ledge and worked his way along the wall to the windows.

Matt shimmied to the first window and tried to push it in, but it was locked. He pulled his closed fist back, got ready to smash the glass, but caught himself, thinking to try another window before risking noise. He shimmied to the second window and tried it. He reached up to push it solidly with his open palm, not prepared for it to give. When it released easily, he lost his footing and stumbled off the ledge. Luckily, he caught hold of the sill, avoiding a fall back down to the garden.

Matt pulled himself back up onto the ledge and up into the window, straddling its opening on his stomach, and let himself fall softly headfirst into the second story of Brian Palmer's home.

CHAPTER 54.

EVIDENCE

Matt found himself in an unfurnished room in Brian Palmer's house. He got to his feet to look and listen. A guard dog or someone to broadcast his break-in would be a disaster. Robbing a house was a severe offense in eighteenth-century London, and repeat offenders had taken the trip to the gallows for crimes like the one he was committing now. Matt had witnessed a three-mile gallows parade the second week he was in London. He had asked Ben why they were celebrating so many men riding in horse-drawn carts, almost as if they'd won some national sporting championship. Ben told him the fifteen criminals were headed to the gallows at Tyburn. Tyburn was five or so miles north of where Matt was now.

Hearing nothing, Matt decided he was alone. He stepped softly toward the closed door and placed his ear against its solid wood to listen. Again, there was only the sound of silence, so he turned the knob and gently pulled the door open. Windows at each end of the hallway flooded it with light. Matt padded into the hall to the nearest door. There was nothing in that room or the next.

Matt tiptoed down the steps to the ground floor and opened the door to the front room, where the drapes were open and it was well lit. A desk was stacked with parchment and old newspapers. He rifled through them fruitlessly. Growing impatient with the large stack, he moved on.

He smiled with satisfaction when he entered the hearth room. A slit in the curtains let in enough light for him to know he'd found Palmer's armory. There were explosives and weapons, kegs of black powder, a box of fuses, three flintlock rifles, two muzzle-loading handguns, and a small cannon in the corner. Four cannonball-shaped bombs still under construction were lined up on a wooden table. Matt slid the curtains open to fill the room with light, hoping to find documents linking Brian to the opera house bombing. There were no papers, diagrams, or anything else that indicated plans, but the contents here might be enough to incriminate. He closed the curtains and left the hearth room with the satisfaction that he was near to putting a cap on Brian's activities.

The next room was completely dark, so Matt opened the door wide to let light stream in from the hall. He jumped back in surprise before recognizing the shape of a tailor's mannequin in the middle of the floor, similar to the one used by Henry Duncan in Richmond to sew men's suits. It wore a formal-looking dark-grey suit of the kind eighteenth-century socialites wore to parties, trimmed in gold bands, complete with a white-and-gold satin glove. One glove was missing.

A table next to the mannequin held a stack of opera programs. Matt began to page through them one after the other. The date on the program from the day of the bombing was circled. Matt's heart beat faster. A floorplan inside the program was marked with an "x" over the wall that held Patrick's box. This was all Matt needed to go to the authorities. He carefully placed the program back into its original place in the stack.

Matt's need to escape almost consumed him, but he made himself walk deliberately and slow as a huge sense of victory flooded his body. He had outsmarted both Brian Palmer and Patrick Ferguson; he had the advantage. The faster he wrapped this up, the faster he'd return home to his injured wife.

I'll never leave her again. The future can go to hell!

Matt double-checked everything, closing drapes and doors, leaving all as he found it. He didn't want to give Brian Palmer any reason to slip away before the police had a chance to surround this place. Matt's couldn't contain his excitement; he'd incriminate Palmer and get Ferguson off his back. Happy that the first floor was in order, Matt tiptoed up the steps. Heavy pounding on the front door froze him in his tracks. Matt stood paralyzed on the stairs at the sound.

"Matthew Miller," a man yelled through the door. "Bow Street Police! Let us in, you rascal, or we'll break the door down!"

CHAPTER 55.

BOW STREET

Pounding on the door of his jail cell woke Matt the next morning. "Wake up, murderer," a voice said through the door. Matt watched the square portal in the door slide open onto a man's face. "Look smart," he commanded. "You're to be interviewed."

Matt pivoted to an upright position on the hard wooden bench that had served as his bed in the spartan jail cell. He wanted to be ready for whoever came through the door. The irons on his ankles clinked musically as they slid down his shins to the grey stone floor. The heavy wrist shackles dug into his flesh and he eased the chains gently onto his lap.

Aside from his restraints, they had treated him reasonably well. One of the guards had even given him a pad for a pillow on the hardwood bench, although no one offered anything resembling a blanket. It had been a mostly sleepless night as he tried to sort out what had happened, but he dozed off for the last few hours of the morning.

"Let me use the pot," Matt said. "I'll be ready. Can I have some water?"

"Make haste," the man said. "There's water out here."

"Food?"

There was no answer.

Matt knocked on the door when he was ready, then shimmied back to the bench before two burly Runners swung the door open.

"Come on," one said, grabbing Matt's underarm to yank him to his feet. The chains slipped from Matt's grasp and the cuffs cut into his flesh again.

"Ease up," Matt said, irritated. "I'm not guilty."

"Who do you think you are, criminal?" the guard said. "Best learn your place."

The guard's tone was enough for Matt to reevaluate his attitude. Matt couldn't afford to have one of these men punch him in the face. Aside from it being a punch in the face, it would bring back the headaches, the hallucinations, and the visions. He needed to keep his wits.

"I'm sorry," Matt replied humbly. The guard acknowledged him with a nod, then motioned Matt to the door. Matt waddled in shackles to a dingy interrogation room. The whole experience of prison was horrible, but forcing someone to walk any distance in chains, in front of an entire room of people, took misery and dehumanization to a new level.

When Matt reached the room, they sat him at a wooden table facing the open door and then stepped outside. His side of the table was worn smooth, no doubt from many years of sweat, oil, and the rubbing of shackles and chains. Matt waited in silence. His nerves were more ragged than he wanted, considering his complete innocence.

****

Matt stood up as soon as William Morley appeared in

the doorway. Morley approached the table and reached his hand out. Matt dragged the chains across the table to meet his palm. Morley noticed Matt's grimace as the shackles dug, once more, into his wrists.

"Irons were never intended to be comfortable," Morley said.

"These are perfect, then," Matt replied. He gave a pained smile.

Morley motioned for him to sit, and Matt gently laid the chains on the table to make as little noise as possible, then sat. Matt looked Morley up and down as he took the chair across from him. He was a balding, middle-aged man of average height and narrow build; his physique contrasted sharply with the burly guards who waited outside the interrogation room. He wore a nearly threadbare tan suit and a discolored cotton shirt. They were the clothes of a man who had grown weary of getting dressed.

Morley looked into Matt's eyes once he sat down, and asked, "What motivated you to murder three people?"

"I didn't murder anyone," Matt replied. "I was set up by a man named Brian Palmer."

Morley had never shut the door behind him, so Matt was still able to see into the lobby of the Bow Street offices. He tried not to look at the men moving around in the hall, but the officers, colorful criminals, and vagrants passing through his line of vision were a constant distraction.

"You expect us to believe you're innocent?" Morley asked. "We've evidence of the man you murdered at the dock and your explosion at the opera house. We recovered everything at your apartments."

"What evidence?"

"Mr. Evans, please," Morley called over his shoulder.

A twenty-something man walked in to stand next to Morley. He was tall and thin with a long mop of dark-brown hair. "Yes, sir," he said.

Morley pointed at a side table, and Matt's eyes followed. A grey sheet covered a pile that Matt hadn't noticed until the moment that Morley pointed. "Please shew the evidence to Mr. Miller," Morley instructed. Evans pulled the cover aside to reveal items that Matt recognized from Brian's house. Morley eyed Matt. "Mr. Evans was at your apartment when the evidence was collected."

"That's Palmer's house," Matt insisted. "Not mine."

"And your purpose there?"

"I broke in looking for this same evidence."

Morley gave Matt his version of an eye roll. Matt reminded himself that Morley had probably heard enough false declarations of innocence to fill a set of bound novels. Nonetheless, Matt was going to defend himself at every opportunity. Evans removed the grey sheet entirely, placed it aside, and then turned to face the stack. He grabbed a white satin glove and then reached it out across the table so that Matt could have a closer look. "This white glove was found at the crime scene," Evans said. "It matches the one on your mannequin."

"It's not my mannequin," Matt replied. He tried to sound confident despite the mountain of evidence sitting on the table.

"Quite your gammoning, Mr. Miller," Morley said. "This is your glove." Morley picked up a black overcoat, trimmed in red with silver buttons. "Found in your carriage. Same coat as was reported by the opera house staff the night Lady Celia Ferguson was murdered," Morley said. "Do you expect us to believe that you and the murderer possess the same coat?"

"It's not mine," Matt said.

"You're a tall man, Mr. Miller," Morley observed. He motioned for Evans to bring the coat. After he had taken it, he dropped it on the table in front of Matt. Matt lifted his wrists to emphasize the shackles. Evans stepped to him with a key and Matt watched patiently as he unlocked the sharp iron bracelets. Matt flexed his wrists when they were off and then swept the chains to one side of the table, hoping to make it inconvenient for Morley to put them back on.

Matt had never seen this coat before. It was made of high-quality wool. The red trim was elegant, striking, and unique enough for someone to remember. There was almost no chance that this type of coat would randomly fit, especially considering that Matt was about four inches taller than the average eighteenth-century Londoner. Matt was somehow sure that it would fit. He put one arm through the coat sleeve, then the other, as he said, "If someone is trying to frame me, it'll be perfect."

"Or, 'tis yours," Evans corrected.

Matt flexed his shoulders around in the coat and then let his arms fall to his sides. The sleeves reached down to just past his wrists. Whoever had tailored the coat had gotten his dimensions precisely. Matt tried to remember if there had been a time when someone could have taken his measurements. *The stolen jacket!* His jacket had disappeared one night when he and Ben were in the pub during his first week in London.

Matt realized, then, that someone had been working on framing him almost from the first day he had arrived. A twinge of panic and a shot of adrenaline made his brain go haywire as it searched for possibilities. Something had triggered his visions. He closed his eyes and let it happen. *Palmer is all over the timeline!*

"Mr. Miller!" Morley's voice brought Matt back to reality.

"It's not my coat," Matt finally said.

"It was in your hackney," Morley replied.

"I borrowed that carriage."

"And the evidence in your apartments?"

"They're not my apartments," Matt insisted. "I'd like to know the extent of the evidence against me." He reminded himself of the gravity of the situation to keep himself from laughing. There were enough items on that table to line his trip to the gallows. Surely, Morley realized that the evidence against Matt was so complete as to be laughable.

"There are programs to the opera," Evans said, "and diagrams of the opera house. We found pieces to build more bombs."

"Dr. Brian Palmer lives in that apartment," Matt insisted. "The landlord's records should tell you this. If they don't, then the man who rented them is your clue."

"We've spoken to your landlord," Morley replied. "The apartments were rented by a crony of yours, who has since left for America—a sea dog named David Sutton."

"What?"

Matt was running scenarios through his head. He sat there with a questioning look on his face.

"Joshua Tucker?" Morley asked.

Matt looked back puzzled.

"Surely you remember the man you murdered."

Matt had heard the name before, maybe from one of Patrick's lists of either conspirators or targets. "I didn't kill anyone," Matt said. "I've heard this name, though."

Morley reached to the pile and slid out a folded and wrinkled piece of parchment. He handed it to Matt and watched as Matt unfolded the note. It was David Sutton's list of the six people he was supposed to investigate.

"Dr. Franklin's hand is unique," Morley said. "We'll soon learn his involvement."

"Franklin had nothing to do with any of this."

"He'll be brought in," Evans replied. "We'll let him confess."

Matt contemplated the list. "Where did you get this?"

"Does it matter?" Morley asked. "You're facing the gallows, and it's black and white."

Matt turned his face to Morley while trying to look into his own mind to analyze the role David Sutton had in his predicament. How could this have happened? *David Sutton?*

"Find Palmer," Matt said. "Bring him in."

"Brian Palmer is known to no one."

"I can take you to Scarlett Palmer's house," Matt said. "She's his lady friend."

"We'll investigate all possible leads, Mr. Miller," Morley replied.

"I didn't commit any of these crimes."

"We found you in your apartments with all of—"

A disturbance at the front office interrupted them. "What's the meaning of this?" Matt heard Benjamin Franklin shout. "I'm an English citizen and postmaster of the American colonies. Take your paws off me!"

Three men surrounded Ben and were shuttling him through the station and to the room where Matt was sitting. Ben finally saw Matt at the table, and his expression of rage morphed to one of confusion. Morley and Evans, who had previously been standing like perched hawks above Matt, now turned to face Ben.

Morley pointed to a chair at the table. "Have a seat, Dr. Franklin," he said. "Three English citizens have been murdered. Why not confess your role?"

CHAPTER 56.

JOHN FIELDING

The Bow Street offices in London continued to bustle with activity. The number of criminals walking through the front entry was growing as Matt sat at his interrogation table. Members of the London police, commonly called the Bow Street Runners, followed behind random suspects as they passed by the doorway. Ben had taken a seat at the corner of the table on Matt's left. He'd retreated from vocalizing his anger and now sat in silence, moving his eyes from person to person, furious at his implication in a murder.

"Your complicity will become manifest shortly, Dr. Franklin," an older man said, entering the room. "Good day, gentlemen. I'm Sir John Fielding, chief magistrate here at Bow Street."

Ben finally broke his silence. "Back-room politics better not be behind my being dragged here and threatened," he said menacingly. "I have fellows in high places." Matt knew the older man wasn't boasting. He did have influential friends.

Fielding didn't give a commanding first impression to Matt. He was thick around the waist, if not portly. Straggly grey hair framed a colorless face that looked bloated and fatigued from years of drinking. He was altogether unimposing and wouldn't have looked out of place sitting on the street in front of a London pub. As soon as he spoke, though, his physical failings disappeared. His eyes opened wide, and his face and voice took on an unexpected prominence and confidence. He was suddenly a man who commanded respect. His strong vocal presence was enough, even, for Benjamin Franklin to take note.

"I can assure you, Dr. Franklin," Fielding explained, forceful but calm. "I concern myself only with stamping out lawlessness, and it matters not whether the purveyors are Whig, Tory, or American." He nodded in Matt's direction. Matt looked at Ben and shook his head. Ben frowned, but continued to remain silent. Someone who didn't know him that well might have misconstrued Ben's frowns as arrogance, but Matt had seen this expression on the older man's face before. It came when Ben felt like someone had backed him into a corner.

"I'm a simple man," Fielding said in response to Ben's silence. "I only want to explain allegations that have been raised against Mr. Miller. Should statecraft play a role in these crimes, I'd not be the origin." Fielding glared at Matt, and there was no mistaking the political undertones of the accusation.

"My role in colonial government has nothing to do with me being in the home of Brian Palmer," Matt said.

"Virginians are proud . . . to a fault," Fielding replied. "You know what our Lord says of pride, Mr. Miller. Confess, and save your soul from damnation."

Matt turned to Ben. "I'm being framed by the bomber.

The evidence against me is almost perfectly complete." He turned to Fielding. "That should give you some pause."

"You still insist that you had no complicity in these crimes?" Fielding asked.

"I was investigating the murder of Celia Ferguson," Matt replied. "The man who committed these murders planned everything down to the smallest detail. It's an incredibly complex ruse."

"Do tell," Fielding said.

"Not until I've had a chance to sort through the evidence."

"Sort through the evidence?" Fielding exclaimed with incredulity. "'Tis overwhelming against you. You'll not repair from this prison until your trial, and we will certainly not risk your fiddling with the evidence."

"I have no motivation to commit these murders," Matt said plainly. He hoped Fielding, a man who knew criminals well, had at least developed some ability to recognize a sincere denial.

Fielding motioned to Morley.

"Mr. Miller," Morley said. "Please follow me."

Matt stood and two broad-shouldered men outside the door made their presence known. Morley pointed, and Matt followed them out of the room.

****

The guards walked Matt back to his cell, a plastered room with a barred window and a solid door with a square viewport wide enough to look through with both eyes at once. He was given a tin cup of water and a clay chamber pot. Matt took the cup and let the man set the pot down so he wouldn't have to touch the nasty thing. He was glad they'd let him use the outhouse next to the building. Matt didn't want to sit inside with his own waste just yet.

Matt should have felt some sense of finality when they locked the door behind them, but he welcomed the solitude. Action had consumed him these last days, and he needed time to think about how Brian Palmer had framed him, and why. The timelines that he could access in his head were blurry. All the blank spots made it impossible to see anything. He'd have to do this the old-fashioned way and write a list.

Matt looked around the cell and chuckled aloud. He had the macabre revelation that he was closer to a death row holding cell than a posh hotel equipped with a writing desk and stationery. Matt walked to the cell door and pounded hard. "Hello," he shouted through the door. "Hello!" When no one came, he pounded again. "Hello!"

Finally, one of the guards put his face to the square hole. "What?" he demanded.

"I need parchment, a quill, and some ink."

"The hell you say."

"I'm a representative of the Virginia House of Burgesses," Matt replied. "Under British common law, you are required to provide me with instruments for note-taking and writing my memoirs."

"British common law?"

"British common law, by order of the king," Matt replied.

"I ain't never heard of such," the guard said. "Go to sleep like everyone else."

"What if I feel like writing my confession?"

"Save us time, it would."

Matt shrugged. His nonchalance made it seem like he was ready to rescind the offer. A few moments later, he glanced up indiscriminately and caught a look of contemplation on the guard's face. The man disappeared without a word and was gone for long enough that Matt almost gave up, but when he returned, he gave Matt a few pieces of parchment, a quill, and a tiny vial of ink. Matt stood from his bed and went to take the writing tools.

"Full confession," the guard said.

"I'll try my best."

The guard peered through the viewport with satisfaction, then was gone.

Matt sat on the chair to use the cot as a desk. "Why would someone from the future frame me for murder?" he whispered as he dipped the pen in ink. He started a list, making sure to use initials for anything that might be incriminating if someone were to read his "memoirs."

Question 1: Why would Brian Palmer murder two people connected to Patrick Ferguson?

1. He knows about Ferguson's plans to stop the AR
2. He doesn't like Ferguson
3. He's a political rival of Ferguson's family
4. He's business rivals of Ferguson's family
5. He wants to distract Ferguson
6. He wants Ferguson to blame me

Matt contemplated the list until he couldn't think of any

additional reasons. He decided to come back to this question.

Question 2: Why would Brian Palmer frame me for two murders I didn't commit?
1. I was in the wrong place at the wrong time
2. He disagrees with my politics
3. He's a business rival
4. Create a conflict between Ferguson and me
5. He's trying to make my life miserable

Matt laughed at the last item. "If it could only be that simple," he thought.

The key to a good brainstorming list was to come up with at least twenty answers or solutions. The first five or ten usually came easily. The last ten made you reach deep for answers and solutions you didn't know were there. Besides his personal experience, Matt had seen examples where brainstorming had netted companies a huge profit.

His favorite anecdote was about the Disney Corporation, though he had never verified it. Disney told a team to figure out how to make more money at the theme parks. They started with simple ideas: charge higher admission, pay employees less, renegotiate supplier prices. By the time they had ten items, all the obvious solutions were gone. One delusional employee called out, "We could print it!"

"Print what?" someone asked.

"Money."

After a good laugh, "print money" went on the list; in brainstorming, every idea, no matter how silly, goes on the list. From this unconventional, brilliant idea, Disney Dollars were born: high-quality Disney-themed paper bills valid anywhere in the park at face value. It soon became clear that once people bought Disney Dollars, they were reluctant to spend them. Over the twenty-eight years that Disney Dollars were available, people walked away with two hundred million dollars in unspent bills.

Matt needed a Disney-Dollars explanation, and he needed it fast.

Question 3: Who is Brian Palmer?
1. Random guy
2. Scientist
3. Businessman
4. Soldier
5. Secret agent
6. A man from the F
7. Renegade T traveler
8. Artifact collector
9. Original scientist who caused the accident
10. Scientist who insisted I return home

A shiver went up Matt's spine. All three lists converged. Matt hadn't given much thought to the scientists who caused the accident and tried to bring him home. They'd told him they had one shot. Only now did he consider why they had one shot and what might have become of them after they took it. Did they have just enough funding to open the wormhole a few times? Were they ordered not to time-travel again?

Question 4: Why would the scientists who insisted I come back be upset with me?

 1. Their careers suffered because of the accident

 2. Their careers suffered trying to bring me home

 3. They never got any recognition

 4. They were charged for murdering four people

Question 5: What's changed?

 1. Brian Palmer has permission to travel to the F

 2. Brian Palmer has gone rogue

If Brian Palmer was on an official mission to bring Matt back to the twenty-first century, he'd trap Matt and open a wormhole on top of him. He might even be obligated to read Matt his rights, or something similar. Matt looked at the wall of his jail cell and blurted out, "He's a free agent."

Matt searched every prescient vision he could remember and knew it was true.

CHAPTER 57.

WILEY OLD MAN

Ben came to Matt's cell after lunch and sat with him silently on the single bench until the guard locked the door and moved away. Matt stood up to check the view portal to see if anyone was standing nearby, but there was no one in the corridor. He turned to Ben and spoke in a hushed tone. "It's the original guy, Ben. He's the one who tried to pull me back to the twenty-first century. It was before I came to Philadelphia."

"How do you know?"

"No other explanation," Matt replied. "Brian Palmer isn't in any of my dreams. He's a traveler, I'm convinced."

"I thought the dreams were disappearing," Ben said. "You welcomed the end of the headaches."

"I got hit in the head coming over."

"Then why were you not able to discern that Sutton was a spy and a scoundrel in these dreams?"

"There's a singular place in hell for that kid," Matt declared. "When I return to the colonies, he's toast. After I saved his arm, he does this?"

"Deception and betrayal are not against the law."

"Either way, I'll find that little bastard. Get me out of here."

"Bail is set at ten thousand pounds," Ben said. "'Twill be some time before I can raise that."

"Ten thousand pounds?"

"They don't want murderers returning to the streets."

"I can sign for it."

"They'll take only gold," Ben explained. "The crisis has affected many of my fellows, but one or two might make a loan. You've been identified in this morning's *Gazette* along with the evidence against you."

"I was only arrested yesterday."

"The *Gazette* was notified of your crimes at the same time as Bow Street."

"I'm being set up."

"John Fielding may not be my favorite Briton, but he's far from corrupt. What could this Palmer character endeavor to gain?"

"It might be simple revenge."

"He must have *some* intent."

Matt shrugged. "He's a murderer."

Ben gave Matt a critical look, but then his expression changed. "If we do manage to secure your release, if only temporarily, where would you start?"

"I'd locate this redhead, Scarlett Palmer. There may be someone at her old apartments who can inform us of her comings and goings. I took her to a jewelry store where she fenced diamonds. Maybe someone there can give us a hint." Matt frowned. "It's like Palmer's thought of everything."

Ben nodded. "If I didn't know you as a son, I'd be certain of your guilt."

"I don't have a motive for these crimes," Matt replied.

"Bureaucrats kill people all the time," Ben observed. "There are plenty of reasons for you to conspire against Ferguson or his people."

"And his wife?" Matt said, irritated.

"Maybe she wasn't the target."

"Are you working for the prosecution?"

"You'll meet the prosecution soon enough," Ben replied. "Fortunately, Sutton's list isn't enough to hold me. I'll do my best for your release."

CHAPTER 58.

ROLLING PIN

Someone called on Ben at his home shortly after sunrise on the morning following his visit to Bow Street. Ben was already sitting in his writing room, trying to rationalize how he was going to save Matthew Miller from an unimaginable predicament. Ben was used to spending these early hours in solitude, so he thrust on a robe and bounded down the steps to the first floor in a state of irritation. The pain in his knees reminded him to slow down. *Damn rheumatism!* The time it took to limp through the short hallway to the front door was enough for him to reconsider his rash desire to scold the visitor. Vigilance overtook him.

At the front door, he thought twice, turned around, and went back upstairs to the second floor. He pushed the drapes aside and opened the window to look down on his visitor. A young man was standing at his front door, and a closed carriage waited on the street. No one was in the coach box. "Who are you?" Ben called down. His tone was a mixture of inquisition and irritation.

"William Spencer, sir," the young man answered. "I've been asked to escort you to Bow Street."

"I'll not step into your carriage," Ben declared. He considered walking to the cupboard to get his pistol. It would help convince this man to step away from his door, but Ben wasn't yet ready to escalate the situation. He hadn't committed a crime and didn't want to start now. "How do I know you're from Bow Street?" he called down.

The young man turned his head to the creaking of a carriage door and Ben followed his gaze. William Morley stepped out of the coach and joined Spencer on the front stoop. They bent their necks upward.

"What do you want with me?" Ben called.

"If you are hiding the heinous villain Matthew Miller," Morley said, "I assure you it's a crime."

"He's not a heinous villain, in any case," Ben said. "Has he escaped?"

"You pretend to have nothing to do with this?"

"I was sleeping until an hour ago."

"Let us in," Morley demanded.

"Only if you give your word that you will not take me from my home."

"I'll confess to no such thing," Morley called.

"Then you'll conduct your interrogation from the cobblestones," Ben replied. "First question, please." Ben looked across the street. People were pulling drapes aside to observe the commotion. "Go ahead."

Morley looked around at the eyes that were now on him and then gazed back up at Ben, exasperated. "You've my pledge," he said finally, loud enough for everyone on the street to hear. Ben closed the window and the drapes and went down to let Morley in.

William Morley, like John Fielding, his boss, was principled and well-intentioned, and Ben sensed that he respected the law. Ben believed such men helped make England the great civilization that it was, and he was willing to hear them out. Ben hopped down the steps again and had to limp to the front door. It took time to undo the heavy lock and swing the door open. "Come inside," he ordered, trying to ignore the pain in his knees.

Ben motioned Morley and Spencer into the front room and then noticed the pistol in Spencer's belt as he stood sentry outside the door. Ben shrugged and joined Marley in the parlor. "Your man can search the house before you go," Ben said. "I assure you that this is as big of a surprise for me as for you." Ben motioned for Morley to take a seat. This wasn't Ben's favorite room in the house, since it got little natural light, but he preferred that Morley not go any farther inside so as not to disturb Margaret.

"You've no idea where Miller has fled?" Morley asked doubtfully as he sat.

"He was in *your* protection," Ben said incredulously. "Do I have the resources to take on Bow Street? You have a small army down there."

"An army that was called away late last night to deal with a riot on the docks. The very livelihood of this city was threatened."

"And someone broke into the jail while you were gone?"

"Miller's cell was open and his shackles were on the table—the same table where our interview took place. He was taunting us!"

"You left an innocent man unprotected?"

"We allowed a criminal mastermind to make his escape."

The screams of a woman interrupted them. "Burglar! Help! Thief!"

Morley gave Ben a knowing smile as they stood to investigate the disturbance. They stepped into the doorway in time to see William Spencer thunder down the steps ahead of Margaret in her dressing gown wielding a giant rolling pin with two hands. She barely missed his head with a swing that looked like a baseball player chasing a ball that was high and outside.

"Thief!" she screamed again.

Spencer scrambled out the front door and Margaret halted in the doorway with the rolling pin cranked back and ready to swing. It took her a moment to notice Ben and Morley standing behind her.

"Dr. Franklin," she said, surprised. "What's the meaning of this?"

Ben turned to Morley. "Young Spencer should have announced that he was searching the home." He glanced at Margaret's maple weapon. "A less-cautious man may have been dealt a fatal blow."

"I apologize, Mrs. —"

"Stevenson," she said, giving Morley a dirty look. "The nerve! Search for what?"

"Mr. Miller has been stolen from Bow Street," Ben said.

"Escaped," Morley corrected.

"He overpowered the guards and found the key to his shackles?"

Morley nodded.

Ben could see that Morley was having trouble believing it himself. "Mr. Morley," Ben said. "I trust that once you ponder the situation, you will realize that you have made a grave error in underestimating a criminal mastermind who lurks somewhere in London. You've been outsmarted."

"By Miller and his allies," Morley said waveringly.

"Utter nonsense! Mr. Miller is a gentleman," Margaret declared. "He's a family man with never a bad word to say about anyone."

"If Miller *was* taken from the jail," Morley asked Ben. "Where would he be held?"

"I don't know," Ben replied. "There are two men, suspects I'd place high atop your list. The first is Brian Palmer and the second is Patrick Ferguson."

"Palmer!" Morley exclaimed. "I no longer wish to discuss a phantom."

"What about Ferguson?"

Morley was silent.

"What about Ferguson?" Ben repeated.

Morley shook his head and glared. "He didn't come home last night."

CHAPTER 59.

RUDE AWAKENING

Matt awoke to a man rooting through his pockets as he lay on a Thames River wharf. It took a few seconds for him to realize what was going on. "Get the hell off me!" he demanded.

"Now you went and woke him," someone said behind him. The first man continued to rifle through Matt's pockets, and so in a single motion, Matt sat up and punched the man hard in the solar plexus, sending him sprawling across the slick wood surface of the dock. The firm toe of a boot connected with Matt's side before he could take his feet and he rolled toward the sprawled man, pain shooting through his ribs.

Haven't felt that in a while!

"Empty your pockets or you're getting a beating," the man who kicked him said.

Matt looked between the two men, trying to determine which one was the biggest threat. In the light of the moon, he could see that they were sailors. Neither was overly broad, but they looked young and athletic. The man poking around in his pockets had smelled of alcohol, and his friend had a slur in his speech. They were drunk, which Matt could use to his advantage. The man who had gone sprawling regained his feet while Matt was trying to do the same.

"I don't want any trouble," Matt said. "You can have everything." He rolled to his belly and went up on all fours.

"Sit," the man who kicked him said. "You're gonna have trouble if you don't give up that purse."

Matt pulled his legs underneath him on the slick surface of the dock and put his hands up. "Don't want any trouble," he repeated. "Let me reach into my pocket." He popped to his feet and retreated on his heels. He was dizzy and there was a sweet taste on his lips.

"Why, you damn—" The man who kicked him charged.

Matt jumped out of his path and swept the man's feet out from under him. To Matt's surprise, the man hit the slick dock at full speed and flopped like a pancake. He hydroplaned across the wood and, as if pushed by some unseen hand, dropped deliberately over the side and into the water, screaming "Help me!"

Matt put his fists up and faced the remaining assailant, who was looking between Matt and the place where his companion had slide from the dock.

"Can he swim?" Matt asked.

"Not too well."

"Help me!" they heard again.

"Better save him," Matt replied.

The man turned to Matt with a pleading look.

Matt scowled. "I'm not going to help you save your criminal friend." Matt kept his fists in the air threateningly, backed away, and sped toward the boardwalk that joined the piers that jutted out into the river.

When Matt was far enough away, the robber rushed to the side of the pier. "Hang on," he yelled over the edge. "I'm coming." The last image that Matt saw in the moonlight was the silhouette of a man searching the dock, most likely for a length of rope.

Matt jogged ahead, trying to put some distance between himself and his potential attackers, but he was almost sure the effort required to fish the man from the water would occupy them for an hour or two. The London wharves were high and old, and a thick, slippery slime covered their water line. A man could hang onto the struts out of the water, even if he couldn't swim, but it was nearly impossible to climb out without help. He hoped the men were close enough friends that the one on the dock wouldn't walk away when it became too difficult.

The price you pay for being a criminal.

Matt rested on a bench when he was out of sight of the men. The last thing he could remember was falling asleep in jail in heavy irons. The shackles alone had made it hard to sleep, but eventually, he'd dropped off. They must have drugged him to unlock the shackles and take him from his cell. He was wearing the coachman's jacket again.

Matt smacked his lips, trying to identify the sweet taste in his mouth. *Chloroform!* He had used it for a couple of months in graduate school and had experienced this same sweet taste on his tongue. This was another clue that he was dealing with a man from the future. The anesthetic properties of chloroform wouldn't be known until the early 1800s, and it wouldn't be commonly used until it was needed in the middle of the century.

Common Name: Chloroform
Chemical Formula: $CHCl_3$
Molecular Weight: 119.4
Natural Source: Seaweed and fungi

Common Name: Cocaine
Chemical Formula: $C_{17}H_{21}NO_4$
Molecular Weight: 303.4
Natural Source: Coca plant

The use of inhaled chloroform played a role in many of the amputations performed during the American Civil War. Chloroform and ether competed for popularity among surgeons, but chloroform was preferred because it wasn't flammable. These two inhaled solvents were widely used as general anesthetics until the numbing effects of cocaine gained popularity later in the century, partially due to some pioneering work by a man named Sigmund Freud.

Matt's purse was there when he reached into his pocket. He pulled it out and found all his silver along with a folded piece of paper: a press-printed map of a section of the River Thames showing streets, watermen's stairs, and docks. A hand-drawn arrow pointed to a building between Fore and Ropemakers Street on the east side of London, before Limekiln Dock. Underneath the arrow was the message, "The intelligence you seek is at #16."

CHAPTER 60.

LIMEKILN HOLES

Matt held the map in the moonlight, adjusting his view so the light hit it enough to show the tiny labels of the streets and stairs. He traced his finger along the river, trying to figure a way he could lose himself between buildings. It seemed a futile exercise, since Matt knew someone was probably watching, and the bright moon made it hard to disappear. Nonetheless, he'd try his best to slink from corner to corner, hoping to shake whoever had drawn the map.

Matt knew he was walking into a trap, but he had to let it snap shut and hope he was smart enough to escape. No one could help him now. Bow Street would arrest him on sight, and he couldn't involve Ben any more than he already had. Matt had some doubt whether Ben was open to helping, anyway. The elder scientist had had a hint of hesitation in his eyes during the interrogation. Ben Franklin had the utmost confidence in English law, and he'd want to give British authorities time to sort it out. It was likely he'd recommend that Matt not go off "half-cocked" before letting Bow Street do their jobs.

Someone had broken Matt out of jail, dumped him on a dock, told him where to go, and now the chess pieces were in motion. He sensed that before the night ended, he'd learn whose game he was playing, and why. It was either Patrick Ferguson or Brian Palmer, working together or separately to ruin him. Patrick Ferguson's perspectives and motivations were a mystery unless Matt took him at face value. Maybe he truly only wanted to prevent the American Revolution, but would he kill to accomplish his goal? There was no doubt that Ferguson was chasing power, but that was a far stretch from being a murderer. Brian Palmer remained a complete mystery. At the very least, one of these men was a murderer.

Matt scanned the dock again. The moon, bright as it was, only lit the streets a block or so in either direction. Seeing no one, he set out along Narrow Street to find the building marked on the map. It was a thirty-minute walk along the northernmost loop of the Thames.

There seemed to be an infinite number of docks and rivermen's stairs at this section of the Thames. They were well marked, though, and so Matt could measure his progress regularly by checking them on his map. The stairs, he thought, were an interesting approach to river access. They extended from the street down into the water. It was high tide now, so the water covered their last steps. The depth of the Thames in this part of London varied five to seven meters, depending on the tide of the English Channel. Rising tide helped boats travel up the river, and lowering tide helped to speed boats back out into the open sea.

Boatmen used the stairs at high tide and the causeways at low. The causeways were flat walkways made out of brick or framed gravel. They looked like roads to nowhere that ran directly into the river. Some even had steps alongside. Matt passed by Hall Stairs, Queen Stairs, and Godwell Stairs, and crossed Limehouse Bridge Dock. According to the map, he was getting close. The moon seemed so bright now that he felt like he was standing in a spotlight. "At least it's a well-lit trap," he muttered.

Matt came to the end of Narrow Street at a three-way intersection with Ropemakers and Fore Street. He looked up at three large warehouses, knowing somehow that one of them contained his final fate.

CHAPTER 61.

R&D

Few boats were floating on the Thames at this hour, so the river was smooth and black. Only the occasional gulps of water against the shore and the low moan of wooden hulls rubbing against the dock interrupted the midnight hush. Matt left the riverbank and walked along Fore Street until he had a full view of #16, a grey monstrosity that seemed to be facing off with the dazzling white moon. The three-story warehouse was tall enough to catch direct light from the moon and its reflection from the Thames.

Matt tried to stay in the shadows, worried about Bow Street and anyone else who could raise the alarm. Trying to hide in this poor excuse for dark was doubly irritating because it had been raining for months; now when he needed clouds the most, they were missing. Nonetheless, even here there were enough buildings, walls, and large objects to eclipse the moonlight. Matt walked in shadows until he reached the warehouse.

The stone wall around the building rose to about eight feet and then slanted another foot to a peak that rose like a two-sided pyramid. The wall was thick enough to crawl along, if it came to that. This wall was a barrier built against vehicles and casual observers, but apparently not meant to be impenetrable. If this was Ferguson's building, Matt would have predicted something more elaborate; barbed wire, at the very least.

Matt pulled on a pair of leather gloves he had swiped from a longboat, reached high, and touched the red brick wall to gauge its height. He crouched, then hopped up to grab the grey mortar at the apex. Matt pulled his chest onto the grey surface and reached for the peak. Once his upper half was nestled against the slant, he pulled higher and straddled the wall like a horse.

He had to rest there for longer than he wanted. When he'd finally caught his breath, he looked over the wall to confirm he wouldn't be falling into a moat, then eased himself over and dropped onto the cobblestones between the wall and the warehouse. He landed in a crouch but still made a loud thump. He squatted there to listen.

Not seeing or hearing any commotion, he stood and began a deliberate walk around the perimeter of the building, searching for an open window, a door, or some alternative access. The doors were solid oak and shut tight; the three windows on the ground floor had thick iron bars. An open window on the second floor caught his eye. He groaned at the prospect of scaling another wall just so he could fall into yet another trap.

The open window was on the moonlit side and exposed to anyone watching from the river, but the light would show ledges and footholds to aide his climb. It was late, and the river was quiet, and there looked to be no additional entrance. Matt measured his position, paced along the building until he was underneath the open window, and hoisted himself back up onto the outer wall.

He wobbled there for a moment to gather his strength, placed his left foot low on the building side of the slant, and thrust his right foot out to the narrow ledge of a barred window on the side of the warehouse. He had misjudged and was now in an uncomfortable forward split between the wall and the building. Matt teetered, then pushed with his back leg to pull himself flush to the brick wall, where he hung there, barely, by his fingertips.

Bracing himself with one hand, Matt reached down to test the barred window; it was solid. Conscious that he was now fully visible against the wall, he committed himself to a rapid climb to the open window. Matt worked his way up ledges and extended bricks on a path that was relatively simple but left his arms aching when he reached the opening. He rested again to catch his breath and regain enough strength to finish. He tilted the window open and pulled himself through, then stepped onto wooden rafters three stories above an expansive room that filled half the warehouse. Bright moonbeams lit the floor through skylights and windows. Tall dividers separated tables, benches, and machines.

Matt was anxious now to see what was below, so he charted a path down. The rafters were a series of interlocked wooden beams that supported the ceiling and skylights and extended all the way to wide struts anchored into the floor. Matt's muscles were already burning from the climb up, and he swore quietly at the long path to the floor, knowing it would take most of his remaining strength.

He swung to grab the first rafter, shifted, and then repeated this motion about twenty times before he finally could drop safely onto the ground. His arms were on fire. Matt braced himself against a thick wood support, stretching his muscles to flush the lactic acid that had gathered in them.

When the soreness subsided, he looked around, trying to identify the objects in this largest room. Everything here said this was Patrick Ferguson's building. Ferguson was a mechanical engineer and a soldier, so advanced weapons were the most natural thing for him to "invent." Matt wasn't surprised to find a cannon in the closest room, partially concealed in a fort of sandbags. He approached it, expecting something modern and futuristic, but it was a standard cast-iron cannon like they'd had onboard the *Norfolk*. Looking closer, he saw that the breech, the very back of the cannon, had separated from the barrel. The metal was charred grey where hot gas had escaped. There was dust on the cannon; it looked like it hadn't been touched for a long time.

Matt knew cannons could weaken and crack, but something about this one made him look a second time. The fissure was charred where the gas had leaked, but it wasn't rusty. *No corrosion. Smokeless powder!* Smokeless powder was vital to advanced weaponry. As likely as not, the formula for smokeless gunpowder was in the chemistry book Patrick stole.

The story of gunpowder was well known among chemists as an example of the iterative nature of science and the incubating effect of human conflict on scientific innovation. Black powder was the most advanced propellant used in firearms in the eighteenth century, but it was inefficient and corrosive. Since it burns at subsonic speeds, it's classified as a low explosive, and it produces byproducts that result in thick white smoke. The white smoke was a huge liability: it lingered around weapons, giving away their positions and obstructing the view of the next shot. In addition, the chemical components of black powder, charcoal, sulfur, and potassium nitrate gradually corroded and pitted even well-maintained weapons.

Smokeless powder, in contrast, is a high explosive: it burns at supersonic speed. A match touched to a pile of smokeless powder makes a bang, while black powder makes a whoosh due to its slower burn rate. Black powder has to burn in a closed space to build up enough energy and pressure to explode, the simplest example being a firecracker.

As Matt examined the damaged cannon, he tried to remember the components of smokeless powder, but nothing came to mind. He remotely remembered something called guncotton, which was accidentally discovered by a scientist who had used a cloth to clean up an acid spill. Matt thought Patrick's experiments with smokeless powder might be a plausible explanation for his interest in Thomas Mifflin's cotton. While Matt couldn't remember the exact formula for guncotton, he did recall that quite a few men had blown themselves up trying to perfect its manufacture and storage.

A wicked smile came to his face as he examined the cracked breech. Patrick had learned the hard way that iron and bronze could not withstand a series of supersonic explosions. Matt appraised the cannon again and felt a sense of relief. Patrick had a long way to go if he wanted to harvest the potential of smokeless propellants. This invention, at the least, was far from changing the balance of power in the Atlantic.

After a quick perusal of the rest of the room, Matt left, almost sure that this was Patrick's research building. He now passed through a door to the center of the warehouse. There he found eight different and oddly configured rifles on a rack. Unlike the cannon, which looked abandoned, the stand of muskets was dusted and orderly. Matt pulled the rifles from the rack one by one to inspect them in the moonlight. He didn't know much about small arms, but it did seem that Patrick was making progress.

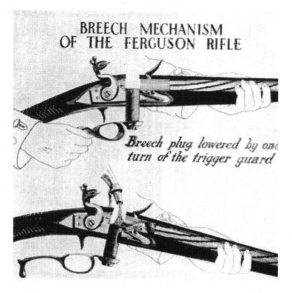

BREECH MECHANISM
OF THE FERGUSON RIFLE

Breech plug lowered by one turn of the trigger guard

British Army Manual Illustration

The second weapon he picked up could be loaded through the breech with a simple rotating mechanism. Another had a percussion cap to ignite the powder, rather than a flintlock, and a third had a revolving cylinder that could be preloaded with powder charges and balls to fire five shots in rapid succession. The barrel was similar to the Brown Bessie that Ben carried while traveling, but the trigger and revolver assembly looked like a primitive version of a six-gun from America's Old West. One musket was strapped to a test rack surrounded by sandbags.

Matt walked softly into the easternmost area of this side of the warehouse. This space was larger, and it was immediately obvious why. It had three prototype carriage frames suspended on different kinds of wheels. Each frame had a unique construction. Only one of the frames had the conventional wood-spoked wheels, while the remaining two had iron wheels that looked like they were made of the strapping used for wooden barrels.

The springs and suspension systems on the carriage frames were like nothing Matt had seen in the eighteenth century. He was curious enough to walk to them, step up on the frames, and use his weight to bounce them slightly. All three were solid under his feet and gave in a controlled fashion as he shifted his weight up and down. Any one of these frames would work for a London carriage.

In the other corner of this room were bike prototypes. Three were displayed on racks in the middle of the floor, while others were casually leaned against the wall, almost as if they'd been discarded and never touched again. For some reason, these discarded bikes attracted Matt's attention, and he walked to them first, before inspecting the working prototypes. Something made him reach out with his finger to wipe the dust from the seat of one. Noticing the swath it made, he used his handkerchief to roughly dust the seat and obscure the mark.

Matt went to the bikes in the center of the room. The frames were shaped like modern mountain bikes, but each of a different material. One appeared to be cast iron, another ground-steel tubes, and a third, oddly enough, used bamboo. The front forks of the bamboo frame were shattered and it was missing its front wheel. The pedal, gear, and chain mechanisms were similar across the bikes and the same as those on the Fergusons that people were pedaling around London.

Matt had not thought much about those bikes before now, but his close inspections made him realize the number of components that went into making a bicycle. The wheels of each were smaller versions of those on Ferguson carriages. The bamboo-framed bicycle had a back wheel coated in a thick substance that was the color of rawhide. It felt like rubber to the touch. The Ferguson bicycles Matt had seen so far rode on either bare steel wheels or rawhide straps; the steel wheels worked fine on unpaved roads and compacted dirt, while the rawhide-strapped wheels worked best on London's cobblestones.

If Patrick were able to perfect rubber, it would be a significant advancement. Matt imagined that Patrick's stolen chemistry book might contain the process for making rubber. Matt didn't know much about rubber, but he had not seen it since he had arrived into the past. The thought of it took him back to his teenage years in Philadelphia growing up with his father. His dad drove a cab in the city. It didn't pay much, they were always struggling for money, so they made frequent visits to the junkyard to buy used tires for the cab. Matt and his father would walk to the back of the yard to unstack and restack tires until they found matching pairs. It was rare to see four matching tires, but they could usually find suitable pairs, and these worked as long as they went together on the front or back axels.

They'd usually pick out two pairs on each visit. Three could fit in the trunk of the cab, and the last went in the back, wrapped in an old beach towel to keep the seat clean. Matt's father had an old tire machine in their garage that he'd use to put them on his cab. Unfortunately, though, there was no convenient way to dispose of old tires, so his dad had a stack of bald tires that went up to the ceiling in the back of the garage, and then another up against the fence in their tiny backyard.

Matt pulled himself out of his daydream. He had seen all there was to see in this half of the warehouse. The inventions in these rooms were respectable, but nothing that would bring Great Britain into a new age. The carriages were of high quality, the bicycles were useful, and the new muskets might help armies incrementally, but none of these things in themselves could fuel an empire.

Matt now found himself up against a wall that went all the way to the top of the ceiling. Two double doors led into the second half of the building. Something about these particular doors made Matt uneasy. He realized that his "spider senses" were tingling, and he smiled, knowing that despite the overwhelming sense that the odds were against him, and that he should run away very, very fast, he'd open these doors and confront what was behind them.

CHAPTER 62.

ENLIGHTENMENT

Matt tentatively touched the door handle, almost hoping to find it sealed—impenetrable, even, by anything weaker than the cannon he had just inspected—but when he tried the brass latch, it clicked open. He pushed cautiously, ready for anything, but no dragon attacked. The room was pitch black. He reached up for the latch that locked the second double door and opened it to let in a paltry amount of light. The windows here were all shuttered.

As he stepped through the door he heard switches. Bright lights flooded the room, blinding him. He stepped back to make his escape.

Spider sense, indeed!

"Mr. Miller," Patrick Ferguson called from somewhere in the ceiling. "Come in, please! Shut the doors behind you. With all the light leaking into the night, Londoners may think the place is on fire."

Matt smiled and shook his head, thinking with some chagrin, "What would Spiderman do?" He stepped into the light and turned to close and lock the doors. Seamus McCalla, his fighting instructor in Philadelphia, had taught him never to sit with his back to a door, especially an unlocked one. Matt heard footsteps descending stairs as he slid the latch into place and saw Patrick appear through a double doorway across the room.

"Make yourself comfortable," Patrick said. "You must be tired from all your climbing." He pointed to a table, and then to a bar cart lined with crystal decanters. "Scotch?"

Matt nodded, smiled, and moved to the conference table. He stood with his hands on the back of a chair. Patrick's civility was unnerving. "You sound like a James Bond villain," Matt joked.

"Ah, that," Patrick said. He was now at the liquor cart. "Peaty or no?"

Matt put his thumb and forefinger together. "Not too much."

"Old men like peat," Patrick said.

"Something about taste buds disappearing with age," Matt agreed. "I think they stop regenerating somewhere around your fifties."

"Aging can be—what do you Americans say—a drag." Patrick turned back to the crystal bottles and spoke toward them. "At least there's whisky." He selected a bottle from the five that were there and poured two glasses, then slid one across the table to Matt, letting his eyes travel over Matt's clothing. "Looks like you were in a bit of a tussle. You don't have a gun on you, perchance?"

Matt shook his head. He opened his coachman's jacket to prove that there was nothing there, then returned his hands to their resting place on the chair back.

Patrick opened his own jacket, revealing a muzzle-loaded pistol in his belt, and then he pointed to a chair. "Have a seat." He took a sip of scotch before he sat. He rolled it around in his mouth. "Speyside single malt from an area known as Dalwhinnie. Maybe you're familiar?"

"As in Dalwhinnie scotch?" Matt asked, pulling out the chair and sitting down. He picked up the chiseled crystal glass, tasted the whisky, and nodded his approval to Patrick.

Patrick raised his eyes. "Hard to tell. It's as capable a guess as I have. I've been there . . . small distillers and such. I buy what I like. You should see Loch Ness. It's easy to imagine a monster in those waters."

"I wouldn't mind going up there with you sometime," Matt said.

"Our relationship grows increasingly complicated," Patrick replied. "Some pieces on the board I control, others, you, and the balance, well . . ."

"How'd you know I was coming here tonight?" Matt asked.

Patrick gave him a sly grin.

Matt looked away, scanning the enormous, brilliantly lit room. He remained jealous that Patrick had sorted out electric lighting while he was still struggling with oil lamps in his Richmond factory. "How long do the batteries last?" he finally asked, breaking the silence.

"Most of the night. We've primitive generators to charge them."

Matt stood slowly and moved closer to one of the egg-shaped bulbs on the wall behind him. The glass was yellow, thick, and flawed, but still a technical marvel for 1772. "What's the filament?"

"Carbonized bamboo, like Edison. Resistance is key.

They don't last long, and I don't have time to perfect them. Either the vacuum is poor from the beginning, or there are leaks."

Matt returned to his chair and faced Patrick. He picked the whisky up again, took another sip, and noted the cascade of warmth that moved along the top of his tongue. "I thought about making a light bulb when I first arrived. Nowhere to plug it in."

"Our challenges have been similar," Patrick said. "Inventions come when the world is ready, and not a moment sooner. I could make the best glass bulbs London has ever seen, but until she has an electrical grid, they are but curiosities that make a fascinating *pop* when you smash them on the cobblestone."

"You could build a grid."

Patrick brushed him off with a slight wave of his hand. "My focus now is on building human capital."

"So no superweapons anywhere?" Matt gave Patrick an emotionless smile. "Something that's, maybe . . . part of your backup plan."

"If you were curious enough to inspect my project rooms as you walked through my building, you've gotten the picture, though I'm quite proud of what I've accomplished."

Matt nodded, trying to acknowledge this commonality between them.

Patrick answered him with a steely look of contempt.

"I didn't kill your wife," Matt said, looking directly into Patrick's eyes. Patrick fixed Matt with a hard glare, caught himself, dropped the emotion from his face, and then leaned back in his chair. Matt used the moment to sip at his scotch. He took only a drop into his mouth, not wanting to cloud his brain.

"I was once obsessed with powerful weapons," Patrick said. "A nuclear weapon is destructive, but its real power is as a deterrent. Right now, you could use nuclear weapons all over the world and not one British enemy would give a whit. Until you can photograph the devastation, such a weapon is inconsequential. Even the most warlike societies want more from conflict than destruction."

"A stick of dynamite could be pretty useful."

"We've done the experiments," Patrick explained. "The tribulations of the dynamite people are well documented. You'd be expected to blow yourself up a few times before perfecting nitrocellulose-based explosives."

"You've made smokeless powder."

"You could discern that by my cannon?"

"Residue with no corrosion."

"I'm an engineer. The cracked metal would have been my first clue. That's the finest cannon they make, and we were only able to fire it three times before it shattered. Smokeless powder is fine, but until metallurgy catches up, well . . ."

Matt looked hard at Patrick across the table. "I'm enjoying our lively conversation; I am. Why am I here?"

"The evidence against you is overwhelming," Patrick replied.

CHAPTER 63.

WALK THIS WAY

Matt Miller and Patrick Ferguson had not moved from their table in the shuttered, electric-lit room in the middle of Patrick's warehouse. Matt remained unsure of the motivations of the opponent who sat across from him. Patrick had gone uncomfortably quiet and seemed more interested in studying his glass.

Matt grew impatient. "Do you know Brian Palmer?" he asked.

"Who?"

"The man who set off the explosion in the opera house."

Patrick's eyes flashed, and then Matt saw him consciously push the anger from his face.

"Did you break me out of prison?" Matt pressed.

Patrick didn't acknowledge Matt's question, but instead studied Matt as if he were observing an animal in a lab experiment.

"You still think I killed your wife," Matt said.

"I believe I was your target," Patrick replied.

Matt tried to read the man, but there was nothing else. The raw contempt in his voice was unburdened by any sort of intrigue. This was true rancor, and it told Matt all he needed to know. "Have you had contact with anyone from the future?" Matt asked.

"The Morris women. You."

"His name's Dr. Brian Palmer," Matt said. "Someone broke me out of jail tonight. They left me on a dock with instructions to come here. I'll ask again: How did you know I was coming?"

"I learned that Franklin was agitating riots along the Pool and hired people to break you out of Bow Street. I knew someone was coming here tonight, though I'm surprised you came alone."

"Why would he agitate riots at the docks?"

"He's the consummate patriot, is he not? Author of the Declaration of Independence? He'll do anything for his revolution."

"He'll do whatever he can to remain British."

Patrick drank the last of the scotch in his glass and walked over to pour himself another. Still working on his first, Matt took another sip. He'd already drunk more than he wanted. It came to him as he watched Patrick that he should go on the offensive. "Sir William Maynard is dead, and I'm sure you had something to do with it."

Patrick shrugged. "Ah . . . that." He sounded tired and disappointed. "An unfortunate misunderstanding that was not to be repeated."

"He's on your list."

"It's not an assassin's list." Patrick went quiet as he replaced the stopper in the decanter. When he turned, his expression was enough to destroy any sense of rapport. "Come," he said, "I'll show you the rest of the building.

You'll be impressed with the artifacts I've collected. There are things I don't display at the manor."

"Artifacts?"

"Of historical significance. We have a unique perspective, you and I. Many masterpieces are available at a reasonable price. There are paintings you may enjoy, and a few sculptures. I hear you're a religious man." There was humor in his voice at the last comment.

"Depends what you mean by religious," Matt replied. "Why would *you* collect religious art?"

"Nothing has inspired or enslaved men like religion. I find the phenomenon fascinating. Plus, the best artists are working for the church."

"Opiate of the masses?"

Patrick gave Matt a bored look. "Let's see the galleries while the batteries are still charged."

CHAPTER 64.

THE PITY

Patrick waved for Matt to follow him through the large open doorway where Patrick had first entered. Matt complied hesitantly.

"I assure you, Mr. Miller, if I were interested in killing you, I'd kill you myself, and I'd *not* do it in stealth. Relax and enjoy the collection."

Not knowing what else to do, and curious, Matt followed Patrick around a partition into the next room. A staircase to either side must have been the source of the descending footsteps Matt heard when Patrick first arrived. Patrick disappeared around the right side of the dividing wall and Matt walked forward to follow him.

They emerged into a room designed exactly like a modern museum with paintings spaced along the wall. There were no skylights, and the only light was from the bulbs mounted above each frame. Four walls, also covered with paintings, formed an inner room containing sculptures. When Matt slowed to look at the paintings, Patrick waved him forward.

"You must see my prize," he declared. The excitement in his voice had a schizophrenic quality when considering his icy-cold cadence only moments before. Patrick pointed to a spot on the floor in front of a large sculpture. "Stand there," he said.

Matt obliged, then chuckled at a vision of a giant anvil dropping onto his head, like in a Roadrunner cartoon. He looked up at the ceiling, but only saw the same interlocking beams he'd used to climb down to the floor.

Matt returned his gaze to the sculpture before him. It was pyramid-shaped and hidden in shadows on a low pedestal made of dark-brown marble. He looked up and could see a woman's face at the top of the sculpture. He turned toward Patrick's footsteps and watched him pull a lever on the wall. Three lights illuminated the sculpture. It was chiseled out of a single piece of white marble: Mary with her dead son draped across her lap.

Matt stepped closer and reached out to touch the smooth surface. The folds of the draped cloth looked so real that he felt like he could pull them up to cover the naked body of the Savior. He ran his hand along Mary's robe and then stepped back. Mary was big enough that her son could fit in her lap. Jesus was supposed to be thirty-three years old at the time, but somehow the proportions made perfect sense.

Michelangelo's *Pietà*

Patrick wandered slowly into the light around the statue. He was now in front of Matt and to his right. Matt thought he was probably still far enough away not to be an immediate physical threat, but Matt still took a cautious step back, as if to get a better view of the sculpture.

"Recognize it?" Patrick asked.

"It's profound," Matt said softly. "Never saw it before."

Patrick grinned his disbelief. "Never been to the Vatican?"

"No."

"Americans don't travel."

"Intercontinental flights still aren't cheap."

"It's Michelangelo's *Pietà*."

Matt barked an astonished laugh. It made sense, though; Patrick was laughably rich, maybe more wealthy than anyone Matt knew on both sides of the Atlantic.

"The Catholic Church has more art than it knows what to do with," Patrick replied. "They're always open to negotiation."

"Why is this your prize?"

"It intrigues me more than any other piece."

Matt looked hard again at the statue. He had often questioned the allure of art. Why did people spend forever gazing at paintings and sculptures? Even now, an engineer and a chemist were standing in front of a carved piece of marble in that unexplainable way that people do as they try to sort out what it means and how it applies to their lives. Matt imagined Michelangelo standing next to them and rolling his eyes. Artists, Matt thought, must have access to some part of human consciousness that defies scientific explanation.

"What do you see in this sculpture?" Patrick asked.

"Two things," Matt replied thoughtfully, remembering his conversation with Scarlett. "The first is the eternal question that all women ask. Maybe men, too, but I think of women, mainly."

Patrick watched Matt, waiting.

"They have the power of creation, and it's a huge responsibility," Matt explained. "Is it right to bring a child into such a cruel and terrible world?"

"Is our Virgin thinking that she made a mistake?"

Matt gazed up at Mary's face. "I don't see the anguish

that you'd expect in a mother who has lost her son. Satisfied is not the right word, but there's a little of that. She knew what would happen and it did. Both of *us* understand the feeling—when what we've predicted comes true, even when it's something bad."

"I dreamed that my wife would be murdered," Patrick said quietly. "The details were missing, but I knew she'd die. I felt no satisfaction."

"My wife will die in the American Revolution," Matt said.

"I think we're done in here," Patrick replied.

CHAPTER 65.

CAIN

Matt walked with Patrick into the next room. Two spotlights lit the center, but unlike those of the gallery they had recently left, the walls were dark. Shapes were lining the black perimeter like shelves or cabinets, but Matt couldn't make out details. Matt moved toward the light while making sure to keep Patrick in the corner of his eye. They were walking on hard polished wood that was very similar to the practice floor they installed in the hay barn on the Taylor-Miller estate. The floor should have been his first clue, but the whole room was making him uneasy. He'd been here in his dreams.

Matt turned to watch Patrick open a closet. It creaked slightly. Patrick withdrew a scabbard and yanked the blade from its sheath, admiring it as the ringing of metal echoed off the walls. Patrick fixated on the resonating metal until the sound was a whisper. "There's a Spanish swordmaker here in London," he said. "He trained at the Toledo factory. His blades are magnificent." Patrick then used his left hand to ceremoniously pull the pistol from his belt, held it in two fingers for Matt to see, then placed it in the closet.

Patrick tilted his glistening blade so Matt could see its full profile, then sliced it through the air to make a whistling buzz that reminded Matt of hornets. "I fancied once that we could be brothers . . . dreamed it, maybe," Patrick said. "You and I would guide the world into a new enlightenment." He reached for the wall and flipped a switch, and electric lights lit up all along the perimeter, revealing practice targets and other martial arts equipment.

Matt saw a red painted rack centered along the wall that contained at least a dozen swords hanging horizontally in two columns. Patrick motioned to the rack. "Pick your weapon, Mr. Miller," he said. "I'll no longer let you stand in my way." He rotated his sword for effect and walked closer to Matt, motioning to the rack with his blade and looking down the edge of the sword. "None, I think, are as fine as this, but you can be assured that they are as sharp."

"I had nothing to do with that bomb," Matt said. "I decided to help you."

"Before or after you broke into my office or shot my man?" Patrick asked. "I'll have no problem killing an unarmed murderer." He stepped forward and slashed at Matt's chest, making him jump back. He had cut through Matt's jacket lapels and shirt and drawn blood. It was all the convincing that Matt needed. He kept Patrick in the corner of his eye as he pulled off his ruined jacket.

The rack held longswords, sabers, backswords, and a rapier. Matt skipped the longsword. He had seen people take advantage of the length and the leverage that came with a two-handed weapon, but he didn't have the necessary experience. His sword instructor, Henry Duncan, owned only one longsword and used it mainly for comparison. Matt was most comfortable with sabers, and the two sabers here looked similar to his own, which was now sitting uselessly at Ben's home. Neither of these sabers on the wall had much of a handguard, though. A smart swordsman would take advantage in a duel and slash away until your fingers were ground meat.

Matt glanced over his shoulder. Patrick was attentive, but he was making no signs of moving closer. He seemed almost content to watch Matt peruse his collection. "Choose wisely, Mr. Miller," he said coldly. "Your very life depends on it."

"James Bond villain, no lie," Matt said. "Listen to yourself."

Patrick charged, swinging his sword. Matt closed his palm around a rapier, pulled it from the rack, and met Patrick's slash at his head with the rapier still in its scabbard. Matt hop-skipped along the red rack, blocking two more slashes, and backed into the center of the room. He dropped his jacket on the floor and used his free hand to push the hard leather sheath from the sword.

Matt's bare blade seemed sleek and nimble once the heavy scabbard was on the ground. Patrick met Matt in the spotlight, grinning. Matt pointed his blade out straight, high enough to look down the edge and into Patrick's eyes. The rapier Matt held was longer and thinner than he liked, but it was perfect for a duel. He tilted it back to balance it in his hand, then slashed it through the air, first above his head, then at chest level, before he thrust it out toward Patrick's feet. Patrick hopped back and knocked the thrust away.

Even in these few parries, Matt felt the fatigue in his

arms from everything he'd already done. He scanned the room before Patrick came forward for another attack. The double doors were wide open, but Patrick blocked his exit. They were his only way out. "If the chance arises," Matt thought, "I'll make my escape." He wanted neither to kill or be killed.

Patrick thrust at him again and Matt swatted his blade away. The Englishman was testing him, but it was helping Matt become comfortable with his sword. A heavy pommel at the end of the hilt added to the overall weight but put the rapier's balance point surprising close to his grip. Matt jumped forward and thrust hard at Patrick's chest, trying his best to stab. Patrick knocked it away, but countered too hard, and Matt took advantage of the misstep, cutting Patrick's face. Blood spurted from Patrick's chin. Patrick backed away to feel his jaw, then pulled his hand away to measure the blood. "Nicely done," he proclaimed, "but I believe it's time we finish this."

Matt pointed his sword again at Patrick's face, put his left hand out with the palm facing the ceiling, and cupped his fingers in a backward waving motion. Matt, too, had had enough. "You're a deranged SOB," Matt said. Patrick flushed with anger and Matt realized he could enrage Patrick into making a mistake. "You've lost your mind," Matt said. "You're not the man to lead the world anywhere."

Patrick charged and slashed at him repeatedly. Matt backed away, but stood firm on the last slash. Patrick's momentum pushed him close and his blade skidded down Matt's and smacked into the guard. Matt's hand went numb from the shock, but he used the tied-up blade to push into Patrick, pivot, and bring his elbow into Patrick's face. Patrick dislodged his blade and backed away. The blow to his face had hurt, but Matt still saw resolve there.

Patrick charged. This time, the rapid blows and momentum got him past the protective radius of Matt's rapier. He slashed twice at Matt's stomach while Matt was turning away and opened a long cut in Matt's side. Matt yelled and Patrick backed off, smiling. A bloodstain was now growing on Matt's shirt. Matt felt the wound, keeping Patrick in sight. The cut was deep, but not fatal. There was only a small spot of bright blood on his hand when he pulled it away.

They parried again, and again, and again, until Matt lost count of the attacks. His arms were weakening, and his reflexes were leaving. He missed a block and Patrick opened another wound on his shoulder, making Matt retreat in some desperation. He hadn't touched Patrick with his blade since he drew blood from his chin.

Matt looked down at the elaborate wire handguard, deciding it was worth a gamble to try it again. He parried twice and pushed forward, leaving his head unprotected. Patrick took the bait, raised his sword, and slashed down at Matt's exposed skull. Matt had his sword up in time and their blades rang as Patrick's sword slid down the rapier and hit the guard. Matt thrust forward, twisting the rapier to entangle Patrick's sword, then thrust upward. Both blades went flying.

Matt used Patrick's disorientation to punch him hard in the face. Patrick blocked the second punch and was on

Matt before he could react. Patrick leaped forward to force Matt off his feet. Matt twisted his knee and fell backward, yelling in pain. He tried to stand, but Patrick was already on top of him, punching him in the head. Matt swung back and drove his fist into Patrick's stomach. Patrick gasped at the blow but stayed on top of Matt, trying to wrap his arm around Matt's neck in a grappling hold.

Matt twisted hard, knowing that once the hold was set, it was fatal. Matt caught a blur of movement out of the corner of his eye and then heard a thud. Patrick collapsed on the ground beside him. In a panic, Matt thrust his arm out and rolled. He struggled to his feet and backed away, his vision sparking from the punches. He squinted.

Nathan Trent was standing in front of him with a leather-covered club. Scarlett Palmer was pointing a flintlock pistol at Matt's face.

"What's this?" Matt shouted. He reached for the slash in his side and felt his shirt, sticky with blood.

"Go!" Nathan commanded. He pointed the club toward the open doors. "Now."

"Why?" Matt said, looking down at Patrick.

"We've been manipulated," Nathan said. "Go before he wakes."

Matt looked at Scarlett. "And you?"

Scarlett flicked the pistol twice toward the door, coaxing Matt to leave. "Noble deeds, Mr. Miller."

"Go!" Nathan repeated.

Matt grabbed his jacket from the floor, limped to the double doors on his twisted knee, hurried through the warehouse, pushed the front doors open, and walked out into the London dawn.

CHAPTER 66.

PICADOR

It was 7:30 a.m. by Matt's watch when he limped away from the warehouse. The morning had burned the dew from the cobblestone, and it was already too warm for an injured man. Stains covered Matt's clothes and he smelled of sweat and blood. There were no cabstands near, so Matt's only hope was to wave one down. Two came by while he limped along, but they sped off once they could see him.

So far, his eyesight hadn't left, though he did push back a few sputters here and there. Besides the occasional carriage refusing to give him a ride, Fore Street was mostly deserted; the stairs and docks here had fallen into disrepair as commerce moved upstream. Bow Street was still searching for him, so maybe it was fortunate that the street was empty. He wasn't sure how much longer he could walk on his twisted knee, but he resigned himself to last until he found a hackney stand. He had nothing else besides putting one foot in front of the other.

A firm punch to Matt's head from the direction of one of the Fore Street causeways sent him crashing to the cobblestones. He automatically thrust his forearm up to protect himself from additional blows, but none came. A man stood behind him silhouetted against the rising sun. The assailant's arm pointed an automatic handgun.

"I calculated that you had a seven-percent chance of leaving Ferguson's building alive," Brain Palmer said. "That's about one in fifteen."

"Thanks," Matt replied, squinting to recognize the man standing before him. "I can do the math." He struggled to his feet. "Multivariate calculation or only a hunch?"

Brian stepped back to keep distance between them. "Wow," he said, waving the gun at Matt's bleeding side. "He kicked your ass." Brian closed his eyes for longer than was normal for a blink and Matt recognized the gesture. Matt did this, too, when his mind was fading in and out during a severe headache.

"The odds were undeniably against me," Matt said.

"You kill him?"

"Go find out yourself."

Brian waved the gun at Matt. "Don't make me shoot you here in the street."

Matt shrugged. "Knocked out, but in better shape than me."

"You walked away?" Brian asked.

"What was the probability of that?"

"Trent must have helped you. I saw the possibility."

Matt stayed silent.

"Good for him," Brian said. "He's smart. Probability was low, though."

Matt was gradually moving in a circle to put the sun at his back. Brian shuffled his feet, waving the gun for emphasis. He'd already looked at his watch twice. Matt saw Brian's long blink again.

"You're wondering why I'm looking at my watch," Brian said.

Matt shrugged.

"I'm less and less conscious of time with every trip through the portal," Brian explained.

"The portal's making you sick," Matt said, tapping his skull a couple of times.

"I'm smarter than anyone who's ever lived."

"How much?" It was a genuine question. IQ was the strongest correlate of success among humans, and a small increase would represent an extreme advantage. If humanity was a horserace, a few extra IQ points was like having the ability to win every race by a nose.

Brian looked at his watch again. "The portal stimulates neuronal growth. I'm smarter than you, by far."

"Have you thought about the consequences?"

"Can you see time?" Brian asked. "I can."

"Could there be any problem with trying to improve on three billion years of evolution?"

"I thought you religious guys didn't believe in evolution."

"Are there any ramifications to trying to improve on God's design?"

"Stupidity is a disease, and I've found the cure," Brian replied. He gave a long blink again and reached up with his one hand to rub his temples with his thumb and forefinger. Matt kicked the gun from Brian's grasp and it bounced across the street. Both men lunged at the tumbling weapon.

Matt swung his fist hard into Brian's stomach and sent him sprawling. He grabbed the gun and pointed it at Brian, who was on the ground, coughing and holding his belly.

"Stand, you son of a bitch," Matt yelled.

Brian struggled to take his feet but remained doubled over, holding his stomach and retching. Even so, he checked his watch and smiled through the pain. "You don't have much time," he said.

"You're coming with me," Matt replied, waving the gun.

Brian, still doubled over, held his hand up. "Dr. Benjamin Franklin and Lord George Beckham have conspired together to give a speech today in front of Parliament. They will present their plan for full representation of the colonies." Brian rechecked his watch. "Speech is scheduled for nine o'clock."

Matt raised the gun. "What else?"

"Don't kill me yet," Brian said calmly. He stood straight now, with one arm still at his stomach. "At exactly nine fifteen, a bomb somewhere near them will go off. The evidence will lead directly to you."

Matt pointed the gun at Brian's head and looked at his Rolex. He had an hour. Matt lifted his eyes to Brian. "Why are you doing this?"

"Because I can."

There was a buzzing noise around them and a feeling of spatial disruption. Matt had never forgotten the sensation from the night they had tried to pull him back to the twenty-first century against his will. He looked around frantically, trying to determine where the portal would open.

"Back up unless you want to join me," Brian said as a

bright green field formed around him. Matt stepped back and cocked the hammer of the gun. There was every reason to rid the world of this man. Brian put his hand up, grinning. "Not yet," he insisted. "You should know this. An assassin left for Virginia on the *Hunter* this morning."

Matt waved the gun. "Who's his target?"

"Thomas Jefferson . . . and you. Ferguson's right, that damn country should never have been formed."

Matt fired the pistol as fast as he could pull the trigger at the same time that the snap of a bullwhip ripped Brian Palmer from the eighteenth century.

CHAPTER 67.

ADMIRAL

Matt's watch said 8:20 a.m. He had fifty-five minutes to reach Parliament and diffuse a bomb. He'd never make it on foot. He ejected the cartridge from the chamber of his gun, put it back in the clip, and thrust the pistol into his belt. Another hackney was coming. He ran out in front of the horses and waved.

"I already have a fare," the driver said threateningly.

"Official business," Matt said. "It's necessary that I go to Parliament—now."

"Official business, hell," the driver yelled. "I'm not driving a beggar anywhere."

Matt reached up and grabbed the bridle of one of the two horses. "You're not going anywhere until you take me to Westminster. A lot of people are going to die if I don't make it."

The driver slapped the reins against the horse, but Matt had a sturdy grip on the animal and it refused to move. Realizing the futility of the situation, the cabbie finally turned to the side to address his passengers. "Make some room; we've pledged to fit another." He looked down at Matt and pointed to the side of the carriage. "Get in."

Matt let go of the horse and stepped to the side.

"Hiya!" the driver yelled as he slapped the animals. Matt jumped back to avoid being tangled in the spoked wheels. He picked himself off the ground and watched the carriage drive away. "Asshole," Matt whispered. He pulled out the gun, chambered a cartridge, and waited behind a mound of abandoned wood that was stacked at the top of some old stairs. A rider on horseback approached after ten minutes. Matt waved his arms and stopped the rider. Both the horse and man were oversized.

"Get the hell out of my way," the man said.

"I need to borrow your horse," Matt replied. "It's official Parliament business. I'll return him when I'm done."

"Out of my way."

Matt leveled the gun at him. "My name's Matt Miller and my friend is Dr. Benjamin Franklin."

"King George is my uncle."

Matt waved the gun again. "Off the horse now, or I'll shoot."

The rider shrugged doubtfully and with some humor. "With that?"

Matt pointed the gun at a water-filled wooden barrel next to the rider and shot twice. The two bullets entered the front cleanly and exploded out the back, and water soaked the man and his horse. The horse reared, shaking the man off. He scrambled to his feet while Matt kept the gun trained on him.

"Back away," Matt said, pointing the gun threateningly.

The rider put his hands up as he moved away from the horse. Matt put his foot in the stirrups while keeping the gun trained on the man as he mounted the horse.

"What kind of gun is that?"

Matt waved the weapon at the man. "Tell me your name."

"No."

"If you want your horse back, tell me your name."

"Oliver," he said hesitantly. "Oliver Pascoe."

"Make your way to Parliament, Oliver Pascoe," Matt said. "Tell them that Ben Franklin has your horse. What's his name?"

"Who?"

"The horse."

"Admiral."

Matt kicked his heels into the horse's sides. "Git!" he yelled, and the horse jumped forward. Matt had forty minutes to cover five miles through the most congested and guarded part of London to thwart the murders of Benjamin Franklin and George Beckham. He wondered what probability for success Brian Palmer had calculated.

CHAPTER 68.

RIVER FLEET

The sound of the horse's shoes hitting cobblestone echoed back and forth between the buildings that lined Narrow Street. The paving stones alternated between uneven, smooth, and slick. Though the road was empty, Matt resisted the temptation to put the horse in a gallop and risk his slipping on the hard cobblestone. The hoofbeats softened as they left the surrounding buildings and entered the fields. It was a welcome change from the clomping, and a small respite, if only for a moment.

Matt turned onto Butcher Row. He was familiar with the roads that lined the river, but the water snaked through London. The only way to reach Westminster in time was to cut a straight path through town. The pavement on Butcher was less treacherous, so he kicked the horse past Broad Street. Butcher ended at a fork in the road that was blocked by a stone guardhouse. Matt eased the horse back to thread him along the left; a few official-looking characters manned the building, but they only stepped out of his way as he approached.

On Brook Street the footing was better. Matt coaxed Admiral into a gallop. "Come on, boy!" Matt had never been on this road before and prayed it wasn't taking him too far from the river. Past a sign for Blue Gate the road turned to dirt and gravel and became better footing. Matt urged the horse forward, now unable to read the names of the streets as they passed.

"Slow down!" a man screamed up at him as he blazed past a vegetable stand. The street was crowding, so he eased into a rapid canter, trying to guide the horse around the wagons that blocked his path. He threaded recklessly between vehicles and horses.

"Arse!" someone yelled.

The Tower of London

Seeing the Tower of London reassured Matt that he was on course. He looked up at the sky and said, "Thanks!" He galloped through the courtyard of the Tower, ignoring the commands of English soldiers on horseback to slow down. He turned to see them confer and give chase. He brushed it off; he had a head start, and they'd have trouble navigating the narrow, congested London streets with three horses.

Matt's best bet now was to stay in view of the river. He heard a commotion behind him as he cantered toward the end of Thames Street. The soldiers were gaining more rapidly than he'd predicted. "Out of the way," Matt yelled at a merchant whose cart took up the whole road. "Official Parliament business!"

"Parliament can go to hell," the merchant shouted back. "Bunch of lazy bastards."

Matt stopped the horse on Water Street, prancing back and forth, not knowing which way to turn. The river blocked a southern path. There was frantic clomping from where he had come, and now red uniforms were visible. Matt gambled on leaving the road eastward on a dirt path, hoping to come out onto another roadway. He galloped across a field and ran into the Fleet Canal. Water completely blocked his path forward.

Damn it!

He pranced again, trying to sort out a route. The canal bridge was far north with no easy way forward. The soldiers were almost on him. "We gotta jump, boy!" Matt said. It was far, and neither he nor the horse would survive a fall into the canal. He turned Admiral and trotted back toward the soldiers, who were coming straight at him.

"Stop! You!" a soldier yelled.

Matt raised his hands and the soldiers slowed. He pivoted the horse again to face the canal and shouted, "Gi *ya*!" as he kicked his heels. "Admiral!" The horse accelerated and jumped. Admiral's front legs came down hard, but there was enough space to land a single back hoof. His other back leg slipped, and he stumbled, but he regained his footing and charged forward. Matt turned to see the soldiers on the opposite side of the canal with their pistols poised. He ducked in time to hear the black powder explosions followed by musket balls whistling over his head.

"Good boy!" Matt shouted, patting the horse's neck and turning him north to pick up Fleet. Admiral was unfazed. Matt galloped Admiral along Fleet Street and then onto Strand, shouting, "Out of the way!" to the dirty looks of pedestrians and people in carts. Admiral hissed like a steam locomotive. Matt finally eased him back at Parliament Street when Westminster Hall came into view. His watch told him he had ten minutes.

CHAPTER 69.

PROCEDURE

Matt hurried the horse through New Palace Yard. It was difficult to thread through the crowd to the entrance of Westminster Hall. Half a dozen soldiers standing guard outside recognized Matt's intentions and blocked him well in front of the elaborate entrance to the meeting hall. Matt hopped from the horse's back while he was still moving and pain shot through his wounded side. He pulled his coat tight to hide his bloody blouse.

An officer rushed behind the soldiers to confront Matt. They weren't pointing their muskets yet, but it was obvious they were thinking about it. Matt checked his watch; eight minutes to go. He pressed the straps of Admiral's bridle into the hand of the first soldier that reached him.

"Hold him," Matt commanded. "I'm Representative Matthew Miller of the Virginia House of Burgesses. There's a bomb in the hall. I want to get in there."

"We've men inside to protect the MPs," said the officer, who had now stepped between his soldiers to confront Matt. He motioned for Matt to stop. "Members of Parliament only. Occasional gathering." The commander glanced back at his subordinates, one of whom was holding Admiral. "Inspect the hall," the officer said. The young soldier dropped the leather straps and the two men hurried inside. Matt watched them open the doors. He could hear Ben's voice echo through the building as he gave his speech.

"It's a time bomb," Matt said. He looked down at his watch. "Slow-burn fuse."

"The hall's been swept, and it's been under guard since morning. If a fuse *were* burning, my men would smell it. They're trained to protect the MPs from Papists and their ilk. You're not in Virginia anymore."

"This bomb won't smell," Matt insisted. "Let me inside."

The officer stood his ground. "My men are doing the inspection."

A moment later, the guards were back. "Looks clear, sir. No sounds, no smells, and no commotion," one reported.

The officer turned back to Matt. He briefly glanced at Admiral's reins, which were dangling on the lawn as the horse pulled up grass. "On your way," the officer said to Matt.

Matt wrinkled his face and swore under his breath. He looked again at his wrist; six minutes. He grabbed Admiral's reins. "It was worth a try," he said to no one in particular. Then he looked at the officer. "Thanks. I feel better there's no threat." Matt bowed to the officer and took his time mounting the horse. Once in the saddle, Matt shouted, "Gi *ya!*" and kicked Admiral toward the doorway of Westminster Hall. He charged into the four soldiers guarding the entrance, splitting them violently back.

Admiral hopped the few steps to the floor of the portico,

through the archway, and hit the partially open doors, thrusting them apart to bang against the walls. A red-brown carpet ran the length of the hall to a series of steps leading to a stage at the south end. Ben was at the podium with George Beckham. Ben ended his speech at the sound of the crashing doors. Surprised members of Parliament turned to watch Matt ride the horse along the carpet that ran between them. Matt was halfway down the length of the hall when Ben shouted, "What's the meaning of this?"

"There's a bomb, Ben!" Matt shouted. "You're the targets. It's Palmer."

The word "bomb" echoed through the hall and a hush went through the MPs. For a moment, the only sound was Admiral's muffled hoofbeats on the red-brown carpet. Then, as if someone fired a starting pistol, a roar went up and people sprinted to the north door. Admiral reared in the panic and Matt dismounted to lead the agitated horse forward. He dropped the reins at the steps but the horse followed him onstage to the speaker's podium to escape the panic.

Ben and Beckham stepped back as Matt charged at them. Matt grabbed the wooden podium and twisted it on its side. The podium tumbled down the steps as a blue-and-white canister rolled out from its bottom. "That's it!" Matt said. He grabbed it before it reached Ben and Beckham, who were back on their heels. The timer said four minutes. "I need to get this out of here," Matt yelled into the noise of the trapped crowd. "It'll take out half of Parliament!"

Matt inspected the north entrance to Westminster Hall, which was now bottlenecked by people trying to leave, then he searched around for somewhere to throw the bomb. The hall was wide open. There was nowhere to hide. Matt latched the bomb under his arm, stepped to Admiral, and put his foot into a stirrup. His hands were sticky with blood, so the bomb almost slipped from his grasp. As he flexed his leg over the saddle, he felt blood ooze out of the slash in his side. He was starting to feel nauseous.

Matt urged the sick feeling from his mind and guided Admiral carefully down the steps, then galloped the length of the hall, shouting, "Clear the door!" The trapped crowd pushed harder into the doorway. The timer now read three minutes.

Matt turned back from the crowd, searching for another exit. He spotted a decorated archway that marked a hall ending in double doors composed almost entirely of stained glass. He kicked hard and Admiral sprinted into the hall. Matt yanked up on the horse's mane, coerced him into the air, and crashed headfirst through the doors. The stained glass shattered around them and they popped out into another room with already open doors. Admiral blasted out of the building into an alley that led to New Palace Yard. The timer read two minutes.

"Out of the way!" Matt shouted as he raced to Bridge Street. He was at the west side of Westminster Bridge with one minute to go when a man tried to wave him down. Oliver Pascoe cried for Matt to stop. Even in the panic, Matt was impressed that the man had already arrived at Westminster to retrieve his horse. Matt sidestepped Admiral around Pascoe and galloped onto the bridge. He had thirty seconds left.

The west side of the river was crowded with boats. He galloped to the center. Twenty seconds! He guided the horse along the railing and threw the bomb into the Thames. It bobbed along the surface as Matt jumped down, thrust off his jacket, wrapped it around Admiral's head, and pulled down. His last vision was of Oliver Pascoe running toward them. The bomb exploded and Matt's world went black.

CHAPTER 70.

TOO LATE

Matt opened his eyes in his room in Ben's house on Craven Street. "What day is it?" he asked to the ceiling.

"Dr. Franklin," Margaret called. "He's awake." She stepped to Matt's bed and spoke kindly. "We knew you'd be fine, Mr. Miller."

"What day is it?" Matt repeated.

"Thursday."

Matt had trouble remembering when he had ridden the horse into Westminster Hall. "How long? How long have I been sleeping?"

"Two days," she said. "Not quite two."

Ben entered the room and came to his side. "You're all right."

"Bow Street?" Matt asked. He tried to sit up, but his head was pounding.

"Take it easy, son," Ben said. "You're no longer a man of interest. Nathan Trent corroborated your story. Bow Street is looking for Brian Palmer."

Matt had to use all his energy to fight his headache and sit up.

Ben went on. "Parliament met again while you were sleeping," he explained. "Beckham was awful amazing. He singlehandedly built a majority. They've drawn articles of representation for the American colonies. We got what we wanted. He'll offer them the same representation as anyone in the kingdom. We'll decide details, logistics, procedures, and communications. American delegates may be required to spend most of their time at Westminster, but I believe—"

"Ben, listen to me now!" Matt said. "Send someone to contact Captain Pearce of the *Norfolk*. They're still taking on cargo in London Harbor. It's the fastest ship in the colonies."

"We don't need a fast ship," Ben replied. "After the impression that you made, they'll not rescind their offer based on a delay of a few weeks. Beckham's contingent is committed to traveling from colony to colony."

"Jefferson's life is in danger," Matt said. "Brian Palmer hired an assassin. He sent him to Virginia on the *Hunter*."

The End of Book Three

LAUGHTER

Matt slept restlessly for his last two weeks at sea. He couldn't escape the feeling of doom, and kept waking up soaked in sweat. The conflict kept moving from one side of his brain to the other, and his usually prescient dreams were flooded with guilt over leaving his pregnant wife unprotected. Father Vincent had said honor, verity, and duty would nourish his soul if he was on the right path; he hadn't said anything about waking up in a cold sweat every night.

I'm the cause of this, Matt thought, *and I have to fix it.*

A sergeant barking orders to the English soldiers behind them made Matt, and Beckham who was riding beside him, turn their heads. Seeing it was nothing, they resumed their silent journey from Richmond to the Taylor-Miller farm. Beckham had proven himself a brave and able statesman. It seemed likely he would achieve full American representation in Parliament.

Beckham, noticing Matt's preoccupation, finally spoke. "Still vexed about the price on your head?"

"No," Matt said. "My wife is ill. I'm anxious to see her. I'd like to say there's something extraordinary about traveling through Virginia while being chased by an assassin, but it's not the first time."

Beckham laughed, and Matt recounted the time Levi Payne hired men to kill him.

After he'd finished, Beckham said thoughtfully, "We live in serious times, and we must always remain diligent. I pray that your wife will be fine."

Matt shrugged. There was nothing more he could say.

"We're escorted by ten elite members of the British guard," Beckham explained. "They're aware of the threat to you and your family, and they'd give their lives before they suffered anyone to be harmed. I pray, too, we have God's speed in locating Mr. Jefferson."

"If he hasn't already been murdered," Matt said, though unconvinced.

He wasn't really so apprehensive about Thomas Jefferson. Nothing in his dreams had ever hinted of his assassination, but Matt knew the assassin's threat would unnerve the young statesman. Jefferson was unfamiliar with violence; Matt reasoned that it was due to his height. He'd have been able to avoid most fights based on his size alone, so he often seemed oblivious to the physicality of men's conversations. Matt had convinced him to study fencing with Henry Duncan, and Jefferson had gained confidence and skill, but he would never be a soldier.

Richmond disappeared behind them as they approached the farm, and Matt's apprehension grew. He could hear the dogs now and see horses running in the pastures behind the white fences. He fought the desire to charge forward. Matt had had no news since the letter announcing that Grace had lost the baby. He wanted to promise never to leave again.

"Corn looks tall," Matt said aloud. "God, I'd love to

walk the fields." Grace's father had treasured his walks in the cornfields. The thought of Thomas Taylor gave Matt a sad smile. He'd been right about being able to hear God's thoughts among the stalks, and Matt needed divine inspiration now more than ever. Matt wondered how Thomas would have dealt with English soldiers attacking his daughter.

Would they already be dead?

"How long do you think it will take to gather the representatives?" Beckham asked.

"One or two weeks."

"I know 'tis a delicate subject with you Americans," Beckham said, "but our protection requires that you quarter my men on your farm."

"I agree," Matt replied. "Most of the meetings will be conducted there, anyway. We have room."

Beckham nodded. "Both the king and Parliament are extending their hands. We must bring the sides together, you and me, before the bond is hopelessly shattered."

"I believe even Jefferson will concur," Matt said. "His dream is for British law to be extended to all citizens of the commonwealth."

"Mr. Jefferson will want to be convinced that our motives are pure."

"He'd be a strong ally," Matt affirmed. "Virginia has much to lose in a conflict." He felt another tinge of guilt at the statement, knowing that he himself had more to lose than most.

As they passed the factory, a mild acetic acid smell emanated from the building, and Matt inhaled deeply. It made him wish for a simpler time when the only thing that mattered was a nicely compressed tablet and enough money to ask for the hand of the woman he loved. Right now, almost every other moment in his life seemed better than today.

Beckham inspected the building as they passed it. "How many do you employ?"

"Over forty. Though we could grow larger."

"Why don't you?"

"For it all to be destroyed in a war?" Matt replied. "No way."

"Even if we fail, how can you be sure of war?"

"I'll relax once we've won the Virginians. The rest of the South can be convinced, but Virginia must lead. Franklin tells me that Pennsylvania will compromise."

"And New England?"

"You'll want to persuade Adams. Boston is about to boil over."

"You speak so ominously," Beckham said.

Matt repeated Beckham's words back to him. "These are serious times, Mr. Beckham."

Near the entrance to the farm, Matt turned again to look at the British soldiers. It had been a long time since he'd had to deal with Redcoats here. This bunch was older and more professional, but that wasn't much of a comfort. Comfort was a luxury now, anyway; he had a price on his head, had lost a child, and his dreams were shouting tragedy.

As they passed through the gate and approached the white farmhouse, Grace's mother opened the front door and stepped out onto the porch. "Hello," she called. "Welcome home."

Matt dismounted and the others followed. They'd been in the saddle for hours now, and shook themselves loose as Matt stepped up onto the porch and hugged Mary as he had since his first days on the Taylors' farm. "A pleasure to see you, Mother. Where's Grace?"

Mary gave him a sober look. She scrutinized the British soldiers. "I assume we'll be hosting these men for the next few days?"

"Two weeks," Matt replied. He looked around. "Where are Grace and the children?"

"The children are with Rebecca," Mary said. "Grace is in bed."

"Still? Where?"

His mother-in-law was grave. "Let her rest. She's had so little sleep. Situate these soldiers. I suspect there are not many here who would help you with that task."

"I must see her," Matt said.

"Settle your men," Mary commanded. Her German accent made her statement strong enough for Matt to step off the porch.

Matt shook his head in irritation as he returned to Beckham. "Let me find Jonathan," he said. "I can trust him to help quarter your men." He pointed. "They'll stay in the black shacks there. We'll have meat for everyone soon."

Matt turned to see Jonathan thundering across the courtyard. He was now taller than Matt and had become a formidable young man. "Jonathan," Matt said, relieved.

"These Redcoats can't stay," Jonathan said. "You should have given us warning before bringing them here."

"I rushed here. Our family may be in danger."

"The danger comes from these soldiers!"

"They're staying." Matt turned to Beckham. "Ambassador Beckham, this is my brother-in-law, Jonathan Taylor, one of the proprietors of this farm."

"You've brought the British ambassador to our home?" Jonathan asked incredulously.

"Jonathan!" Matt scolded. "He's here to help Virginia obtain representation in Parliament."

"I no longer wish to be British," Jonathan said. "This scum can stay in Richmond." He said it loudly enough for the guards to hear; Matt saw them grow agitated. Beckham raised his hand at their commander. "How can it be that both you and Will have become shills for these tyrants?" Jonathan asked as Matt yanked him across the dirt road into an equipment shed.

"I don't like these soldiers any more than you do," Matt said as he slid the door shut. "The threat to our family is real."

"Have you seen your wife? Or does the company of your new fellows consume you?"

"Grandmother said Grace was sleeping."

"Are you going to tell my sister more soldiers are staying at her home?"

Matt looked at the door. "Everything I'm doing now is to keep your sister alive and this farm from being burned to the ground. Beckham is here to negotiate a peace."

"Let it burn," Jonathan replied. His voice had steel in it.

They turned at the sound of the door. David Taylor stood in the doorway. "Mr. Beckham told me the situation," David said. "I'll take care of the soldiers." He looked straight at Jonathan. "These aren't the men who attacked your sister. Those men will get the noose."

Jonathan glared at his uncle. "Like in Boston? Did those men?"

"Calm yourself," David replied. "Do you plan to fight a whole squad of British soldiers?" He looked furiously at Matt. "Why would you bring them here, knowing what they did?" He shook his head and left, sliding the door shut behind him.

Matt spun to face Jonathan. "You will not say another word to these men or Ambassador Beckham. I will not let this farm and family be destroyed."

Jonathan held Matt's glare. Matt accepted it as his acknowledgment.

Matt left the shed and hurried across the yard to Beckham. "My wife is ill, assaulted by British soldiers. I trust you can find your way."

"Your uncle told me," Beckham replied. "I appreciate your hospitality and understand your family's dismay." Matt nodded, backed away, and strode toward his home. He sprinted up the staircase to the master bedroom.

Grace was sitting up in bed, reading a book in front of an open window. The room was cool and fragrant. He went to the bed to pull her into his arms. "They told me," he said. "When did this happen?"

"A month after you left," Grace replied. Her voice had a cold finality. "I lost our baby. It was a little girl."

"The men will be brought to justice," Matt said. "I'll bring them there if the law does not."

"An eye for an eye," Grace said.

"We cannot—"

A gunshot echoed outside.

"What?" Matt jumped from the bed and out onto the balcony.

Jonathan stood in the courtyard holding a smoking pistol. Twenty yards away, David Taylor was trying to keep Beckham on his feet. Bright-red blood dripped from Beckham's head.

"What's befallen?" Grace demanded.

Matt turned to her. "The British Ambassador has been shot."